"A clever conceit, with a surprisingly moral center. Lots of fun, deftly witty, and one of the most appealing central characters of recent years."
—*New York Times* bestselling author Simon R. Green

"If you want your life saved, you call the cops. If you want your *soul* saved, you call Jesse James Dawson, a modern-day samurai who has it all over an Old West gunslinger and then some. But with demonic double-dealing, enemies old and new lining up to take a shot, and every battle to the death, you'd better buckle up for one helluva ride. Humor, action, and a one-way trip straight to Hell, this book delivers it all."
—National bestselling author Rob Thurman

"K. A. Stewart's Jesse James Dawson is a modern-day warrior who can tie up his ponytail with one hand and use a katana in the other to fend off the forces of evil. Equal parts heroic, dark, and funny, *A Devil in the Details* is a welcome addition to the urban fantasy genre, pickup truck included."
—Anton Strout, author of *Dead Matter*

"[*A Devil in the Details*] hits the trifecta of strong story, characters, and prose. . . . Stewart's wisecracking hero is smart and thoroughly 3-D. The tight, terse style honors but doesn't copy Jim Butcher's Harry Dresden books, and urban fantasy fans looking for something new will happily devour Stewart's debut."
—*Publishers Weekly*

continued . . .

Jesse James Dawson Novels
by K. A. Stewart

A Devil in the Details
A Shot in the Dark

A SHOT IN THE DARK

A JESSE JAMES DAWSON NOVEL

K. A. STEWART

A ROC BOOK

ROC
Published by New American Library, a division of
Penguin Group (USA) Inc., 375 Hudson Street,
New York, New York 10014, USA
Penguin Group (Canada), 90 Eglinton Avenue East, Suite 700, Toronto,
Ontario M4P 2Y3, Canada (a division of Pearson Penguin Canada Inc.)
Penguin Books Ltd., 80 Strand, London WC2R 0RL, England
Penguin Ireland, 25 St. Stephen's Green, Dublin 2,
Ireland (a division of Penguin Books Ltd.)
Penguin Group (Australia), 250 Camberwell Road, Camberwell, Victoria 3124,
Australia (a division of Pearson Australia Group Pty. Ltd.)
Penguin Books India Pvt. Ltd., 11 Community Centre, Panchsheel Park,
New Delhi - 110 017, India
Penguin Group (NZ), 67 Apollo Drive, Rosedale, Auckland 0632,
New Zealand (a division of Pearson New Zealand Ltd.)
Penguin Books (South Africa) (Pty.) Ltd., 24 Sturdee Avenue,
Rosebank, Johannesburg 2196, South Africa

Penguin Books Ltd., Registered Offices:
80 Strand, London WC2R 0RL, England

First published by Roc, an imprint of New American Library,
a division of Penguin Group (USA) Inc.

First Printing, July 2011
10 9 8 7 6 5 4 3 2 1

For the Jewell Pack
Who never doubted, even when I did.

ACKNOWLEDGMENTS

First and foremost, thanks to Anne Sowards, Kat Sherbo and Chris Lotts, without whom none of this would have been possible. A huge thanks to my beta-slaves: Janet Yantes, Geoff Glover, Jesse Phillips, Jenn Wolfe, Will Sisco and Auggy. Thanks to Elysabeth Williams, Lisa Brackmann, Alice Loweecey, Rob Thurman, and Stacia Kane, who are not only amazing authors, but also amazing friends. To Dr. Gita Bransteitter, for invaluable medical advice and for feeding my nail polish addiction. For Purgatory, all hail The Junk! For the Badger Blades crew and their epic weaponry. And a special thanks to Sensei Dave Elam, who didn't blink an eye when I asked, "Can you show me how to knock a guy out?" As always, for Scott and Aislynn.

1

Two years ago . . .

"**F**ire in the hole!" I grabbed the kid by the front of his shirt and dragged him into the water, falling on top of him to protect him further. Problem being, there was room for one man at the bottom of the pool, but not two. Half submerged as I was, the explosion was enough to deafen me, the sound wave skipping across the top of the water to smack me upside my very thick skull.

As I felt things pelting down on me, splattering my shoulders and the one arm I couldn't get under the water, I was forced to admit that this had *not* been one of my better ideas. I pressed my forehead against the kid's, trapping him under the water, and held my breath until spots danced before my eyes. Pondering just how I'd gotten to this point, I was pretty sure that somehow, it was the poodle's fault.

Now, I hate poodles. They're not even real dogs. They're more like rats in sheep's clothing. The constant "yip yip yip" should be blared over loudspeakers to end police standoffs. And no cute fluffy animal should be pink. It's just wrong on so many levels.

So I hope you can understand the amazing amount of restraint I exercised, not half an hour earlier, as someone's pink, yappy, woolly rat barked and snapped around my ankles. One quick stomp with my heavy boot and it'd be all over for the glorified rodent. I had a feeling my client, the dog's owner, would object to me murdering her darling Mitzi or Bitsy or whatever the hell its name was. She seemed the objecting type.

"Now you're certain you can do this? You come highly recommended, but . . ." It was the umpteen thousandth time she'd asked the very same question.

"Ma'am, I can't promise anything. Yes, I think I can do this. But there is always an element of uncertainty. Anything could happen." I was tired of pointing out to her that the contract was already set, so she was stuck with my services whether she liked it or not. If not for that, and my own personal honor, I might have bailed a long time ago myself.

She sniffed, her jaw tightening in displeasure. I got the feeling that she was used to getting absolute answers. From her dyed hair to her real pearl necklace, from her trimmed-in-real-mink coat to her purse by some designer I'd never heard of, Mrs. Effingham was a lady. The kind that expects you to use the word with a capital L like some kind of title. When she snapped her manicured fingers, she expected the world to come running. Guess that explained how her kid wound up like he was.

Junior was standing behind Mummy, shoulders stooped sullenly. He obviously didn't want to be here, despite the fact that he was the guest of honor. His very expensive haircut was ruined by the fact that he probably hadn't showered in days, and with his hands stuffed in his pockets, he practically oozed teenaged angst. Occasionally, he would look up at his mother and this flicker of absolute hate would pass through his eyes, but most of the time he gazed vacantly into space.

The breeze carried a faint hint of lilac and the promise of a spring shower. From the manor house behind us, I could catch the smell of something in the soup genre being prepared for dinner. Though, it probably wasn't soup, it was something fancy like bisque or . . . whatever rich people eat. Nothing out of a can for this family, no way.

It was definitely the fanciest backyard I'd ever been in. Tall stone walls marked the borders, stately and dignified. The elaborate koi pond put my own water garden to shame. I mean, what they called a pond, I'd call a pool and me and my buddies would be swimming in it. And I would forever be envious of the barbecue grill (apparently unused) sitting on their expansive patio. The gas grill was almost big enough to require its own garage.

Dressed in my tarnished mail, with a sword hanging on my left hip, I stood out on their carefully sculpted lawn like one of those tacky yard ornaments. Maybe the one of the old farmer mooning. Damn good thing their neighbors couldn't see into the yard. The high walls prevented that, and cast long shadows across the grass, creeping slowly toward us as the sun made its way downward in the sky.

Beyond the walled garden where we stood, down

the hill in some quaint New England village, a church bell tolled the half hour. The time was drawing close.

"Mrs. Effingham, if I could have you return to the house while we do this. I only need Elliot here with me." *And take your gawd-awful yappy dog with you.*

"I prefer to remain with my son, thank you."

I finally turned to face her, drawing up to my full height to make sure I got the "looking down" part just right. Scruffy and uncouth as I am, I know how to be intimidating when I need to be. "That wasn't a request, Mrs. Effingham. That was an order. This is not a spectator sport."

Splotches of color flared under the caked-on makeup on her cheeks, not an attractive look at all. "How dare you? I am paying you good money—"

"You are paying me to be an expert in what I do. So we either do this my way, or I walk now, and your darling little boy goes to Hell. With or without the handbasket." Sometimes, I'm just an asshole. I admit it. I couldn't have walked away, not with the contract set, but she didn't need to know that. She gaped like a landed fish for a few moments before jerking the poor poodle into her arms and stalking across the landscaped lawn to the house.

Only then did I get a faint smile from Junior. "Man, you royally pissed her off."

"I have that effect on people." With Mummy gone, I could feel some of the tension go out of my shoulders. Sad when I'd rather face a demon than an upstanding social matron. Guess I could understand some of Junior's rebellious tendencies. "How are you doing?"

He shrugged his shoulders, finding the grass infinitely more interesting than looking at me. "Okay." Not much on public speaking either. I figured it just never got to be his turn to talk with his mother around.

"Do you understand what's going on here?" In all my negotiations for this particular challenge, I'd had very little chance to actually talk to the kid. Mummy had handled most of the details.

"Yeah. Guess so." He shrugged again and kicked a bare patch in the grass.

"Do you understand that this is your only chance? If I fail, your soul is bound for Hell when you die. No getting out of it, no reprieve." There ought to be an age limit on demon contracts. A sixteen-year-old shouldn't be able to just wish away their soul on any little thing that catches their fancy.

Scuff scuff went the sneakers.

"Do you even want your soul back?"

His fidgeting stopped, and after a moment, he nodded. I was just happy to get something that wasn't a shrug. "I'm cold all the time now. I want to warm up." Most likely, the chill was in his mind, but whatever worked.

"Even if I win, if you do this again, you're on your own. Mommy can't buy you out of this again."

Junior nodded once more, his dark brows almost meeting above his eyes. "Yeah, I got it. She's been screaming it in my ear for weeks now."

"She's just worried about you."

Junior snorted. "No, she's worried that I'm gonna

embarrass her. Can't let anybody know that Ava Effingham's boy sold his soul for a freakin' car. Somebody else's kid probably sold theirs for a Harvard degree or something, much more respectable."

I had to give the kid a teeny weeny bit of credit. He'd sold his soul for a '72 Corvette Stingray. I mean, at least he sold it for a *car*, not some piece of crap. Of course, I'd only seen pictures of the vehicle. It was currently in a pile of scrap in some auto yard, chunks of the telephone pole that killed it still embedded in the metal. The boy was lucky to be alive.

See, that's the thing about demon contracts. They never say what you think they do. Just because the demon promised you a car, or whatever it was, doesn't mean that it said how long you get to keep it.

I also had to give him credit for the most words I'd heard him string together. There was no mistaking the bitterness in his voice. "Sounds like there's issues there."

That earned me another noncommittal shrug. "Just usual stuff."

The shadows from the wall had reached the toes of my boots, and I loosened my katana in its scabbard. Flexing my left wrist, a small item dropped out of my thick leather bracer into my palm. I examined the coin—just some worthless carnival trinket I'd dragged home from somewhere—and rolled it over the backs of my fingers a few times 'cause it looked cool. The metal made my skin tingle. It was almost time. "Where's your dad in all this?"

"He died. Three years ago. Mom says it was cancer,

but I know better. It was . . . that liver thing you get when you drink too much. What is that?"

"Cirrhosis?"

"Yeah, that's it." Junior shrugged yet again. He had a very limited body vocabulary. "We weren't really close."

"You know, in ancient Japan, if a boy's father died, the boy became the head of the household. Kids even younger than you. They were expected to armor up and go fight as knights, just like their fathers had."

"That had to suck."

"They were treated like adults. They were given great respect."

He snorted. "That'd never happen here. Mom's a control freak."

"No?" The shadows oozed over the toes of my boots. Almost there. Flip flip flip went the coin, back and forth across my knuckles. "You were grown-up enough to sell your soul, even if it was for something stupid. I figure if you're enough of an adult with that crowd, you're an adult for me. You want a bit of advice from a total stranger?" Shrug. "Well, you're gonna get it anyway, 'cause I might be dead after this and then I won't get to say it."

That caught his attention and he finally looked up, puzzlement in his eyes. I suppose it had never occurred to him that a man may die today because of him. For kids, death is something that happens in movies and video games, or hidden away in sterile hospitals. It doesn't happen in your backyard, with somebody's guts spilling out on your Chuck Taylors.

"Your dad is gone. You're all your mom has. Even if she rides your ass sometimes, it's only because in her own warped way, she loves you. Man up, grow a pair, and earn that respect you want."

Junior didn't seem to know what to say to that. I didn't expect much. Hallmark moments don't really happen, and I highly doubted there'd be some miraculous change in him no matter how the next hour or so turned out.

My boots were cast in full shadow. The church bell tolled again. Quarter 'til. Time. With a flick of my thumb, I launched the coin into the air and watched as it sparkled on its descent, sinking into the bottom of the koi pond with a tiny splash. Smirking to myself, I murmured, "No magic on my person. Yessir, Mr. Demon, whatever you say."

Next, I turned to Junior and offered him a respectful bow. "With your permission, sir, I'll get this show on the road."

"Um . . . yeah, sure . . . What do I need to do?"

I adjusted the heavy leather bracers on my wrists, rolled my shoulders to loosen them up, and did one or two deep knee bends. My armor jingled faintly. I was ready. "You don't need to do anything but stay out of the way. And whatever you do, keep out of the shadows."

With a startled look at his feet, Junior took two big steps back from the wall's advancing shade. Me, I stood right at the boundary, that wavering line between light and dark.

As the last distant bell died away, the shadows in

front of me . . . rippled. It's the only way I could think to explain it. Like tiny waves lapping, they rippled in a way that had nothing to do with the texture of the ground beneath them, or the breeze that still stirred the evening air. With each subtle pulse, the darkness gathered substance, grew, solidified. Something oozed up from the earth itself, and the grass turned brown and withered as I watched.

And up from the ground come a-bubblin' crude. Oil that is. I smirked at my own humor, but kept it to myself. The kid probably wouldn't know what I was talking about anyway.

The oily-looking substance took on form, rising up like a liquid serpent, and swayed in front of me, its "head" at eye level. A sickly parody of a rainbow colored the dark surface, shifting and changing with the viscous fluid beneath.

It was a Snot demon, as I classified them, lacking the power to hold a more complex form, and barely sentient enough to negotiate for the souls it required. The amorphous head dipped and turned as it eyed me, the body stretching out into the yard nearly to the wall. It had to be a good twenty feet long, and as big around as my thigh. The smell of sulfur and ozone overrode the lilac in the air.

I slid my katana out of its scabbard and took one step forward. "I am Jesse James Dawson, here to champion the soul of Elliot Eugene Effingham." The kid's mom musta hated him. I vowed to never bitch about my own name again. "Are we in agreement?"

The black tattoo covering my right arm from knuckles to elbow said that we were. The contract had been negotiated as tightly as possible, considering the Snot's lack of communication skills. I'd even managed to work in a few sly tricks of my own. I hoped. I flexed my left wrist, feeling the empty place in the bracer where the coin had once been. I had to trust that I'd bargained well, or this was going to be a short fight.

The ooze creature rose up to tower over me, no doubt to be intimidating, but it misjudged the height of the wall behind it, and the last rays of the setting sun caught it. It ducked back down with a hiss of displeasure that caused tiny bubbles to rise from its innards and pop on the surface. The smell of sulfur got stronger, and I had to hide my smirk.

Yeah, these things weren't too bright, and as long as the sun was in the sky, this thing was confined to the shadow of the wall. It could advance only as quickly as the sun set, following the absence of light over the grass. It would take time to get it where I wanted it, but hopefully it was enough time to let me really piss it off, which was just what I needed.

A face formed at the end of the long serpent, with barely enough definition to even be called a face. There were indentations that could be eyes, an opening that might be a mouth. The nose was ... well, a lumpier lump among the rest of the lumps. The faux face stretched into a broad smile, appearing inordinately cheerful. Okay, that was just plain eerie. "We are _____. We are ready."

First off, the mere sound of the creature's name, impossible to spell or pronounce with any human tongue, made things inside my head seize up and quiver, quietly calling for Mommy for a few moments. And second, the oily sheen on the creature's surface seemed to taint its voice as well, and my stomach rolled as the strangeness slithered into my ears and coated my tongue. I forced myself to swallow the sour taste at the back of my throat. The first time I heard a demon speak, two years ago, I'd puked. I was past that now.

The kid wasn't. I could hear him ralphing up his breakfast behind me. It may have even been last week's breakfast. And his sneakers. And someone else's sneakers. Ew.

"Elliot, if you could move back toward the patio when you're done?" The shadows were creeping ever forward, and I needed room for what I had planned. It was either going to be freakin' brilliant, or the stupidest thing I'd ever tried.

"You must come out of the light." The thick serpent's head bobbed up and down, feeling out the limits of its shadowy confinement.

I couldn't help it—the smirk finally made its escape. "Go into the light, Carol Anne." And I struck.

It wasn't a hard blow by any means. More of a love tap, really. But when I drew back, a thin slice of demonic ooze flipped off my blade, vanishing into a wisp of black mist before it hit the ground.

The oil serpent reared back more in surprise than pain, then whipped its tail around to take a swipe at my legs. I jumped and it missed, passing beneath my feet. The demon recoiled out of the stinging sunlight, massing for another attack in the safety of the wall's shadow. Me, I was just impressed at my air time, considering how much my gear weighed.

When it lunged at me again, I sidestepped and flicked my sword, slicing off another thin layer of . . . whatever it was made out of. The wound just filled in, leaving no trace, but that wasn't the point. The second tiny wisp of blight vanished, but I knew it wasn't gone. When there was enough of it, free-floating demon essence, we'd have a portal, and then I could get rid of Monty here.

Y'know, Monty? As in Python? 'Cause he's like a snake? Oh come on, that was funny.

To the untrained observer, it looked like I wasn't doing much at all. A slice here, a nick there, dodge, duck, parry. To a trained observer, it was blatantly obvious that I wasn't doing much at all. The damage I was inflicting was healing up as soon as the blade came free, and the blight I was draining out was minimal at best.

But the sun kept setting, and the wall's shadow kept advancing. I lurked at that edge, careful to never dart into the darkness for more than the length of a thrust, retreating across the carefully manicured grass one step at a time.

The Snot demon left a trail across the greenery, burned dead and brown like a snail trail from Hell. (Mrs. Effingham wasn't going to be pleased at all when she saw that.) Twice, it braved the waning sun to try to wrap me up in its slimy coils, but I was too fast and it was too wussy to handle the light. Bubbles rose to its oily surface, bursting against the air with the stench of sulfur, the sound creating a distinctive hiss of frustration. It was getting pissed off.

Good.

The sky was sunset red when my heels hit the tile border around the koi pond, and I had to grin. Sure, I had no more room to retreat, and in about ten seconds, the sun was going to drop down below the top edge of the wall, casting the entire yard in darkness and giving the demon free rein. I had Monty right where I wanted him.

In an eyeblink, the sunlight was gone, and the angry demon rose above me, swaying as it towered. The face at the end was pocked by bursting bubbles of agitation, but there was no mistaking the snarl on the mockery of a mouth.

Come get some, bitch. I took one step back, into thin air, holding my sword safely to the side as I fell back.

I hit the water hard enough to almost knock my carefully gasped air from my lungs and sank straight to the bottom. From there, I watched through the riled waters as the enraged oil serpent dove headfirst after me.

It intended to crush me, I think, the heavy mass of black sludge spreading out to fill the shape of the pond, its entire body pouring into the water. For a split second, I thought it was going to succeed, and I know I felt my ribs creak under protest. The natural human demand for "Air!" registered in my brain, certain I was about to be smothered or drowned, or both, but before I could even think of flailing in panic, the weight suddenly lifted, and the demon launched itself out of the koi pond with an inhuman shriek.

I fought to the surface despite the weight of my armor (and the padding beneath that had soaked up its own weight in water), to see the Snot demon writhing on the grass like a salted earthworm. Over and over the coils rolled, like it would tie itself in knots, and a thick oily smoke rolled off its transparent skin.

I'd be lying if I pretended I wasn't a little smug. "That's right. Holy water, bitch. Suck it." The glint of gold caught my eye, and I bent to retrieve my coin from the bottom of the pool. My fake, absolutely worthless, magically blessed coin. *Thank you, my love.* One of my wife's brilliant ideas. I couldn't wait to tell her it had worked.

A hand entered my vision, and I looked up to find Elliot offering to help me out of the koi pond. Probably not a bad idea, considering how much heavier I was now than when I'd gone in. "Thanks, kid."

I grabbed his forearm, intending to haul myself out, when I heard it. It was the sound of bacon sizzling, the sound of water boiling furiously. I looked over, dreading what I already knew I was going to see.

There was Monty, swelling up like the world's biggest blood blister, its surface straining to contain the rolling boil within. Even as I watched, a thin slit appeared, and the oil slick spurted from it, driven by the unbelievable internal pressure. Monty was about to blow.

"Fire in the hole!" I grabbed the kid by the front of his shirt and dragged him into the water, falling on top of him to protect him further. Problem being, there was room for one man at the bottom of the pool, but not two. Half submerged as I was, the explosion was enough to deafen me, the sound wave skipping across the top of the water to smack me upside my very thick skull.

I waited as long as I could, until bits-o-Monty stopped raining down on me, before I fought my way into standing, letting Elliot scramble for air. Drowning the client would be bad, m'kay?

He threw himself facedown at the side of the pool, gasping and coughing, while I examined the state of my demon-splattered self. Already, the boiling droplets had eaten through my leather bracers, and were currently burning into the skin beneath. With a hiss, I plunged my forearms into the water, sighing at the soothing relief. I dunked the rest of me for good measure, surfacing with a splutter and shaking myself like a wet dog.

"You okay, kid?" I glanced at Elliot who had become strangely quiet, then turned to follow his stunned line of sight.

The portal was there, hovering just against the back wall, swirling in shades of black and blacker. All over the yard, tiny gobbets of Snot demon were dissolving into their base component, blight, and drifting through the planar tear. It looked like an eerie black river running uphill, finally slowing to a trickle before the portal snapped shut with an audible pop and the reek of ozone.

Just to be sure, I stripped off my right bracer, and

scrubbed the remnants of the tattoo flakes off with the blessed water. "There we are, Elliot, all nice and shiny again."

He examined his left arm, bare now too, then bent to scour it off as well. He scrubbed and scraped until the skin of his arm was blistering pink and I was afraid he'd draw blood. I caught his hand. "Hey. It's cool, okay? It's all over."

He stared at me with wide, shock-filled eyes for a long moment, then nodded. There were tears glimmering in his eyes, but he refused to let them fall, and I pretended I didn't see.

Instead, I turned to eye the destruction left in the wake of my battle. The yard was essentially burned barren, the grass withered and downright charred in places. I was still standing knee-deep in the once-pristine koi pond, which would probably never support life again. Already, the large ornamental fish were starting to float to the surface, eyes gone cloudy in death.

I managed to clamber out of the pool, flopping on the dead grass with a wet squishing sound. It was going to be days before the padding under my mail dried. Hell, it might be days before I decided to stand up again.

The arrival of my archnemesis, Mitzi the poodle, was heralded with a string of high pitched yips and yaps that threatened to burst my eardrums. The vicious little rat came streaking out of its doggy door, tiny needle fangs bared and aimed right for my face now that it was within its short little reach.

I waited until it was almost on me, then roared "Boo!" at it. The pink dog almost flipped itself completely over, scrambling to reverse direction, and it disappeared back inside with the high, "yi! yi! yi!" of fear. I laid my head back on the ground, folded my hands across my chest, and just watched the dim light of the stars appear overhead.

I hate poodles.

2

Now . . .

Nothing says the end of summer like the annual Daw-son family barbecue and snarky T-shirt contest. I won, by the way. I always win. It's my contest. (We used to have a dirty T-shirt contest, but that got awkward once the kids started learning to read.)

My own little five-year-old censor, Annabelle, was playing on the patio with her cousin Nicky, closely supervised by my brother's wife, Stephanie. Mira, the light of my life, and Melanie sat close by, the women no doubt having some in-depth and disgusting discussion about Mel's very large belly, due to pop in about three months.

The sire of said impending spawn, Marty, hovered in a small protective circle of other males, made up of myself, my brother Cole, our friend Will, and my live-in student Estéban. The general theme seemed to be making sure Marty knew just how that happened, and much off-color advice on how to prevent it again. But really, we teased. Marty was gonna be an amazing dad.

He wasn't what you'd think of as the quintessential "dad" figure. Short and squat with biceps the size of my damn thighs, Celtic tattoos from wrist to shoulder on both arms, scruffy black beard and a shaved head . . . Honestly, if we lived in some fantasy world, he'd be the surly dwarf character and that's the truth. He's even a blacksmith, an honest-to-God blacksmith. How's that for a stereotype?

But what most people didn't see was the genuinely good heart and fierce loyalty he could show. Marty was good people.

He'd dragged me aside earlier in the day to get some of my deep thoughts on being a daddy. Personally, when I'm being held up as the bastion of fatherhood, the world's in sad shape, but I did what I could, and he seemed grateful. Nervous as hell, but grateful.

The winning T-shirt of the day proudly proclaimed MEAT IS MURDER. TASTY, TASTY MURDER. Evidence of my convictions was sizzling on the grill, and I stood over it like a king over his domain. Or something.

Estéban reached out a hand toward the lid and I swatted him with the flat of my spatula. "Ahht! No touchy the burgers!"

"But I'm starving!" My seventeen-year-old protégé had hit a growth spurt sometime over the summer, topping my own six feet by a good couple of inches now, and it was entirely possible that he was about to faint dead away from not eating in the last thirty seconds.

"They're not done, but if you think you can get past me, by all means, take one." I smirked and picked up a pair of long tongs in my other hand, dropping into a fighting stance.

Will started up a chant of "Fight, fight, fight!" and

Estéban made a grab for the long grill brush, arming himself. We moved out into the yard, never taking our eyes off one another. This was not the first time we'd done this. Hell, this wasn't even the first time we'd done this *today*, much to my wife's annoyance.

Right from the start, I had Estéban at a disadvantage. Sure, he had the longer reach on me, and both of my "weapons" were much shorter than my preferred katana. But I had two weapons to his one, and I hadn't even started teaching him how to counter a dual-wielding opponent. Not many demons used swords; it didn't seem a priority skill to teach.

The teen eyed me for a moment, trying to figure out the best way around my double threat. I stood, balanced on the balls of my feet, and just waited. He had no patience; it was one of his key flaws. He'd make the first move.

He tried to go on the offensive, I'll give him that. But there was no way I was gonna let the upstart get the jump on me. He feigned a lunge that I pretended to fall for, and when he tried to reverse under my guard, I whacked the brush aside with the tongs and went for his throat with the spatula.

Just like that, it was over. He blinked, feeling the edge of the utensil pressed just below his jaw. If I'd put any force behind it at all, I could have drawn blood. I wouldn't, of course, and that wasn't the point. He understood the lesson. In a real fight, he'd be dead by now, just that quick. His shoulders slumped in defeat and he dropped his eyes to his sneakers.

"Hey." He looked up. "You can't be expected to

know everything yet. We'll work on dual-wielding next week, okay?"

After a moment, he nodded, and I pulled him into a headlock to noogie him good. Trying not to laugh, he pushed free and rolled his eyes, pretending to be too cool for such antics.

It had taken us the better part of the summer to get to this point, where he didn't get all pissy and butt-hurt when I beat him and where I realized how to work around his stiff pride. I hadn't killed him yet. Things were looking up. Now if I could just repair things with the rest of my crew.

Jesse hadn't been the most jolly of sorts this summer for a variety of reasons. Okay, really, I'd been a right bastard for a lot of it. My temper flared at weird times, and even I'll admit I was surly on my good days. Part of the object of this party was to convince the guys I really wasn't a raging asshole. Maybe to convince me, too. It had been a rough six months, since that mess back in March.

I guess, no matter what kind of badass you think you are, having someone try to murder you kinda takes a toll on your mental processes. More than one person had mentioned PTSD, but never where they thought I could hear.

I caught Cole handing Will a five-dollar bill as we came back to the patio, and raised a brow at my little brother. "Et tu, Brute?"

"Someday, that kid's gonna take you."

"Not today." I wiped the tongs on a towel and went about flipping the burgers over. "Hey, can you grab me the—" A chorus of new voices interrupted my train of thought, and I looked up to find Dr. Bridget arriving with date in tow.

At least, I assumed it was a date. It was a strange person of the male persuasion. A date? Since when was she dating? Granted, she was my wife's best friend, but only my doctor. I guess she wasn't required to file her itinerary with me, but . . . A date? Really?

"Who the hell's that?" Will asked as we all turned to watch this new male in our territory.

"No clue. She didn't say she was bringing anyone . . ."

This new fellow was . . . not like us. That much was obvious. We were proudly part of the long-hair-and-tattoos club, my brother excluded. Marty had a kilt on and his tattooed arms were proudly displayed. Will's mop of curly hair was barely confined under his ball cap, and my own ponytail was there only to keep my hair out of the grill.

This new guy was clean cut (okay, I can't hold that against him given that Cole keeps his hair cop-short too) and there was gel in his dark hair. And a polo shirt? Khaki shorts? Loafers, for the love of little fishes! The moment he accepted a mango daiquiri from my wife, we knew this was a creature unlike any we knew. I mean, no straight guy drinks a daiquiri, let alone anything in mango. Not in Kansas City, the most "mid" of Midwestern cities.

"Guys, this is Cam." Bridget presented him with a smile, but there was that hint of unease lurking in her eyes. She knew how ruthless we could be, if provoked.

"He just moved to the area recently, and he doesn't really know a lot of people yet, so be nice." Her eyes were fixed on me at that point, and I held my hands up defensively.

"I'm a perfect angel!" Will and Marty both took turns choking, and I glared at them. Dr. Bridget glared back at me.

"I mean it, Jess. Oh, and he used to be a priest. Watch your language." And with that she abandoned the newly dubbed "Cam" and retreated back to the female section of the patio. He watched her go for long moments. If he was smart, he was willing her to come back and save him.

The five of us looked at him, and he looked back, all of us trying to figure out the other. Finally, Will broke the silence. "So . . . Cam?"

"Short for Cameron."

"And you were . . . a priest?"

Cam-short-for-Cameron fidgeted with his glass uncomfortably. "Not really. I went to seminary, but I left before I took my vows."

The burgers were going to burn if I didn't start paying attention, so reluctantly, I went back to tending the food and left the interrogation to my buddies.

"Does that mean you automatically go to Hell?"

"Will!"

"What?" He looked at Marty, all bewildered-like, truly having no idea that it wasn't an appropriate question. I often think that Will was born without that little voice in his head that says "don't."

"Welcome to the area." Cole finally took the role of

responsible (and sane) adult, and stepped forward to offer his hand. Cameron shook it with a grateful smile, obviously pegging my little brother as a kindred spirit.

"Thanks. It's hard, moving when you don't know anybody."

That led to the questions of why he moved, yadda yadda, and I might have actually listened with more than token interest if the last party guest hadn't turned up just then. A totally uninvited party guest that I was not at all happy to see.

I didn't know the name of the man who walked around the corner of my house with a broad smile, but I'd always called him Axel. Y'know, like "Sympathy for the Devil"? He wasn't a Jagger, for sure, and that just left . . . oh never mind. It made sense when I did it, trust me.

On the surface, he looked rather normal. He wore faded blue jeans, a plain white T-shirt, and scuffed black boots. Granted, there was the blond Mohawk, the totally excessive piercings, but when you work at the kind of clothing store that I do, his appearance was rather tame. I knew it was a mask, a cover for what was truly underneath.

Axel was a demon. He was my demon, actually, intent on collecting my soul if he could. I hadn't seen him in months, since I cast him out of my yard last spring. To say we were not speaking was putting it lightly.

He spotted me and made a beeline in my direction. "Jesse! I tried ringing the doorbell, but no one answered . . . Are we having a party?" For one horrifying moment, I thought he was going to hug me, but he stopped short. "Ooh, burgers!"

Everyone was giving me that "Who's this guy?" look. Everyone but Mira. She was on her feet, watching me with tension on her face. She knew. She knew, and she was waiting to see what I wanted her to do.

For a brief (*very* brief) moment, I wanted to see what would happen if my wife the witch threw down against my own personal demon. But Axel was more powerful than I wanted to truly admit, and any kind of major magic work would take a horrible toll on Mira. So, no, not really an option.

Not to mention that there were civilians here, people who had no idea that real demons walked the world. My sister-in-law, the kids, Dr. Bridget and her new boyfriend . . . All potentially collateral damage.

I pasted a smile on my face and jerked my head toward Marty. "Beer me, Marty." My stocky friend tossed me a bottle and I passed it to Axel. "This is Axel. I work with him at It." Lies suck, and I hate doing it, but sometimes they come in handy. And Axel could pass for one of my tattooed, pierced, punk coworkers easily enough.

The man-demon twisted the bottle open and took a long drink, then sighed with satisfaction. "Good stuff." He looked around at the crowd, which was still mostly staring at him. "Do I have something on my face?" He felt around on his face with mock alarm, touching the gold rings in both eyebrows, the stud in his nose, the labret piercing just below his lower lip.

The buffoonery worked, and everyone laughed. Well, almost everyone. Mira and I exchanged worried looks, but what was I supposed to do? Any tussle I started here would be in full view of people I didn't want hurt. There was no choice but to leave him be, for now.

And my day just got weirder after that. For no reason I could discern, Axel stuck around, introducing himself to my friends and family with a charming smile and witty conversation. He avoided Mira without seeming to do so, and after straying too near my daughter once and coming face-to-face with my wife's cold expression, he avoided the little kids, too. That worried me. He was being entirely too accommodating. And what the hell did he even want? He wasn't the "social call" kind of demon.

Estéban was too perceptive for his own damn good, too. He caught me when everyone else was distracted. "I've seen him before. At It, but he doesn't work there." He raised one dark brow at me, daring me to disagree with him.

"You're a smart kid." I handed him the first platter of burgers. "If I say move, you grab Anna and Nicky and get your ass in the house, *entiendes*?"

"*Entiendo*." His jaw firmed, taking his duty very seriously.

"And Estéban? If that happens, I'm gonna need my sword."

"Yes, sir."

Estéban was a good kid, from a good family. A good family who also happened to be demon hunters for generations going back. It felt a little weird, relying on a teenager to be my backup, but of everyone here,

I knew I could trust the kid to follow orders, and to never back down. We'd fought demons together before.

Cam-short-for-Cameron tried to blend too, making small talk with Cole mostly, while I went through the motions of rustling up grub for everyone. I tried to keep an eye on both him and Axel until I gave myself a headache.

The almost-priest seemed like an all right sort of guy, if a little strange. More than once, I caught him watching me, though he'd look away the moment he realized I was looking back at him. It did also occur to me that maybe he was just watching me to figure out why I was staring at him, too.

He had a very faint limp when he walked, like maybe his right leg wasn't entirely sound, and when he wasn't staring at me, he was very attentive to Dr. Bridget. The smiles they exchanged from time to time made me feel like a peeping Tom. It was that smile that said, "I'm totally head-over-heels in love with this person."

I had to admit, it was a bizarre feeling, watching them, and I finally decided that this was how I'd feel when Annabelle started dating someday. If Bridget had warned me, I could have been cleaning a shotgun or something when they came in. *"She's my only daughter . . ."* Which is probably why she didn't warn me.

The burgers came off the grill and the brats and hotdogs went on, and the party partied on. If not for my own voice carrying across the patio as Axel laughed at someone's joke, I might have even forgotten that he was there. Did anyone else notice the voice, I wondered. Or did he sound like me to only my own ears? It was almost disorienting, hearing myself speak from yards away.

Some clouds drifted across the sun, dropping the temperature by a few degrees, and we all started watching the sky warily. Estéban and I in particular had an aversion to stormy weather. That's what happens once you get a firsthand look at the inside of a tornado.

The moment the first droplets hit the ground, Mira marshaled the troops into moving the party inside, everyone grabbing what they could. In moments, the backyard was empty, save for me and Axel. He lingered near the patio table, fingers walking across the neat tile squares in the tabletop. Marking out chess positions, I realized, from the last game we played. Before I'd packed the set up and taken it inside, of course. Because I was mad at him.

Being reminded of that made me feel petty, which then made me feel ashamed. And my response to shame is to get defensive, which comes out in a rather vicious brand of humor.

I smirked and asked him, "Not coming inside?" knowing full well that he couldn't. Mira had long ago placed magical wards on the doors and windows, specifically to keep Axel out. I didn't know what would happen if he tried to pass through them, but I'm sure it wouldn't be pleasant.

Axel gave me a smirk in return, but it faded. We both stood uncomfortably in the rain, looking everywhere but at each other. Finally, he said, "How've you been, Jesse?"

"I'm still upright and breathing. Why?"

He shrugged. "Just asking. Been a while since I've had to try to make small talk."

The rain picked up, the pleasant shower promising to become a downpour in short order. And since this was getting way too chick-flicky for me, I decided to cut straight to the meat. "What do you want, Axel?"

"What makes you think I want anything?"

"Because you always want something." He always wanted *one* thing: my soul. Which was why I'd booted him out of my yard about six months ago. Big jerk nearly got me killed with his hints and taunts and sly smirks. "And what's with the getup?" I gestured at his all-too-human body. Normally, his appearances involved possessed squirrels, and once a really nasty opossum.

"You ever think maybe I just wanted a burger? And a beer. Oh that beer was wonderful." He paused a moment, a blissfully dreamy expression on his face until I cleared my throat. "It's almost impossible to drink out of those bottles when you're six inches tall, you know. And a beer-drinking squirrel is a bit conspicuous." I just raised a brow at him. We both knew he hadn't answered my question yet. "I was in the neighborhood, all right? Thought I'd swing by and say 'hey'."

I had to chuckle at that, and he gave me a surprised look. "Come on. You really expect me to buy that? You used to be better at this."

For a moment he tried to find something to say to

refute me, but . . . well, you just can't. He finally chuckled and shrugged again. "Yeah, I did. Guess my heart's not in it right now."

"Maybe you need a vacation."

"Ah, wouldn't that be grand? Somewhere warm, with a beach . . ." There was that wistfulness to his face again, for all of about three seconds. Then something in his eyes became more . . . pointed, somehow. Sharper. "Aren't you taking a vacation here soon? Your annual camping trip thingy?"

"Yeah." He obviously knew, already. It wasn't like I was revealing trade secrets. "We're leaving day after tomorrow." Immediately following the annual Dawson family barbecue and snarky T-shirt contest always came the annual guys' paintball extravaganza, in the wilds of Colorado. Yet another attempt to make all the amends I needed to.

"That's good! You should definitely go do that." He did everything but clap his hands in glee. "A vacation might do you a world of good, and all that fresh air out in the middle of nowhere should be exhilarating . . ." He paused in his enthusiastic babbling when I frowned at him. "What?"

"Since when did you become a travel guide?"

"What, just because I'm a demon, I can't appreciate nature's bounty?"

I winced and glanced behind me, but they'd all gone inside. Only Mira remained in the kitchen, cleaning up and looking over her shoulder to check on me just a little bit more than necessary. I waved to her, but she didn't wave back. Her gaze went to Axel, then back to me with a very clear "Get him out of here" message.

Yeah, cause I *wanted* to be standing out in the rain chitchatting with a demon. "You need to go."

"Yeah, figured as much. She hates me." He leaned to the side to look around me, offering Mira a smile that I know she wasn't going to return.

"*I* hate you."

"If you truly hated me, you'd have had her ward the yard." He grinned at me.

"I didn't actually expect you to come back."

"We always come back." His smile vanished instantly, and his eyes flared red for a heartbeat. It seemed more an unconscious thing than his usual posturing. "You should remember that. We *always* come back, Jesse." For a moment, I thought he'd say more; then he just stuffed his hands in his pockets and wandered off around the corner of the house, shoulders hunched against the steady rain.

I waited for longer than was probably necessary, to make sure he was really gone, and Mira handed me a towel as I came inside.

"What did he want?" Worry warred with outright hostility in her green eyes. My wife was ready to go to war, if need be. God, I loved her.

"I don't know. He was . . . being strange." She raised a brow at me. "Stranger than usual. Did anyone else realize?"

"No. Why would they?"

And that was a huge relief, really. Even my friends who knew what I did in my spare time—Will, who patched me up; Marty, who crafted my weapons; and Cole, whose soul I'd saved—knew nothing about Axel. I suppose, deep down, I was ashamed of myself for even talking to him. I'd never told anyone but Mira. And Estéban now, I guess. The circle widens.

"Here, take these into the living room. They've got the football game on." Mira plopped a bowl of tortilla chips into my hands and shooed me out of the kitchen.

Over the course of the evening I couldn't forget Axel, but I did manage to push him to the back of my mind for the most part. I had more important things to do. Things like laughing at Will's truly horrific impressions, teasing Marty about his upcoming foray into fatherhood, just spending time with my little brother, which seemed to happen so rarely anymore.

We watched football. We mocked the commercials. We discussed world events like grown-ups ought to. Seemed like there was something going wrong in every corner of the globe, lately. Riots. Droughts. Unrest and discontent, fledgling conflicts that promised to grow into mini-wars and disasters just poised to strike. Is it any wonder that I'd been in a crappy mood for the last few months? Every time I flipped the TV on, the world was going to hell, and . . .

See, that's what I'm talking about right there. The sudden dives into dark thoughts, the overwhelming sense of impending doom. Like there was this giant boot somewhere, and I was just waiting for it to drop on my head. It wasn't like me, and even I knew it. That's what I was supposed to be working on. I would enjoy my friends, dammit.

And if I fell into a brooding silence, I had Anna and Nicky there to clamber into my lap, chattering about anything and everything. It didn't matter what. It was nearly impossible to be glum with the pair of them in close proximity.

I had Dr. Bridget there to threaten electroshock therapy (and of course the guys knew just where to get a spare car battery to make that happen, if she was serious). Her keen eyes watched me when she thought I wasn't looking, the medical professional in her always analyzing, diagnosing. I couldn't blame her. It's what she did, and she was good.

I had Mira. And she was just perfect, hiding her worry much better than I did, touching my shoulder lightly every time she walked past the couch. More than anything, that tiny bit of contact did me a heap of good. Just that reminder that I wasn't alone, and someone amazing loved me. I glanced over my shoulder to give her a grateful smile.

And somehow, somewhere, Mira and Bridget got their heads together, and before any of us realized just how it happened, Cam-short-for-Cameron had been invited along on our camping/paintball trip.

Oh how wonderful.

3

Nothing can put a dent in a man's dignity so quickly as being forced to parade around a doctor's examination room in nothing but a paper sheet. But after my injuries last spring, Mira insisted that I get Dr. Bridget's okay before I went traipsing off into the wilds of Colorado. So, here I was doing laps while my friend the doctor watched me critically.

Not that I mind good-looking women staring at me, normally. Dr. Bridget was curvy in all the right places, even in the tailored suit she was wearing for the day. Funny how she looked so different here at her office, her dark hair all pulled back and tamed, than at my house with her hair in pigtails and wearing shorts and a smart-ass T-shirt. The two sides of Dr. Bridget.

"Are you having any more pain?" She jotted down some notes in my file as I hopped back up on the table.

"Nope. Everything seems to be fully functional." Her hands were ice cold when she started groping my calf, and I jumped. "Geez, Bridge! Did you go juggle snowballs or something before coming in here?"

She smiled sweetly at me over the rims of her new glasses. "Iced them down just for you, Jesse dear."

The scars on my calf were still nicely pink and hairless, circles the size of fifty-cent pieces adorning both sides where a crab-demon had stabbed me last January. I didn't think that was a body-piercing fad that was going to catch on. Innocuous in appearance now, that wound had almost cost me my leg, the demon's poison invading my body despite all medical intervention. Only my wife's magic had kept me from having Stumpy as a nickname.

Of course, it was the torn muscle on the inside of that same leg that had landed me back in Dr. Bridget's office. That particular injury was earned by falling on my ass on a wet floor (speaking of bruised dignity). Well, and the running around fighting hellhounds and dodging tornados after that hadn't helped either.

But I'd been a good boy ever since, I promise! I'd given up walking with a cane (most of the time) only two months ago, and I'd been diligent with my physical therapy. I was hoping I'd get credit for time served.

I wasn't sure what Dr. Bridget was looking for with the poking and prodding, but she found it. Or didn't find it. Whichever one was the good one.

With a sigh, she stood up and leaned against the counter. "You know I'm not in favor of this trip, right?"

"You may have mentioned it once or a thousand times." I put on my best begging eyes. Hey, it works on Mira. Sometimes. "C'mon, Doc, please? Pleeeeeeease?"

She tried real hard not to laugh, and finally managed to keep it to an exasperated chuckle. "You have no shame, do you?"

"None."

"Yeah, I guess you can go. Just make sure you pay

attention, and if it starts hurting, take it easy. Go get dressed."

I gave a little "woo-hoo!" of celebration, and ducked into the tiny curtained alcove to get my pants back on. I expected to hear the door open and close as the good doctor left the room, and when that didn't happen, I knew she wasn't done with me. "Something on your mind, Bridge?"

"Mira says you're still not sleeping well."

"Why is it that I always seem to come up in conversation between you two?" Annoyance made the words a bit sharper than I'd meant. But dammit, why was my business everyone's business? *Deep breath, Jess. No reason to rip her head off, she's just doing her job.*

"She's worried about you." Even without seeing her, I could hear the frown in her voice. Part of it was the doctor in her, being irritated at a stubborn patient. Part of it was my wife's best friend, being pissed at me for upsetting said wife. "Are those sleeping pills not helping?"

Fully clothed, I pulled the curtain aside so I could at least look at her while we were talking. "Wouldn't know, I didn't take them."

She sighed again. "Jess—"

"No. Just, no. I'm not going to drug myself out of my gourd. It's not that bad." Truth was, I hated the fog the sleeping pills caused. I was still very aware that someone had tried to run me off the road last March. That person was still out there. I couldn't afford to be anything less than alert.

Of course, the lack of sleep wasn't helping that cause either. I always dreamed about my fights. It's just the way my brain processes my bizarre excuse for a life. But in the past few months, the nightmares were getting worse. One of them was being particularly persistent, and when that one ripped and clawed its way through my head, there was no sleeping for the rest of the night. I called him the Yeti. It was almost four years ago that I'd faced him, and while he hadn't killed me, I sure as hell hadn't gotten out unscathed. There wasn't a single night in the past month that I hadn't woken up in a panic, flailing against something that wasn't even there. In general, I was averaging about five hours a night. On a good night.

And doctor or not, it was none of her damn business. "Am I cleared for the trip?"

She eyed me for long moments, pursing her lips like she really wanted to say no, but eventually she nodded. "Yeah. Knock yourself out." With one last scribble in my file, we were done.

I was bending to lace up my combat boots when she paused again. "Hey, Jesse?" There was a change in her voice. Hard to describe, but in my mind it always signaled her change from Dr. Bridget, to just plain Bridge. I looked up. "Thanks for taking Cam along. It's been hard for him to meet folks here."

This was the moment in those strained conversations where you either continued the argument, or let it go. I took a deep breath and opted to let it go. Part of me was absurdly proud of myself over that. I offered her a small smile, showing her I had no hard feelings, before turning back to my bootlaces. "He met you, didn't he? How'd that happen?"

"Church." That made me chuckle, though I carefully hid it. I was not surprised at all.

Finished with my boots, I stood up, flipping my hair out of my face. "Well, just remember, he does anything hinky and I'll whup his ass. You just say the word."

The doctor chuckled, and even blushed a little. "Thanks, Jess." That even earned me a one-armed hug. Go me!

I followed her out to the front desk to do all the pertinent paperwork, signing my name with a flourish to celebrate my release from doctor's care. I hadn't had insurance for months, and while Dr. Bridget didn't really expect me to pay full price, I felt guilty about shorting her any. I mean, this was her livelihood. Not her fault insurance companies didn't cover demon slaying.

"Bridget!"

"Cam!" I looked up in time to see Cam-short-for-Cameron appear out of nowhere and sweep my doctor into a deep kiss. Quickly, I averted my eyes. Just . . . don't wanna see stuff like that, y'know? After a suspiciously long time, I heard her giggle—actually giggle!— and assumed it was safe to look up again.

"I thought I'd see if you had time to go to lunch, since I'm here." Mr. Romance. Ugh.

Bridget patted her dark hair back into place and straightened her shirt a little, blushing bright red. "Is Lisa done with you?"

The tall former priest nodded. "Clean bill of health. She says I should be able to get up and down the trail just fine." Finally, someone remembered I was standing there. "Oh! Hey, Jesse!"

"Cameron." I was polite. Civil. I even smiled. I just couldn't bring myself to greet him with the same kind of enthusiasm he showed me. I'm sure it was some kind of psychobabble alpha male BS, but . . . I still wasn't sold on Mr. Not-a-Priest. Not yet.

He looked my T-shirt over and chuckled. "TRUST ME, I'M A JEDI, hmm?"

"These are not the droids you're looking for." Look, I could joke, see? "You ready for tomorrow?"

"Yeah, looks like it. Marty said that he had some paintball equipment I could borrow. I've never played before, so I'm really looking forward to it." His dimples showed when he grinned. Could he look any more preppy?

"We're gonna head out real early in the morning, so be ready when we swing by."

He nodded. "Marty gave me all the details. It sounds like a lot of fun. It's great that his uncle lets you use his cabin."

Marty's uncle Douglas, though well beyond any age to go hiking into the wilds himself, was more than happy to let our bunch of miscreants crash there for a few days every year. We'd even made friends with the caretaker's family, and they'd be joining us once we got up there. It usually made for hijinks and hilarity.

"It's a goodly walk, but if I can make it up there, I'm sure you can." I tilted my head to look at his leg, though under his khaki slacks it was impossible to see what was causing the limp. "It didn't seem to hold you up any when you were at my place." Bridget slipped away while we talked, presumably tidying things up before her lunch, and inconveniently leaving me without a good way to escape. *Dammit!*

Cam nodded. "It's a lot better than it was when it first happened. I was on crutches for months." That at least I could sympathize with. When I didn't say anything else, he seemed compelled to fill the silence. "Car accident. Last spring." With one hand, he lifted his gelled spikes away from his forehead to reveal a small pink scar disappearing into his hair. "Head, meet windshield. I was lucky."

"I can tell." Obviously, he expected me to elaborate on my own injury. I didn't feel like it. "Well. Guess I'll see you in the morning."

"Sure thing!" He grinned at me with perfectly white teeth, and some small, petty part of me wanted to punch him in the mouth.

The good doctor chose that moment to join us again and I used it as my excuse to duck out.

Okay, he seemed like a good guy. A really good guy, and Dr. Bridget obviously had the hots for him big time. So why did I have the urge to snatch him up by the collar of his designer polo shirt and shake him like a rag doll?

The strangeness of my reaction bothered me the rest of the day, enough that I looked at my punk-haired boss halfway through my short shift at my real job and asked, "Am I an asshole?"

The music was blaring some kind of death-metal-techno crossbreed crap, and of course I had to repeat myself three or four times before she could hear me.

Kristyn grinned at me from under her locks of pumpkin-orange hair. "Is this an essay question?"

"Come on, I'm serious." I stuffed my armload of novelty T-shirts on the appropriate shelf and reached over to turn the music down. "I'm pretty easygoing, right? I don't fly off the handle for no reason, do I?"

There was a long pause there, one of those that answered more than her words could. "You've . . . had your moments, lately. Why?"

"Yeah, but . . . general grumpiness aside, do I normally dislike people immediately? I mean, I like to think I give people a chance, y'know?"

She paused to think that one over, clicking her tongue piercing across her teeth. "Nope. Normally, you are one of the mellowest people I know, old dude." She tilted her head curiously. "Why?"

"Just . . . thinking." I went back to rearranging the novelty wall, and she let it drop. I, on the other hand, couldn't.

I pondered on it all the way through a really domestic dinner with my wife and the kids (It was just easier to think of Estéban as ours. It saved time in the long run). I mean, I'm normally an easygoing guy. You don't bother me, I don't kick your ass. That kinda thing. But the events of last spring had changed me, and not for the better.

A guy tried to kill me. That was a given. Two people, actually, though only one of them remained at large. So I suppose I was entitled to a bit of natural wariness. But somewhere along the way, this cynical, borderline paranoid grouch took my place, and he was starting to annoy even me. I was trying to manage it through my usual meditations and katas, but . . . it wasn't working. So, was my reaction to Cam just a by-product of post-traumatic stress disorder, or was there really something wrong with the guy? God, I hated not trusting my own instincts.

Later that night, Mira and I lay in bed together, her head nestled in the crook of my neck where I could smell the strawberry-ness of her hair. Still bogged down in my brooding of the day, I mentioned my less than charitable feelings toward Cam-short-for-Cameron.

Mira chuckled softly, her breath warm on my chest. "It's like a new dog in your territory. Go sniff each other's butts, you'll be fine."

"That's . . . distinctly unappetizing." I tilted my head to look down at her and she gave me a grin. "But seriously, you don't get a weird vibe off of him or anything?"

She rolled her green eyes. "I don't scan every person that I run into, Jesse. Next thing I know, you'll be having Cole run a background check on the guy." I know my eyes lit up, and when I opened my mouth, she put her hand across it. "No. Do *not* do that."

There was a very disappointed little boy deep inside me. "But it would be cool!"

That earned me another roll of her eyes. "Leave it alone. This is the first guy Bridge has dated in forever, and I kinda like seeing her happy, okay? Try to get to know him before you call out the dogs."

My head flopped back to the pillow and I sighed. "I'm just being a jerk again, aren't I?"

"I wasn't going to say that . . ."

"You were thinking it." I rubbed my gritty eyes, trying not to think about all the sleep I would *not* be getting that night. "Maybe I should skip this trip. Stay home, get some sleep, do some stuff around the house."

Mira sat up and looked down at me, her wealth of sable, curly hair falling around my face like a curtain. "Jesse, I'm going to say something, and I want you to understand that it comes from a place of love, okay?"

Slightly worried, I said, "Okay?"

"If you don't get out of this house for a few days, I'm going to do you grievous bodily harm." She leaned down and kissed me once, then rolled over and turned off the bedside lamp.

In the darkness, we curled up together, both of us knowing it was only a matter of time before I woke us both with my nightmares and spent the rest of the night on the couch. Mira's fingers traced up and down my forearm where it rested across her waist, like she could memorize it just by touch.

She was right. I was being a jerk. I'd been a jerk all summer, touchy and quick to anger. Part of it I could chalk up to frustration at being injured, but . . . not all of it. I mean, I'd been hurt before, and worse. I'd been blown up, stitched together, taped down, and stapled shut. I couldn't blame it all on that.

Deep down, I knew it was the fear of the unknown.

It was the lingering mystery of who tried to run me off the road a few months ago, of where my last client had disappeared to after the tornado took us on our brief tour of Oz. It was the uncertainty, the inability to *do* anything. I was great with an enemy to fight. Just point me and I do the slice and dice thing. But with just doubts and what-ifs? Not so much.

That's where the dreams came from. Always the same one, with silver claws and red eyes materializing out of nothing, killing me again and again because I simply couldn't see it in time to save myself. He was the Yeti, and the ugly scars down the left side of my rib cage were only a small part of what he'd left me.

I'd tried to find something in my *bushido* texts, some snippet of wisdom or piece of advice to set me back on track. The *Hagakure* said that a samurai should never joke about being afraid, lest their true heart be revealed. Since humor was one of my chief defense mechanisms, I was pretty much screwed.

Of course, it also said that in order to ease nervousness, you should rub spit on your ears and kick everything in your path. Hadn't tried that yet. Maybe next week.

"What did he really want?" Out of the darkness, Mira's voice startled me, and I jumped a little. She sounded smaller somehow, and I held her tighter without really knowing why.

"Who, Cam?"

"No. Him. The . . . thing, yesterday."

"Ah." She wouldn't say a demon's name, not even the mocking one I'd assigned to him. But I knew who she meant. Last night, we'd carefully avoided mentioning Axel and his party crashing, but I guess my reprieve was over. "I don't know. Like I said, he was being weird, even for him."

"What did he say?"

I frowned a little, though she couldn't see it. "Not much. He seemed really excited that I was going on vacation. Enthusiastic, even." Too enthusiastic. Yet another thing that had bothered me ever since.

"How do you feel about that?" Her hand was still stroking up and down my arm, and it finally occurred to me that she was looking for goose bumps. I was and always would be the magic-less wonder, but my early-warning system was finely tuned.

"I don't know. My first instinct is to do exactly the opposite of whatever makes him happy. But then I think, maybe that's what he *wants* me to do, and I should go after all, and then I get all confused after that." I nuzzled her ear a little, hoping to distract her. "Ignore him. He's a douche."

She turned in my arms, facing me though neither of us could see in the darkened room. "You'd tell me, right? If you thought something was wrong, you'd tell me?" Her fingers stroked through my hair, combing the strands out straight over and over.

I had to think long and seriously about that. Lying by omission had become all too easy for me of late, and I'd promised myself that I wouldn't do it anymore—not to her. So, was something wrong?

I really thought about it, bringing Axel's face to the front of my mind, rolling the idea of the vacation trip through my head. There was no twisting of my innards, no painfully cold goose bumps along my arms. Just my natural antidemon revulsion where Axel was concerned.

"I got nothing, baby. No shivers, no nothing. I think we're okay. Besides, you've got like fifty layers of protective spells on me. What could happen?" That seemed to appease her and we both settled down to sleep.

Well, Mira settled down to sleep. I lay awake, watching the streetlight outside cast weird shadows through the blinds and replaying the strange conversation with Axel over and over. My brain kept coming back to one sentence again and again.

"We always come back, Jesse."

Then the goose bumps came, peppered over my skin like tiny needles of ice. I didn't know why that one statement triggered my danger-sense, but I was pretty sure I'd get a chance to find out.

4

Morning comes damn early on two hours' sleep, especially when "morning" starts at three a.m. But we had a long drive ahead of us, and the early bird gets the . . . oh screw it. It was freakin' early.

I kissed Mira's forehead and slipped out of bed without waking her. Bonus points for me. I'd packed the night before, and left my clothes in the living room so I could dress without waking anyone else.

Walking down the hallway, I poked my head into Annabelle's room. It took me a moment to locate her head of red curls, pillowed between a giant pink frog and a worn wolf plushie. Even in the darkness, I could see the faintest pink tint to her cheeks, her face flushed with the heat of sleep like kids' do. Aside from her coloring, strawberry blond hair and blue eyes, she was the image of her mother, right down to the shape of her mouth and her pert little nose. She was the most beautiful thing in the world.

"Sleep well, button. Be good for Mommy," I whispered, then moved on.

The only other thing I really needed to do *would* involve waking someone, but considering that someone was living in my house rent free, I figured ten minutes of lost sleep wouldn't hurt him.

Our spare bedroom had been converted from Mira's

personal sanctuary into Estéban's room when he came
to live with us. Not that the kid had much, but he'd put
up a few posters, and some letters from home were
taped to the wall above his bed.

Unfortunately, Mira's computer was still set up in
there, mostly for the kid to work on his homework.
(Mira was a stickler about grades. Who knew?) But it
was also how I kept contact with the other champions, like myself. And since Estéban was nominally
one too, he was allowed to peep at my conversations.
A little.

Mira's brand-new, custom-built computer had enough
lights and whizzers on it to light up the entire room, so
I didn't bother with flipping the overhead on. I parked
myself in front of the green glowing monitor and proceeded to jump through seven kinds of hoops to finally
access the Web site I was after in the first place. Our
Webmaster was downright paranoid when it came to
security.

Just because I could, I left the volume up when the
sentry-bot screamed "BOOBIES!" at supersonic deci-
bels.

Estéban said something like "Grnf?" and rolled
over, yanking his comforter over his head.

The Webcam window popped up on the screen, and
I smirked at Viljo. "Boobies, hmm?"

"I thought you were Estéban." The hacker-turned-
Web-security-expert rattled around on his keyboards
without even looking up at his screen. "I do not want
him surfing for porn on my baby, and he is surprisingly easy to embarrass."

Due to unexpected motherboard meltdown a few months ago, we'd been forced to replace Mira's old computer. Viljo had taken great pride and care in building this new monstrosity before us.

"But enough of that, down to business. Password?" He finally peered at his screen, eyes narrowing suspiciously. The wispy mustache he'd been trying to grow for the better part of a year looked like it might actually have enough hair now to warrant shaving. Or at least a good plucking.

"Viljo, you're looking right at me. It's me." The new computer came with a shiny new Webcam. I wasn't sure how I felt about that, yet. The improved technology did confirm that Viljo really was as pasty as I'd always thought, though, and that his dyed black hair was even stringier.

"Do not care, new protocols. Password?"

"Viljo, I'm going to come through this computer and kick your ass." Which was, oddly, my password. "And shouldn't it be pass *phrase*?"

"Password accepted. Hold on to your socks." Viljo hit a few keys, and suddenly my computer screen blossomed into sights and sounds and colors not known to mortal man. Okay, not really, but that's how he wanted me to feel about it.

I hunt-and-pecked my sign-in ID into the right fields and finally got logged into Grapevine, flipping to the ITINERARY tab. "I'm gonna be out of town for a few days, Vil, and nowhere near a computer."

"Does Ivan know you're going?"

"I mentioned it, a long time ago, but I doubt he remembers. That's why I'm filling out the nice little form, right?" I was almost thirty-three years old. I was fully capable of leaving the house without "daddy's" permission.

Don't get me wrong. I have the utmost respect for Ivan Zelenko and the network of champions he has created out of nothing. Without Ivan's knowledge and training, most of us would have been dead years ago. But I draw the line at letting him govern my "off hours."

"Business or pleasure?"

"Pleasure, in theory. Camping trip with my buddies."

The computer geek paused in his furious typing and blinked at me, owl-eyed. "Like . . . outside?"

"Yes, with the big glowing ball of death in the sky. Y'know, the sun?"

He snorted. "Now you are just making words up."

I had to chuckle. I highly doubted that Viljo was as blatantly stereotypical as he pretended to be, but he still made me laugh with some of his nerd outrage. "I'm gonna be in your neck of the woods, actually. Just west of Fort Collins." Viljo was hunkered down somewhere south of my impending vacation, near Pikes Peak last I knew.

"I will be sure to wave in your general direction, from safely within my tightly closed curtains."

I finished updating my expected whereabouts— after last spring, I was damn lucky they didn't want me to let them know when I went to piss—and hit

SEND. "I should be back on Saturday. If I'm not, send in the cavalry."

"Will do." Viljo grumbled to himself. "Not like I am doing anything else at the moment."

Work technically done, I settled in the comfy chair for a chat. "Still slow?"

"Not a single contract since April, across the board. Nothing for me to do but sit here and polish my connectors."

That sounded . . . never mind how that sounded. "There have been dead spells before though, right?"

Viljo shook his head, his matte black hair falling down into his eyes until he pushed it back irritably. "Not like this. And even the two contracts in April were negotiated long before the incident. So really, there have been no new ones since . . ."

"The incident." That's what we were calling it now. He really meant since Miguel and Guy died. Two champions down in the space of a month, and it would have been three if it hadn't been for major luck, and (I was fully willing to admit) Estéban's timely arrival. Six months since I banished the thing that stalked them, killed them. Tried to kill me. And not a peep out of a demon in all that time. Axel didn't count.

"What's Ivan got to say about it?" I hadn't heard from our revered leader-ish person in a couple of months, and even when I did talk to him, he kept things pretty close to the vest. It was just his way.

The geek shook his head, frowning pensively. "He

does not say much, anymore. I think he is worried, but I do not know about what."

Yeah, I got the same feeling from the old man, but trying to get him to talk was like hugging a rabid wolverine. You could do it, but you wouldn't like what came next. "Maybe I'll try and poke him a little, when I get back."

"Would you? I would appreciate that." There was very real relief in Viljo's voice, and it occurred to me suddenly just how very devoted the little geek was to our Ivan. "Is Estéban going with you on your vacation?"

"No, he's staying here to hold down the fort." I glanced back at the sleeping lump in the bed, trying to decide if he was really asleep, or just faking. I finally settled on faking. No one really snored that evenly. "Listen, if he tries to log in a contract while I'm gone, send someone to find me, okay? He's not ready yet." *Yeah, kid, hear that? I'm always watching you.* I felt rather pleased with myself at being two steps ahead of the kid.

"I do not know who I would send, but I will do something." Windows on my computer screen started shutting down on their own. Viljo was obviously done with our conversation.

A thought occurred to me, belatedly. "Hey, Vil?" He looked up. "Have the Knights Stuck-up-idus had any contracts?"

The geek pursed his lips thoughtfully. "I have not talked to Father Gregory in some months. I do not know. I will try to find out if you think it is important?"

"Yeah. Just . . . call it morbid curiosity." The Order of St. Silvius—holy knights operating in the name of a Catholic saint who did not exist—wasn't what you'd call friendly with us, the more secular champions. Still, if prodded, they'd usually share information. I wondered if they were having the same dry spell as the rest of us.

"Have a good trip, Jesse."

"Thanks." The Grapevine window shut down, redirecting me to some site with nauseatingly cute kittens and poorly spelled captions. I sat in the semidarkness for a few more moments, scratching at the beard stubble on my chin.

Estéban's sheets rustled as he rolled over to look in my direction. "What does it mean, that no one has been asked for a contract?"

I shrugged my shoulders at the little faker. "Dunno. Maybe nothing. Maybe we scared them all off." Fat chance.

Estéban knew that as well as I did. The kid's family had been fighting demons for more generations than I could even imagine. Between his mom and Ivan, we had at our fingertips an amazing catalogue of demon knowledge, and at no point in history had they all just . . . vanished. I'd asked.

"Maybe you shouldn't go. Maybe you should stay here."

"Why, you scared?" I had to grin at the instant frown I got from him. He was so easy to mess with.

"Someone should be here to take care of Miss Mira, and Annabelle."

"That's what you're for, isn't it?" I stood up, cross-ing the few steps to roughly mess up his hair. "You take care of them for me, Estéban. Like the big bad champion I know you're gonna be someday." Some-day would be never, if I got my way, but the grave duty seemed to appease him. "And since you're awake, roll out. We're gonna go do forms."

He grumbled and retreated under his pillow again, but while I gathered up the weapons, he clambered out of bed and met me out in the front yard. Something else we'd worked on over the summer, the idea that he could expect lessons at any time of the day or night, rain or shine, sleepy or not.

Sometimes, I wondered what my neighbors must think of us. There we were at oh-dark-thirty, out in the front yard waving blades around like a couple of luna-tics, the kid in just his pajama pants and bare feet de-spite the early-morning chill.

Estéban's weapon of choice was a machete, passed down through his family for . . . Well, I had no idea how long. Suffice to say that he had at least two broth-ers and a father who had used it before him. He had two younger brothers waiting to take it up when the inevitable happened.

The metal of his blade was dark with age and use, only the edge gleaming brightly where he kept it honed to a razor-sharp finish. The grip had been wrapped in leather so long that the original layers had rotted away and just been covered over with more, sweat and grime melting it into a hard finish. It was a blade with personality, with life in it. Not unlike mine in its own way.

She wasn't anything spectacular. She'd been one of Marty's earlier works, when he first started his whole weapon-crafting experiment. Just a plain blade of polished steel, with blemishes where we'd had to grind out hard-won nicks. The guard was an octagon of solid brass. The pommel was brass too, and heavy enough to crack a skull if need be. The hilt was wrapped in cord of my favorite blue. This sword and I, we'd been through a lot, and I trusted her with my life.

Together, Estéban and I moved through various katas, both of us slender to the point of scrawny, but him a taller, darker shadow to myself. The kid had picked up the forms easily, I'll give him that. His technique wasn't quite as polished as mine, but I'd been doing it for years compared to his six months. I'd give him a couple more before I started hounding him about it.

We'd had to adapt a few things for his shorter blade, but if his arms kept growing the way they were, he'd make up for the difference in reach in no time. I watched him from the corner of my eye as we blocked, parried, struck, all in slow motion. His dark brows were drawn in concentration, eyes fixed on his feet. Without breaking stride, I spun and swatted him across the ass with the flat of my sword. "Eyes up! Unless you're fighting some foot fungus demon I don't know about."

He growled, jerking his head up, but corrected his posture instantly.

I slid back into the proper place in the kata without really thinking about it. "Tell me the way of the warrior." This too was part of the kid's education. If he was going to learn to fight, he'd learn to fight my way. He'd follow the *bushido*. And this was how I'd been trained back in the day, working my mind and my body at the same time. I often quizzed him while we sparred or ran katas.

"The way of the warrior is the brave acceptance of death." His movements faltered for just a moment as he wracked his brain for the correct information. "That's in *The Book of Five Rings*, by Miyamoto Musashi."

"Right. It's also found in the *Hagakure*." The next move put his back to me, and I eyed his stance critically. Not too bad. So far. "How many times should you be rōnin, according to the *Hagakure*?"

"Seven." That answer came immediately. "Fall seven times, get up eight."

"And what does that mean?"

"It means . . . it means if you don't learn to deal with the bad times, you won't learn how to get back up from them. If you fall, you always get back up."

Very good. His brain was working pretty good, considering that I'd rousted him out of bed. Now, how were his reflexes? With a small grin, I slipped up behind him and thrust my scabbard between his feet.

Instead of tripping, he picked up his right foot and spun on his left, landing in a crouch with his machete pinning the scabbard to the damp grass. He smirked at me. "Gotcha."

I smiled, nodding my approval. "This time." We both stood, bowing from the waist to each other. "Go get a little more sleep—you've got school in a couple hours."

Estéban hesitated a moment, but finally nodded. "Have a good trip."

"Thanks." He disappeared back inside, leaving me alone on the lawn. With nothing else to do but wait, I went through a few more katas on my own. It felt good, the balanced weight in my hands, the smooth glide across the grass. It centered me. I needed centering.

Marty was supposed to pick me up around four thirty, but it was nearly five when the ancient Suburban pulled into my driveway. I gave my buddy a questioning look as I went to toss my gear in the back.

"Two friggin' tires were flat this morning, man."

"You drive through a construction zone or something?"

"Nah, there was nothing in them. More like someone let the air out. I had to air them back up." He half hung out the window to talk to me as I walked past. "Then dumbass over here, his alarm didn't go off." Will, sitting in the front passenger seat, winced as Marty punched him in the shoulder (I'm guessing not for the first time).

"Well, maybe we're getting all the bad luck out of the way at the beginning, hmm?" I swung the back doors open wide and was greeted by a giant muzzle full of slobbering wet tongue. "Gah!"

Duke, Marty's behemoth of an English mastiff,

slurped up my cheek and wiggled in happiness so hard that the entire truck shook. "Marty! What's the monster doing here?" It was almost impossible to defend myself with my hands full, so I got drenched again as I was tossing my backpack in with the rest of the gear. "Ugh, off! Sit, Duke!"

Obediently, the brindle mastiff sat, and the springs on the truck jounced a little.

Marty turned around to holler over the seats. "Mel was trying to walk him last night, and he accidentally knocked her down. I didn't think it was safe to leave her alone with him, in her condition."

Now, that may sound like Duke is some slavering machine of destruction, but in reality he was the biggest teddy bear I'd ever seen. He let Annabelle ride him, for Pete's sake. But I could totally see how the big lummox could barrel over someone in his affectionate enthusiasm. He'd be totally devastated if he realized he'd hurt someone. He was just that kinda dog.

"Why'd he knock her down?" It took some doing, but I got a very enthusiastic Duke shoehorned back inside and managed to shut the doors.

Marty fired up the old diesel engine and backed out of my drive. "She said he was after a squirrel."

Duke's breath was hot on the back of my neck as I tried to get settled in the middle seat. "Your dog's afraid of squirrels, man." And birds, and mice, and thunder, and his own shadow . . .

"Maybe he's growing up on me."

"Dude, if he gets any bigger, I'm planting a flag on him and claiming him in the name of Spain."

We managed to pick up Cole without incident, and he brought with him a thermos of police-station sludge, otherwise known as his self-brewed coffee. We all politely declined and tried to ignore the distinctive aroma of scorched coffee beans that filled the truck. (I swear, I caught Duke pawing at his nose and whining.)

Last on the list to fetch was Cam-short-for-Cameron, and while the guys decided to rearrange the packs in the back to make room for one more, I was elected to go up and fetch the ex-priest. Ex-almost-priest? Whatever.

The apartment building was one of a dozen similar buildings within view, one of those identical little enclaves where I was certain people walked into the wrong apartment all the time by mistake. It was a place for college students, recent newlyweds (I should know, I'd been one once), and itinerate drug dealers. Cheap, easy to get in, easy to abandon.

Of course, Cameron's apartment was on the fourth floor, and there was no elevator. I hiked up the four flights of stairs, grumbling under my breath and watching the chipped concrete under my boots warily. If one of those steps gave way, the rusted-out railing wasn't going to save me. When was the last time this place had even seen a maintenance man?

There was no door marked 4D, but I took a chance and knocked on the blank door across from 4C. I was ready for anything when the door opened, but thankfully, it was just Cameron.

His smile looked almost relieved. "I was starting to worry about you guys."

"Yeah, Marty had some car trouble." Cam stepped back and I took that as an invitation to come on inside.

I crossed the threshold and almost tripped over my own two feet in surprise. Tiny prickles rose up on my skin as I passed through the doorway, the hairs on my arms standing at attention. I waved my hand back and forth through the open space once or twice, feeling a distinct barrier glide up and down my arm. I recognized that sensation; I felt it every day when I went in and out of my own house. It was the feeling of magical wards, a protective spell set up to keep the bad things out and the good things safe.

Trying to be casual, I bent down to tie my boot and rubbed a finger across the floor. It felt faintly gritty. Salt, maybe? Mira used salt sometimes. Or it could have been just plain old street dirt. Only one way to be sure, and in this neighborhood, there was no way I was gonna taste it. It could just as easily be meth or rat poison, too.

If Cameron noticed my sudden distraction, he didn't say, only gathering up his stuff with quiet efficiency. "How long a drive is it going to be?"

"Um . . . normally, about ten hours. But Marty had to bring his dog, so I imagine we'll be stopping more often."

There was no way to tell who set those wards. They could have been left by the previous owner, for all I knew. Once you knew what to look for, it's actually amazing how many people manifest some basic magical ability without truly realizing it. And Mira had said

A SHOT IN THE DARK

that thresholds were the easiest things in the world to ward. Granted, without someone to keep them up, they'd fade away eventually, but if the previous owner hadn't been gone very long . . . maybe . . .

Still, maybe I needed to pay more attention to my new "friend." I stood up and turned a critical eye on the man, and his apartment.

Cameron himself looked obsessively neat. His dark hair was gelled into very fashionable (I'm sure) spikes. He had on jeans that were obviously brand-new, and a pair of hiking boots that probably just came straight out of the box. That was going to cost him some blisters on this hike. His shirt was still a button-up, but in plaid this time. Next to my I LIKE YOU, I'LL KILL YOU LAST T-shirt, he looked positively refined.

Aside from him, there wasn't much to see. The apartment was largely empty, even for a bachelor's pad. The carpet was typical renter brown, worn and matted from years of foot traffic. The linoleum at the front door was some generic shade of hide-the-dirt.

There was a lawn chair in what passed for the living room, and one of those do-it-yourself coffee tables. That small piece of furniture was covered in neat piles of books, but the only one I could see well was the enormous Bible on the top of the stack.

There was no TV, and I couldn't see into the tiny kitchen to see if there were any dishes in the sink. Through what I assumed was the bedroom door, I could see an inflatable air mattress, bare of any sheets. No posters. No pictures. No half-broken beer light on the wall. No smell. Every lived-in place has its own smell, the scent of the person who lives there, of their food and their cologne and the mustiness of their books. This place was sterile, untouched except for the faint aroma of whatever cleaner they'd scrubbed the place down with between tenants.

This wasn't a bachelor's apartment. This was the apartment of someone who expected to bail on short notice.

"Pretty pathetic, isn't it?" Cam shouldered his backpack, and apparently noticed my critique of his home. "Right before I moved, there was a fire. Lost everything."

"That sucks, man. A car wreck, then a fire? What universal power did you piss off?" It didn't . . . feel right. I had no reason to think the man was lying to me, and yet . . .

"I know, right? But hey, it saved me on moving costs." He grinned and shrugged. It was charming, disarming . . . and something cold slithered across the back of my neck. Not quite my danger sense blaring, but it was at least perking up and taking notice. Hm.

"Always look on the bright side, I guess." I led the way back out the door, watching as Cam stopped to lock it behind us.

There was no pause in his movement, no indication that he felt anything strange at all. Granted, most humans wouldn't know the wards were there. They'd light up like neon for a magic user but most people would go about their merry way, none the wiser.

For me, caught somewhere between magic and mule, it was like having my nose pressed against the glass of a five-star restaurant. I could see it, smell it, but actually having any? Not so much. The feast was there, tantalizingly just out of reach.

Ivan and Mira both insisted that my magic ability was just buried, but I had my doubts. Just because the rest of the champions had mojo didn't mean all of us had to. Right? So far, I'd done just fine without it.

It did occur to me on the way down the stairs, that regardless of who had set the protective spells, Cameron passed in and out of them unharmed. I guess that had to count in his favor.

And he had no tattoos. I remembered that from the barbecue. Now, most of my buddies had ink. Mine, the first two lines of the *Tao Te Ching* tattooed down each biceps. Marty's, full sleeves of stylized Celtic animals. Will's, a hookah-smoking caterpillar not visible without him taking off more clothes than anybody was comfortable with. Those things I didn't care about. Those were safe tattoos. Normal tattoos.

But there were some I always, *always*, took a second look at. Tribal markings especially, the black vines and barbed wire that were so popular a few years ago. I look, because sometimes, just sometimes, those tattoos would wriggle under my vision, like heat waves off asphalt. They'd twist until my brain ached from trying to follow the impossible knots and whorls. Those were demon brands, marking someone who had sold their soul.

Oh yes, I checked for tattoos now. People passing me on the sidewalk, customers that came into the store, random drivers next to me at stoplights. I looked for that telltale smudge of black on the inner left arm. Because you just never know.

But Cameron had been wearing shorts and short sleeves at the house, and there had been no incriminating black scrawls on his skin. His arms were perfectly clean, like every other aspect of his life.

You're getting paranoid. Yeah, well, that didn't mean they weren't out to get me.

5

*M*y breath fogged the air in front of me, misting my eyes until I blinked them clear. My hand was numb on the hilt of my sword. I had to assume it was still there, because I could no longer feel the wrapping cord against my palm. "Quit stalling. I know you're there."

The red eyes gleamed in the darkness, always out of the corner of my eye, never where I could get a good bead on it. I knew what it was. I knew it would come from a direction I never expected. The dream never changed.

Even knowing I was dreaming, I was trapped there for the duration. I knew that too. Trapped in the darkness, in the silence, senses straining for the slightest hint, for the tiniest warning that would never come. "Come on! Come get me!" My voice echoed against . . . something. Unseen walls, penning me in place. Confining me with . . . that.

There was the faintest sound to my left, the sound of something soft, sliding across a smooth surface. Fur on stone. Knowing it was a mistake, I turned anyway, my dream self compelled to walk suicidally into the attack like every other night. My eyes straining against the blackness, I braced for a charge from the front.

And it came from behind. It always came from behind. No matter where I looked, what I heard, it was always behind me. Silver claws, gleaming in a light that had no source, sank through the links of my mail armor. Fangs sank into my *neck and shoulder, ravaging flesh for the sheer joy of causing pain. It lifted me above its massive head like so much luggage, and it bellowed its triumph. Ribs cracked and broke under its viselike grip. Things in my chest burst under the immense pressure. I choked on my own blood, drowning in it.*

The white-furred muzzle invaded my vision, the black nose quivering as it sniffed me all over. There was a guttural chuckle from deep within the barrel chest. With a negligent heave, it tossed me away, my body flailing helplessly through the air. I fell forever . . .

Waking from that dream was always a jolt, but this time I managed to stop myself from screaming. Instead, my eyes snapped open, and I kept my ragged gasp to a nicely controlled inhale. No one around me would be the wiser. My hand found the rigid line of scars that went down my left side from armpit to hip, and I rubbed the thick tissue, easing away aches that weren't really there.

The black lanes of the highway rushed by the window, the glass just inches from the tip of my nose. The hum of the tires was a blessedly mundane background noise, normal and totally based in the real world. I clung to that for a few moments, forcing my mind to embrace reality and reject the craziness in my own head. Even knowing it was only a dream, I couldn't suppress a shudder, and part of me still felt the warm, thick trickle of my own blood down my neck.

No . . . wait . . . Something warm and thick *was* trickling down my neck. "Ew, augh! Get off, you nasty beast!" With a canine grumble, Duke turned his drooling self around and squeezed between the piles of luggage in the back to lay down.

"Duke! Sit!" Marty snapped, a bit belatedly, from the driver's seat. The dog just sighed as if to say, "I *am* sitting."

"Have a nice nap, did we?" Beside me, Cole smirked in my direction.

I rubbed my face, trying to get the grit out of my eyes. "How long was I out?"

"Half an hour, maybe? Not long."

Damn. This was going to be a long friggin' trip.

A samurai, a blacksmith, a cop, a paramedic, and a priest all cram into a beat-up old Suburban and head for the Colorado Rockies. It sounded like a bad joke, but it was my life. And I was stuck in it for a twelve-hour road trip.

Other than my brief exchange with Cole, silence reigned in the cramped vehicle, not our usual modus operandi at all. In fact, I couldn't remember the last time Will went this long without babbling about anything and everything that popped into his head. I blamed Cameron, sitting on the end of the seat farthest from me. He kept his nose buried in a book—a *book* for Pete's sake! Who takes a book on a paintball/camping trip??—oblivious to the guilt I'd assigned him.

Cole caught the look and elbowed me in the side with a scowl. I shrugged. This was *not* my fault, dammit. It was Mira's, or Dr. Bridget's or . . . *not* my idea.

It didn't help that the crisp morning had given way to a hot and muggy day—not unusual for the first week of September on the great wide Kansas plains, but still unpleasant. Once we got to the mountains, I knew it would cool down, but being wedged into the Suburban with no air conditioning was miserable at the moment. We all smelled like sweaty dog. I tilted my head to glance at Cole's watch. Only eight hours left to go. Great. I got up before the butt crack of dawn for this?

My head ached already, and my stomach did a slow roll, expressing its displeasure. Long car trips had never agreed with me, at least when I wasn't driving. The heat, the constant motion, terrifying nightmares . . . Yeah, it was no wonder I wasn't feeling top-notch. And of course, my general discomfort with Cameron's presence didn't help either.

Y'know, I could have just asked the guy. *"Hey, you happen to cast any magic spells lately?"* Definitely would have been an icebreaker. But you don't just go saying that kind of stuff to people. And while trying to figure out a way to tactfully drop that question into conversation, I'd fallen asleep.

Cole elbowed me again. "They'll be fine. Would you relax? This is supposed to be a fun trip."

I was puzzled for a moment, before realizing that he assumed my antisocial demeanor was from worrying about Mira and Annabelle. True, it *had* been my chief argument for skipping this trip altogether. And I *was* worried about them a little.

Estéban was there, to be sure, but despite what training he'd had with me over the summer, he was just a kid. Sometime in the last few months, he'd remembered he was only seventeen. He'd discovered girls, and music, and cars (after I taught him to drive). He was athletic enough, and devoted to our lessons, but he really lacked discipline. Despite my promise to teach him as best I could, any lack of focus on his part was actually fine with me. If I could keep him away from the demon-slaying profession, so much the better.

Even though I'd given him the responsibility of watching over my family, it made me nervous that he was their only means of physical protection. What could he really do, hormone something to death?

I grunted in response to Cole and stared out the window, watching the lines of I-70 go whipping past. My brother was most likely right. The summer had been quiet. No one tried to run me off the road; no one tried to hack my computer. No body-hopping demons had showed up in my backyard to taunt and heckle me (well, until a couple of days ago). I hadn't had any phone calls from potential clients since the disaster back in March. No one had. To anyone on the outside, these were all good things!

Part of me felt like an idiot for being such an old worrywart. It wasn't like I was the only guy who left family at home. Cole's ailing son was valiantly starting kindergarten, like Anna, and Marty's wife Melanie was six months along with their first. Neither of them were obsessing about it. Just me and the knot in my stomach. Of course, no one had tried to kill either of them in the last year or so. I'd had more close calls than I liked to think about.

You know how that one guy in the Western who

always says the place is *too* quiet? Yeah, that's how I felt. Something was brewing, it just hadn't come to the surface yet. And the farther we got away from home, the more it tickled at the back of my mind, an insidious little whisper that said, *"We always come back, Jesse."*

"Rest stop!" Will announced from the front, and even I could feel a twinge of relief. I just needed to get out of the truck and away from my thoughts.

We all piled out, everyone stretching and groaning including the dog. The five of us made an interesting troupe. You had me in all my wiry-scrawny glory with my shoulder-length blond ponytail and the beginnings of scruffy red beard stubble.

Shorter than me by a good foot, Marty's head was shaved totally bald, and he'd cut the sleeves off his T-shirt to show off his ink. At least he wore cargo pants today instead of his usual kilt.

Will's curly hair was pulled back in a ponytail, and he took a moment to wipe the smudges off his thick glasses. My height, probably, though a good seventy-five pounds heavier if not more. Wicked smart, though he did a bumbling idiot impression really well.

Cole . . . well, Cole looked like a cop, and there was no way out of it. Clean cut, clean shaven, perfect posture, good boy. That's my little brother.

And of course, Cam-short-for-Cameron, who was trying to make lumberjack into the new fall chic.

Marty tossed me the end of Duke's leash and vanished in the direction of the restrooms. How exactly did I get elected official dog walker? By the time I pondered that for a moment, the guys had vanished, leaving me and Duke alone.

The big goofball gave me his best pleading look and leaned against the leash just enough to get his message across. *I gotta go, boss!*

That was all well and good, but I suddenly realized this was a chance to do a little snooping. Cam's backpack was on top of the pile. Maybe I could just peek inside, real quick like. "Hang on, boy, Uncle Jesse's being a bad person."

The backpack itself was brand-new, still stiff with creases in it from where it had been boxed at the store. Glancing around once, on the lookout for the guys coming back, I unzipped it and went poking.

Jeans, jeans, socks, more socks, two shirts, boxers—ew! I grimaced and kept pawing my way past someone else's underwear down into the depths of the bag. And I came up with nothing. No esoteric trinkets, no mystery bottles or vials. Nothing sent any tingles along my skin, evidence of magic derring-do.

Duke, not nearly as fascinated with my detective work as I was, tugged harder on the leash, whining softly.

"Hang on, almost done." Each garment was tidily folded; it was easy enough to get everything back in the pack like I'd never touched it. Easier that than explaining to Cam why I was rummaging around in his drawers.

The spell hadn't been his. Couldn't have been. I'd never seen a magic user yet, my wife included, who didn't carry something on their person, some shard of their own power. Sometimes it was a talisman, sometimes it was just tools of the trade. Hell, even with no magic to call my own, I carried charms and spells with me almost all the time, courtesy of Mira.

Mira's was her pentacle necklace. Miguel's had been a gold hoop earring in his left ear. Estéban's was a silver ring on his pinkie finger. Ivan's was the gold cross he wore religiously, pardon the pun.

A cross . . . Did Mr. Not-a-Priest wear a cross? I tried to picture Cam in my head, but couldn't pull up that particular detail. It would be fitting, and magic passed for faith often enough . . . Okay, so it was looking like he wasn't responsible, but I couldn't rule him out completely. I'd have to get a better look.

Duke butted his head against my hip, rocking me. "All right, all right. Let's do this." I tucked Cam's pack back in with the rest—mine had a suspicious damp spot, and I gave the dog the evil eye—and we went in search of facilities.

I found a nice big patch of grass, suitable for the occasion, and a very relieved Duke did his business quickly. I cleaned it up like a good citizen, but there was nothing in the world that would compel me to get back into that truck before I absolutely had to. Every part of me was stiff.

Glancing around, I realized I had a fairly decent open area and I decided to stretch out. Sword katas were all well and good—those I do for love. But to get myself limbered up, there were a few others I could run through real quick, work the kinks out of my muscles and joints.

Duke cocked his head in puzzlement as I looped his lead around my wrist, and set about going through a few slow stretches. I could feel my muscles loosening immediately, and for a few moments, I closed my eyes and just flowed through the motions. It was so easy to lose myself in the movements.

"Am I interrupting?" Cam-short-for-Cameron's voice made me open my eyes, and I very nearly came around swinging. Thankfully, the ex-priest didn't notice, more intent on feeding half his ham sandwich to the dog. "I thought he might be hungry."

Duke scarfed it down in one bite, then looked hopefully at his new best friend. Cam chuckled and rubbed the dog's head. In my mind, I glared at the mutt for being a traitor. "Um, I heard Marty and Will talk about leaving you here for being grumpy. They are joking, right?"

This was my chance, I realized, to get a better look at our new buddy. I finished the kata with one last motion, a slow spin that ended in a low crouch, then stood up with a hop. Was Cameron wearing a necklace? Couldn't tell. Stupid collared shirt. "Nope. We left Cole at a rest stop for two hours one time before we came back to get him." I tugged Duke's lead and got him moving. "But Marty won't leave the mutt, so I'm not too worried."

Cam blinked and followed me back to the Suburban. "I don't think I got a chance to thank you for inviting me along. I still don't have a lot of friends in the area."

I gave a noncommittal shrug. He knew he was here

only because my wife insisted. No point in rubbing his nose in it. "Hope you have a good time. It's a long hike up there, but the cabin is nice and we always have a ton of fun running around like loonies in the woods."

"And by the way, do you have any supernatural powers at your disposal? Just one of those questions I ask everyone." Somehow, I just couldn't make that conversation sound sane, even in my own head.

"Still, I know this is kinda your time with your buddies. I do appreciate it." Thankfully, he went back to eating his sandwich, and that was the end of the touchy-feely stuff. It was also the end of my chance to question him alone, and I mentally kicked myself as I got Duke loaded back into the truck.

It's impossible to leave someone at the rest stop when they beat you back to the vehicle. Marty and Will were visibly disappointed to find Duke and me firmly ensconced in our seats when they got back, and Cole smirked at me as he slid in beside me. "Cam narced, didn't he?"

"Yup."

In the front seat, Will and Marty exchanged devilish looks. I had a feeling Cam-short-for-Cameron was getting left at the next rest stop. I think he felt it too, 'cause he didn't make any effort to leave the car for the rest of the trip. Dude wasn't stupid, I'll give him that.

Needless to say, I wasn't going to get out of the car either, and that effectively trapped Cole between us. He wasn't going to be the happiest of campers by the time we got to Colorado.

I have to say that Kansas is very flat. And very uni-
form. Mile five looked just like mile five hundred and
five, and the only thing that changed was the fact that
we lost the music radio stations about halfway across
the state. That left us with only the news chatter one,
and after more tales of woe—everything from floods
to wildfires to revolutions—Marty reached over and
snapped it off. All that remained was the sound of
Duke snoring, and the engine growling.

Finally, the silence became unbearable, and Will
broke. "So, how do you *almost* become a priest?"

Cam stuck his finger in his book so he could answer.
"Well, I was about two weeks away from taking my
vows, and I realized it just wasn't for me. I still believe
in God, but . . . I wasn't meant for the priesthood. I told
them so, and I walked away."

"So what do you do now?"

Cam actually hesitated a moment before answering.
"I handle acquisitions for the library system."

Will turned all the way around in his seat, almost
getting choked by the seat belt to do so. "Wait, wait . . .
You're a librarian?"

"Well . . . sort of."

We tried. I'll swear on anything you like, we really
did try. But Marty broke out in snickers first, which set
Will off, and then . . . Yeesh. Just so you won't think
we're all heartless bastards, Cam laughed right along
with us.

"Yeah, it sounds a bit . . . lame. But I do like my job."
He shrugged and grinned a little.

"There's things to be said about doing a job you

love, no matter what anyone thinks." Everyone agreed with me there, and the awkwardness seemed to ease in the truck. Will grilled Cam about things you should *never* ask a virtual stranger, and I went back to staring out the window at the mountains on the far distant horizon.

They looked murky, a deep purple pall settling over them despite the scorching sunshine. They were brooding, like I had been all summer.

I wondered what mountains had to brood about, and rubbed the lingering ache in my right leg. The hike up the mountain was going to be the first real test of my newly healed self. I wondered which of us was going to win.

"Dude, will you snap out of it?" I flinched, but it didn't keep me from getting hit in the face with a piece of ice from Will's cup. "Geez, you'd think somebody died."

Goose bumps sprang up along my arms and my stomach gave a painful wrench. Something cold and slimy slithered down my spine, and it had nothing to do with Duke and his saliva problem. "Don't say stuff like that, man. Not cool."

Will seemed to realize he'd overstepped, and the smile in his eyes faded behind his round glasses. "Sorry, dude. My bad." Great, now I felt like I'd kicked a puppy.

The others, at least the ones who knew me, took the conversation in a new direction and left me alone. The goose bumps refused to fade, and despite the sweltering heat, I found myself rubbing the chill out of my arms several times. Something had shifted, and not in my favor.

I stared at my own blue eyes in the window's reflection, and I saw lines around them that were only recent additions to the topography of my face. A few white hairs in my reddish beard stubble caught the sunlight and gleamed like beacons. There was a tiny scar on my cheek, one that would fade with time but for now was pink and shiny. My blond hair, pulled back in a ponytail like always, seemed to be receding just slightly. That could have been my own vicious imagination, though.

It was my eyes that kept my attention. They were haunted eyes, hunted eyes. They said that something, somewhere, was out to get me. I knew that just as surely as I knew the sun would set tonight. The only two questions that needed answering were when, and how many of the people I loved were going to get in the way?

Dammit, Jess, you're doing it again. In my own constant state of worry and paranoia, I'd blown the guys off almost all summer. I knew this. I had been a crappy friend for months. (We're not even going to talk about how frustrated Mira was with me.) I had been hoping that this camping trip would make up for some of it, but my innate sense of impending doom said otherwise. I should have stayed home. I just knew it.

I didn't realize my hand was clenched into a fist until Cole touched me and I jumped. He gave me a look, but didn't say anything. He understood, at least better than anyone else in the car. He was a cop; they dealt with life and death on a regular basis. And he knew demons. If anyone in the world was going to know how I felt, it was my baby brother. After a moment, I nodded slightly. I would try to relax. I'd promised.

I caught Cam-short-for-Cameron watching the silent exchange from the other side of the car. The rest of the way to Colorado, I felt him glance at me from time to time, trying to figure me out.

Good luck, buddy. Better people have tried and failed.

6

The last outpost of civilization before we headed up into the mountains was quite a ways west of Fort Collins, Colorado, and consisted of a small grocery store proudly named Ericson's. Marty knew the owner, and that's where we'd be parking the Suburban before heading out on foot.

As everyone ducked inside the store for last-minute supplies, I snuck around the corner to call home one last time before I lost my cell signal farther up the mountain.

Mira answered on the second ring. "Hello!" There was water running in the background. Doing dishes, maybe? Laundry? I couldn't help but try to picture what she was wearing today, how she had her hair done. Okay, I'd been gone twelve hours, and I missed her already.

"Hey, baby." I leaned against the side of the store, gazing at the state of Colorado spread out all hazy clear to the distant horizon. "We're getting ready to head up the mountain, and I wanted to give you a call before I left my phone here."

"Well, we're fine. Estéban's mowing the yard and Steph took the kids to the movies, so I'm getting some paperwork done for the shop."

"Oh." That made me sad, actually. For some reason,

I'd really wanted to hear my daughter's voice. "Well, tell Anna I love her, okay? When she gets back."

"I'll do that." She paused a moment, and I could picture her chewing her bottom lip thoughtfully, her green eyes dark. "Jess, are you okay? You sound a bit off."

"Yeah . . . same shit, different day." She knew what I was talking about. Lately, we'd been having rather . . . energetic discussions about my life outlook. "I fell asleep in the truck on the way out, and the dreams came."

I heard her wince on the other end of the line. "Screaming?"

"No, thankfully. But didn't make for a happy road trip." I rested my head against the side of the building for a moment. "I'm trying, baby. I really am."

"I know. And it's okay. You'll have fun and maybe you'll be feeling more like yourself at the end of the week."

"I hope so." At this point, I was starting to wonder about seeing a shrink, and for me, that's saying something. "Listen, if you need anything, call Ivan. Or Avery. The numbers are in my notebook."

Avery Vincent, the champion out of San Francisco, could be on a plane and in Kansas City before anyone could find me in the wilds of Colorado. At least, that's what I told myself.

"I know, Jess. We went over this like fifty times. We'll be fine. You guys just watch what you're doing, and don't fall off a cliff or anything, okay?"

There was a squawk of indignation around front,

and I peered around the building in time to see Duke tangle his leash around Will's legs and send him sprawling off the wooden porch. Once downed, the big dog proceeded to try to drown his victim in wet slobbery kisses, despite Will's vain attempts to shove the mammoth mutt off. "Maybe you should do some of that voodoo you do so well? I think we're gonna need it."

She chuckled. "Will's hurt already, isn't he?"

"Not yet, but he's working on it."

"I'll put some protection spells on you all. Except Cam. I haven't had time to ask his permission."

"Then we'll be extra careful with him." I had to wonder, if Cam already had his own protection spells in place, would he notice the addition of Mira's? There are times when I kick myself for not studying up on this magic thing more.

It did make me feel better to know we'd have my wife's protection spells laid over us. Like a security blanket. One of those big fluffy ones with the satin binding around the edge. What? I have a five-year-old daughter. Daddies know about these things.

I said my good-byes and I-love-yous and tried to sound upbeat and cheerful. Mira wasn't fooled, but I was hoping she'd appreciate my efforts.

In the store, Cameron and an upright-again Will were poking through bags of dried fruit and trail mix, and I headed straight for the rather large selection of Ericson's homemade jerky, shouldering Cole aside in an attempt at playfulness.

"You got room in your pack for this?" Cole tossed

me a package of jalapeño buffalo jerky. "Mine's stuffed full already."

"Yeah, I can probably manage." I grabbed a pack of teriyaki for myself.

We took very few edible supplies up the mountain with us. Paintball gear plus sufficient ammunition wasn't light, and we'd be walking several miles up rough terrain. Marty's uncle was always good enough to stock the place for our arrival every year, so we could get away without packing staples. However, we would always make room for Ericson's jerky. It was practically a food group in and of itself.

Marty was trying to struggle into his backpack and hold on to Duke at the same time when Cole and I came back out. My brother grabbed the dog, and I helped out with the luggage. "The clerk says the Quinns were by yesterday real early. Bet you money Zane's waiting to ambush us on the trail."

The Quinns were old family friends of Marty's, and they looked after the cabin in the off season. Every year, they joined us up there to roughhouse and play paintball. We'd watched the only child in the family grow up.

"That means you get to go first." Will pointed at Marty.

"Wuss."

The rest of us hauled our backpacks out of the truck, struggling into the heavy monstrosities while Duke did his best to knock us all on our backs. As Will had proven, if the dog ever got us down, we'd be just like turtles, stuck there for the duration of whatever mockery would be sure to follow.

Cole was pawing through his things, looking for a place to stuff the extra pack of jerky he just *had* to have, and I spotted his holstered gun in there. And I don't mean his paintball marker, I mean his real I'm-a-cop-and-I'll-shoot-your-ass gun. "Um . . . little brother? You really think you're going to need that?"

He glanced up, first at me, then pointedly at the hilt of the katana sticking up over my shoulder. Yeah, okay. Pot, kettle, all that. "Mine's for exercise."

"So's mine. I want to do some target shooting while we're up there."

I left it at that. It wasn't worth arguing over, and honestly I don't know what to say to Cole ninety percent of the time anymore. Another goal for the camping trip: figure out how to talk to my once demon-sworn little brother. I was coming too close to dying too often to let things go unsettled between us.

"Guys, check this out!" At first, I wasn't sure what Marty had in his hand, but I was pretty sure you could buy it only at a shop where you had to be eighteen to even walk in the door. It had rubber hoses and metal brackets and a flat leather pocket all attached by metal grommets.

Marty strapped the doohickey to his forearm, and I finally recognized it as a slingshot. A very powerful, lethal-looking slingshot. To demonstrate, Marty drew back on the leather pocket (it had a finger loop, how convenient) and let it go with a snap that echoed.

"They say you can hunt anything up to the size of a coyote with this. I wanna do some target practice with it too."

These are my friends. Give us a weapon of individual destruction, and we're like kids at Christmas.

"Aren't those illegal?" Cole raised a brow at Marty, who just grinned. My brother groaned and turned away. "I can't know this."

I elbowed him a little when the rest of the idiots weren't looking. "Hey, you're not a cop just now. Relax, remember?" He just rolled his eyes at me.

I don't know whose brilliant idea it was to haul all the paintball gear up a mountain once a year, but there are times when I think they need a kick in the shin. It's not the markers that are so heavy, really, as it is the air tanks and the actual paintballs. Granted, we'd probably be out of air and paint both within the first couple of days, so the trip down would be a lot lighter.

We didn't really go hiking so much as prepare for all-out war. Girding our loins, or something. Air tanks were affixed to guns, hoppers were filled with paint, masks were adjusted to fit properly.

We were a scary-looking lot. The paintball masks covered our entire faces, giving us a kind of anonymous storm trooper menace. (Except mine, which sported a smile made of silver spikes.) Even in borrowed equipment, Cam managed to look like he knew what he was doing, and once everyone was packed and loaded, Marty tossed the Suburban keys to the store clerk. We did a quick round of paper-rock-scissors to see just who got the honor of heading out first. Cole waved as he left the parking lot, disappearing almost instantly in the thick foliage. With his uncanny direction sense, he could be counted on not to get lost, and he'd break a trail for the rest of us on the grassy path.

Lucky me, I got to go last.

The way the plan worked was thusly: We would head out at ten-minute intervals, up a well-mown grass path through the woods. You could hide beside the trail and wait to ambush folks, you could jog to try to catch up with those in front of you. If you got shot, you had to wait where you were for another ten minutes before moving on again. Sure, it made the trek to the cabin drag out forever, but we always had a great time.

While we waited, I tossed my cell into Marty's glove compartment along with everyone else's. There'd be no signal at the cabin, and if I lost and/or broke one more phone, Mira was going to kill me.

"Just stay in view of the trail. It leads right up to the cabin. You can't miss it," Marty assured Cameron, who was the second to depart. "And I'm coming right behind you, so once I'm done lighting you up, you can follow me." He grinned and thumped Cam on the shoulder, sending him off.

One by one, the guys (and Duke) headed out, and when my time came, I shouldered my pack and sword, and flicked the safety off my paintball marker. Last year, Cole had stayed just inside the trees and shot me in the face the moment I left the parking lot. I'd be ready this time.

No one jumped out at me when I stepped off the

asphalt, and I took this as a good sign. Maybe I'd get a chance to admire the scenery for a few minutes before I was blinded by unnaturally colored blobs of paint.

This was damn beautiful country. The trees towered over me, branches blocking out the slowly darkening sky as the day drifted toward early evening. About a million different kinds of birds chirped and called all around me, and in the underbrush, small furry things scampered and rustled, fleeing before the terror that was me, I'm sure.

I loved this place.

I also established within the first few minutes that my injured leg seemed to be functioning as intended. I even broke into a light jog, determined to overtake Will, who should have been about ten minutes in front of me. No way he'd be running; I could catch him.

I paused often to listen for any movement up ahead, but it was hard to hear with my own breath whooshing in my ears. I kinda felt like Darth Vader, all wheezy in my mask.

Once, though, I stopped at just the right moment to hear the soft thud of a paintball marker up ahead of me. Hunkering down, I let my eyes relax until the forest blurred into fuzzy shapes that made no sense whatsoever. Only then could I see the motion that didn't belong, the sign of something foreign moving through the trees. Quietly, with the stealth of a ninja (no really, a ninja!), I started tracking.

It took me about ten minutes to work my way up behind my prey without alerting him. The curly ponytail said it was Will, and I grinned as I took aim.

Thup-thup-thup, a perfect bright green line right up the middle of his back. "Ack!" He whirled, trying to find the source of his attack, and flipped me the bird when I waved from my concealment.

I made my way to his side. "I heard you tag someone, who'd you get?"

"Either Cole or Cameron. Short-haired and tall, couldn't tell the difference."

We nodded and parted ways, Will parking where he was with his marker over his head. He was out for ten minutes, but whoever he'd tagged earlier should just be moving again. I ducked into the brush, grinning inside my mask.

Somewhere up ahead of me was my little brother—or Cameron, which was just as good—and I was on the hunt.

Twice more, I heard the distant sounds of brief paint-splattery battle, but it was a good half hour before I found anyone again.

Coming around a large oak, I spotted Duke standing in the middle of the trail, looking rather bewildered. There was no sign of Marty anywhere, and the big dog stood as if frozen.

A cold chill slid down my back, and I scanned the underbrush for signs of my friend. Had something happened? Was he hurt? I strained my ears for any sound of movement, but even the wildlife had fallen silent, no doubt spooked by my own clumsy passage through the brush.

Risking giving away my position, I called out in a hoarse whisper, "Marty?" Just as I debated on abandoning the paintball gun for my sword, I took four hits to the chest and one directly to the mask. Blue paint smeared my vision and splattered through the grille enough that I could taste it. (Let me assure you, the paint may smell like hot chocolate, but it tastes like crap.)

Wiping the paint off my mask, I finally spotted Marty in his camouflage gear, lying right under his own dog to fire off a few shots. No wonder the poor animal looked confused.

"No fair using the dog as a shield, man!" By the way his shoulders were shaking, he was laughing his ass off. That's how he wanted to play it, hmm? "Duke! Sit!"

Obediently, the two-hundred-pound mutt sat, right in the middle of Marty's back.

"Jesse, you rat bastard!"

"You're welcome!" I gave him a jaunty wave and found a nice fallen tree to sit on and wait out my time-out. He wrestled his way out from under his dog, and the pair of them disappeared up the path.

Of course, yelling out like that put Marty and me on everyone's hit list. Cole got me from behind not twenty yards up the mountain. I managed to tag Will and Cam both before they saw me, and somewhere along the way, Marty closed the distance and lit me up again. It got so I was spending more time sitting than walking.

I was taking advantage of my enforced rest stop to answer nature's call when I heard a soft "Hsst!" behind me. Thinking one of the guys was about to ambush me, ten-minute rule or not, I pretended not to hear it, taking the time to zip up my jeans. No way I was gonna let them surprise me like *that*.

I bent down, pretending to tie my boot, but really, I was reaching for my own marker. Maybe I could get a shot off first.

"Hsst!" There was a bit more insistence in the noise this time, and when I refused to respond, it was followed with a hissed, "Over here!"

That . . . didn't sound like the guys. In fact, if I didn't know better, I'd say it sounded like me. *Oh hell*. I yanked up my mask and perched it on the top of my head to get a clear view. "Axel?"

"In the flesh." There was a skittering sound and I looked up in time to see a fat gray squirrel disappear around the trunk of a tree and reappear on the other side, bushy tail twitching spastically. The furry beastie gave me a red-eyed grin. "Who did you expect? It's too early for Santa."

The animal was a dark charcoal gray, almost black, and it had to outweigh my squirrels back home by a good chunk. Its ears were adorned with enormous tufts of hair. Looked like my great-uncle Walt.

"In someone else's flesh, you mean. Nice ears."

"Yes, they are rather nice, aren't—" He preened with one front paw until he realized what he was doing; then he looked at his offending foot in horror. "Oh hell no. Wait there." With a flick of his brushy tail, he disappeared around the tree again.

"Slipping into something less furry?"

"You could say that." The face that appeared around

the tree a few moments later was all too human looking, Axel taking his usual pierced, Mohawked guise.

How he did that, I will never know. I mean, most
demons, they can hide their true form, make an illusion over it that looks human. Even the weaker ones,
the Snots and Scuttles can manage that much. Guess it
helps them relate to their victims. Touch them, though,
and your hand will go right through it, like a holo-
gram.

The true forms, the actual demon bodies, are constructed of solidified blight. That's how we're able to
banish them, cutting away bits and pieces until they
lose concentration and the ability to hold themselves
together. Demons come in a lot of different forms: the
Snots, barely more than brainless oozes; the Scuttles,
often insectoid and a bit more intelligent; the Skins,
usually some kind of fur-bearing animal, strong and
cunning; and the Shirts, the ones who have evolved
enough to look vaguely human. I'd fought them all, at
one time or another. I thought I had a pretty good handle on what to expect.

But Axel . . . If he was a Shirt, he was the most
human-looking one I'd ever seen, and his constructed
body was rock solid. Which meant that he was either
way more powerful than any demon I'd ever seen
or . . . or I don't know what. Yet another of those mys-
teries I was unlikely to solve anytime soon.

The squirrel, now unpossessed—dispossessed?—
shot out of the underbrush like a gray rocket and up
the nearest tree, chattering its displeasure.

"What are you doing here?" I stood up, glancing

around warily. The last thing I needed was one of the guys catching the demon here. I'd never be able to explain that away.

"Looking for you." Axel rubbed at one of his ears, then frowned at his hand. "Damn rodents."

"I'm not that hard to find."

The squirrel was still scolding him from the branches above, and Axel shot a red-eyed glare. "Watch it, or I'll eat your entrails." His answer was a walnut launched at his head with surprising accuracy. I liked the squirrel already. Axel bared his teeth at his former host, then turned his attention back to me. "I'd have caught up sooner, but that damn mutt was too close."

Okay, supreme beings, bless Duke in all his furry glory. I was so getting that dog a huge rawhide bone when we got home. "Stalker much?"

"Oh that's nothing. I almost mistook your brother for you, until I heard him speak. That could have been . . . awkward."

I went from being creeped out to pissed off in zero seconds flat. "You stay away from him. He's off limits and you know it."

Axel held up one hand to forestall my incoming rant. "Now, now, no need to get feisty. I didn't come here for that." Another walnut pelted him in the head, and he snarled at the branches above. "You're a furry hors d'oeuvre, I swear . . ."

I snapped my fingers to get his attention. "Focus, Axel. Why *did* you come here?" The more I looked at him, the more I thought there was something . . . off. Something in his usual smile, some tightness around his mouth, or his eyes. The way he sagged against the tree, almost like he actually needed it to keep himself upright. "Are you okay?" Part of me wondered why I even cared.

He ignored my question but seemed to take it as a challenge, pushing off the tree to stand on his own. It didn't escape me that he wrapped one arm tightly around his ribs, holding himself in pain. "I came to give you a message."

I saw how he stayed close to the tree trunk, dodging as much of the fading sunlight as he could. Now, I'm pretty sure the light doesn't physically harm them, but man, demons don't like it. The forest canopy provided just enough shade where he was standing to throw his face into darkness.

"Step into the light." Unlike most demons I'd dealt with, Axel had never made special efforts to avoid the sun. Something was wrong. Well, more wrong than usual.

"I'll stay here, thanks."

"What's up, Axel?"

"Let's just say I'm not at my best today, hmm? Now shut up and let me give my message." His eyes flashed red and stayed that way. I was pissing him off.

"From who?"

"Doesn't matter." He moved one step closer, and as his face passed out of the tree's shadow, I could see it clearly for the first time. His lower lip was split and swollen, and the right half of his face was a lovely shade of eggplant purple. Axel had obviously had a very bad day.

"What the hell happened to you?" More importantly, *how* the hell had it happened? I'd never seen a demon with visible injuries. At least ones I didn't cause myself. Damn, how much damage did it take to bruise blight?

He managed a pained grin, running his tongue over his teeth. "A fairly accurate description, actually. You ever see those videos of family Thanksgiving dinners that turn into all-out brawls? Think of it like that."

"You had a family food fight?"

He chuckled. I will never get used to hearing my laugh come out of a demon's mouth, and the muscles in my back twitched as I tried not to shudder. "I guess you could call it food. If it's any comfort to you, I came out on the winning side."

"I'd hate to see the other guy."

"Oh yes. You would." The smile faded quickly. "You need to get off the mountain."

Normally, I would laugh in the face of any order Axel gave me, but there was something in his eyes, something in his borrowed voice. It sent another wave of chills down my back. "You're the one that told me to come up here."

That earned me a frown. "You ever hear of reverse psychology?"

"Yeah, and you suck at it." I finally closed the distance between us, just so I could lower my voice. Who knew where the guys were? "Did you flatten Marty's tires?"

His mouth twisted as he contemplated the answer. "I can neither confirm nor deny that."

"And turn Will's alarm clock off?"

"Hey, that was just him being a moron. I had nothing to do with that."

I could feel the beginnings of a headache, somewhere behind my eyes. "Any particular reason why?"

"You'll find out. But get somewhere public. Somewhere you can put your back against something solid."

"That sounds like a threat, Axel."

He shook his head. "Not from me. I'll swear it if you like. Just . . . do as I ask, this one time."

Everything in me screamed no. You don't do what a demon asks, period, the end. Even if (especially if) they phrase it to be for your own good. I eyed him warily, as if I could drag secrets from him with the power of my charismatic gaze. Or some shit. "What's in it for you? You don't give out information for free."

The demon's eyes flared red again in the dappled shadows, and he spat a curse in a language I didn't understand. Even so, the single word made my vision swim and the trees around me tilt at bizarre angles for the space of two breaths. Demonic speech is not meant for human ears. The cussing that followed in English was easier to follow.

"Damn you for your stubbornness, Jesse Dawson. You are the most infuriating creature on this planet."

"You been talking to my wife?" When in doubt, resort to being a smart-ass.

Axel was not amused. His gaze swept the forest around us, and he finally pointed at my feet. "There. Pick that up."

"That" proved to be a small branch, probably fallen

off one of the trees overhead. Small, nondescript, definitely not something that could be used as a weapon. I bent to retrieve it, carefully keeping my eyes on him.

He held his hand out to me as I straightened up. "Hand it to me." Cautiously, I extended the stick out to him, and he snatched it out of my hand. "There, now you've given me something. We're even."

At the risk of sounding mushy . . . where was the Axel I had come to know and hate? He would never have let a potential deal go without at least trying to bargain for something bigger, and his insistence on it had almost cost me my life last spring. "Axel, what's going on? You're not usually this . . . accommodating."

"Don't worry, Jesse. I still want your soul. But for right now, I need to keep it attached to your body until I can come collect."

"So you're saying I'm in danger. From what?" He stepped away from me, started to retreat into the trees. "Dammit, Axel, you can't just drop this on me and bail!"

"I can't say more. My hands are tied. If I could—" Whatever he was going to say next was lost as he suddenly stumbled.

I admit, it's instinct. Someone falls, you catch them. I jumped forward, caught his arms and eased him down as he sagged toward the ground. A bout of wracking coughs shook his wiry frame, ending all conversation for a few long minutes. Eventually, he turned his head and spat something dark and sticky off to the side, wiping his mouth with the back of his hand.

"Are you okay?" I asked again. It felt strange, asking him that. Why should I care if the demon was hurt? Damn, could he even *be* hurt? They could be banished, yes, evicted from whatever physical form they'd taken. But actually injured? That opened up a whole new realm of "evil things Jesse can do to demons" if it was true. I made a mental note to roll this over in my brain later. There had to be something here I could use.

He took a few deep breaths, testing, before he nodded. "Yeah. Just a bit more banged up than I realized." He raised a brow, glancing at my hands still on his arms. "Are you gonna kiss me, or let go?"

"Fuck off." I released him immediately, but I had to stare at my hands, rubbing my fingertips together. There was nothing there. No tingle of magic, no scent of cloves, no electric spark. Under normal circumstances, I should never have been able to touch the demon, not with my wife's spells of protection laid on me. But they protected me only from someone who meant me harm . . .

"Get off the mountain, Jesse. That's all I ask." The voice, my stolen voice, was distant suddenly, and I looked up in time to see Axel fade from view before my eyes. There was a faint scent of sulfur and ozone, and he was gone. His last words were whispered from thin air. "They're coming."

Well . . . fuck. That was as deep and meaningful as I could manage. Who was coming? When? Where? I cussed Axel up one side and down the other as I stood and debated my options. This was all pertinent information I could have used, dammit!

A nut bounced off my paintball mask with a loud clack. Glancing up, I saw my irate rodent friend still watching me. "Yeah, I know. I know. And you better git too, before he does come back and eat you."

The animal gave me a firm chitter and vanished in a swoosh of fuzzy tail.

I couldn't just "get off the mountain." My friends were out there in the woods, and they'd freak if I didn't show up at the cabin in pretty short order. Not to mention that the Quinns were already up there, and if something bad was coming for me, I couldn't just leave them.

"Okay, first things first. One, stop talking to myself. Two, gather up the guys." I'd figure out what to tell them when we were all in one spot. *Hey guys, I got a message that we need to go.* "*From where?*" "*Um . . . little bird told me?*"

I mean, here I was with an enigmatic warning from a creature I couldn't trust any farther than I could throw him. Except . . . the spells hadn't tripped. I should have zapped the hell out of him when we touched, pun intended, but nothing happened. What did that mean?

I quickly dismantled my marker and stowed it in my pack, suddenly preferring to leave my hands free for my sword if need be. I found my way back to the trail through a few yards of intervening scrub brush, then set out at a determined jog. I had to find my friends, and fast.

7

The cabin was a wonderful sight, when I finally burst from the trees into the large clearing. Now, let me explain that when I say cabin, I don't mean some little shack in the woods. It was a two-story bungalow with porches in both front and back, running water, a fully stocked bar, and a generator-driven fridge. The second floor was mostly a loft where we could spread our sleeping bags and crash, and downstairs we could sprawl out in front of the fireplace and play cards or shoot the breeze, or whatever.

Oscar Quinn was stacking firewood on the front porch, laughing and chatting to my friends who had all beaten me there, to a man. "Oh, and there's the last one. Hey, Jesse!" Oscar was in his midfifties, if I had to guess, but lean and wiry as only an outdoorsman can be. His skin was dark and weathered, and his hair was whiter than it had been, last I'd seen him, but the smile was the same. It made his eyes crinkle.

As I trotted across the open area, I did a mental head count, relaxing a little when I realized everyone had arrived safely, if paint-splattered. If anyone noticed that I had my sword in my hand instead of my paint-ball gun, they didn't comment.

By the time I got inside, everyone was claiming a chunk of floor in the loft or jostling over the kitchen sink as they tried to wash the paint out of . . . every-where. I tried to get Cole's attention, to get him away from the others, but he was either intentionally ignor-ing me, or I wasn't putting enough effort into it. "Cole. Cole! Hey, dumbass!" Nada.

It would wait, I told myself. Axel had said to get off the mountain, so surely that meant I had time to do so. Right? Right?? Besides, the sun would be down in the next half hour. Traipsing down the trail in the dead of night was just asking for an accident.

To convince myself, I walked to the window where I could see the glory of the Colorado wilderness spread out before me. Night was falling, the sky already deep purple to the east, and the color of day-old nacho cheese in the west. Things looked peaceful. They looked normal. It looked totally alien to me, I realized. When normal looks weird, your life is pretty messed up.

"Martin, check the refrigerator, make sure it's on." Oscar frowned and wrinkled his nose as he came in the door. "Smells like the eggs have spoiled. Would be just our luck, yet another thing going wrong."

A quick check established that the fridge was work-ing, but I quit paying attention to what was going on behind me sometime after that. I could smell it too, the distinct odor of rotten eggs, very faint on the mountain air. *The scent of sulfur.*

I craned my neck to peer out the window, searching the tree line for . . . what? I didn't know, but the goose bumps were suddenly marching up and down my back, keeping time with my heart as it sped up. Was it just me, or was there something out there, watching us?

Someone moved at my elbow, and I glanced long enough to see that it was Cameron. He looked out the window with the same dark frown I knew I was wearing. There was something rotten in Denmark, and I was pretty sure it wasn't the eggs.

"Oscar? Where's Zane?"

Oscar looked up from his discussion of generator mechanics. "I sent him out to get more firewood. He should be back any minute; he's been gone awhile."

Any minute wasn't soon enough. I walked out the door, taking my sword with me. I felt the guys' eyes on me, all of them wondering what was up. Cole said, "Jess?" but I ignored him. I didn't have an answer yet anyway.

Cameron joined me on the porch, and I swear he raised his head to sniff the air, which might have been odd if I hadn't just done the same thing. The faint scent was gone . . . no, wait. I breathed deep again, and caught just the hint of it. Sulfur on the fitful breeze. The icy prickles across my arms were painful, and I drew my katana free of its scabbard, flexing my fingers on the hilt.

It could be Axel. I already knew he was in the area. But it didn't feel like Axel. Maybe it made me an idiot, but Axel didn't strike this deep chord of terror that I felt coiling around in my guts. He had never triggered my "danger sense," not like this.

I strained my eyes at the tree line, as if I could make

Zane Quinn materialize by sheer force of will. "Come on . . . get back here . . ."

His voice preceded him, sounding garish and out of place in the suddenly silent wood. As he broke the tree line, I could see the boy's head bobbing as he sang off-key to whatever music was playing on his player. His arms were loaded with chopped wood, high enough that he could barely see over the top.

Far to our west, over the mountains that blocked our view, into an ocean we couldn't even see from here, the sun set.

"Behind him . . ." I saw the movement even as Cam breathed the words. Something was moving in the trees behind Zane. Something dark, coming on fast in odd leaps and bounds from branch to trunk to forest floor.

"Zane! RUN!" I was off the porch and running before I realized it, and the teenager blinked at me in surprise instead of obeying. The hesitation cost him instantly.

In those first horrifying seconds, I couldn't tell you how many there were, or even what they were. They were shapes, lean, lithe, springing across the open area in inhuman leaps. I demanded more speed from my feet, but it wasn't going to do any good. I was only human, and I knew those things weren't. I'd never reach him in time.

Two of them burst from the brush to my right and bowled into Zane. The firewood went flying. The copper tang of blood burst into the unnaturally still air, and the boy screamed in pain. Four more pounced down out of the overhanging branches, landing on their fellows, on Zane, without thought for safety. After that, I lost count, but there were more. So many more.

Without breaking stride, I waded in with my sword, feeling the resistance as it met solid forms, sliced yielding flesh. I had to clear them fast, before hitting the kid became too great a risk. There was no beauty to it. I hacked and slashed where I could, my momentum carrying me through them and out the far side. I figured at least a few would pursue me, but not a single one did. Like sharks in a frenzy, they swarmed to that blood scent.

"Here! On me!" I yelled. I stabbed, I sliced, and it was like kicking at the Rock of Gibraltar. I didn't have what they wanted, so I didn't exist.

The one on top of Zane reared up and I thrust through its shoulder, my blade appearing a good three inches out the back. The creature's face drew up in a rictus of pain, but it made no sound, even as I kicked it off my sword. Its face was smeared almost black with fresh blood, what remained of its rotten teeth coated and sticky with it. And worst of all, it looked almost human. Whatever it was, it seemed to suddenly understand fear and pain because another slash from my sword had it hopping backward, moving on all fours at times, and on two legs at others.

Things got tricky after that. The kid was in there somewhere, thrashing and screaming, and the things on him were getting in their own way more than not. It was like sorting through the football huddle from Hell.

Finally, I caught a glimpse of bright fabric and made a wild grab with my free hand. It was the collar of Zane's jacket, and I bodily dragged him out from under the writhing pile. There was no time to get him on his feet, and I didn't wait to see if he even could. Getting a good grip, I started dragging, taking swipes at the creatures that got too close. There were more than I'd thought, swarming out of the trees, massing at the dark pools of Zane's blood that gathered in the grass. Those that couldn't get near those delectable morsels were flanking me, intent on retrieving the meal I'd just stolen from them.

Zane was still functional enough to kick with his legs, either in defense or scrabbling desperately to put distance between himself and his attackers. His heel connected with a shrunken, skeletal nose, the bone crunching wetly.

A hand reached for me, dark with filth and God knows what else, and I severed it at the wrist. The thing recoiled in silence, but its fellows closed the gap.

Out of the corner of my eye, I saw the things circling, trying to get between me and the cabin, and there was nothing I could do to stop it. Instinct, that primal lizard voice in the back of your brain, told me to drop the kid, to bolt for the cabin. Damn good thing I was an evolved primate. I kept moving, hauling Zane back over the rough ground as quickly as I could, hoping to God I didn't trip on something and go down. It would be the end for both of us.

An explosion shattered the eerie silence, and it took me a second to recognize the sound of Cole's gun. One of the things on my left was ripped away, sent asshole over appetite by my brother's shot. Some part of me could hear him shouting my name, screaming for me to move move move! And not just Cole. All the guys were scattered across the front porch, caught somewhere between "What the fuck?!" and "Lemme at 'em!" 'Cause face it, I'm the only one dumb enough to run headlong into something like that.

Another shot sounded, but there were too many of the things scrambling after me to see if it did any good. Three of them charged from my right, more than I could take at once, and just as I braced to take one or two of them out before they got me down, I was nearly flattened by two hundred pounds of brindle mastiff as he hurtled past me. Duke's bellow added to the chaos, and the big dog tore into two of my attackers with a raging fury I never imagined he possessed.

I heard bones snap in those massive jaws, and not once did any of the creatures make a noise. The only voices I could hear were my buddies, Cole screaming at me and Marty shouting at Duke, and a panicked breathy shriek from the kid I was dragging across the clearing.

Duke seemed to grasp the idea of a fighting retreat, and as soon as he'd beaten the creatures back, he was at my side, a rumbling growl in his barrel chest but backing up step by step just as I did.

My heels hit something solid, and for a split second, I just knew I was done for. Then hands reached past me to grab Zane, to haul him up the porch steps and inside. Somehow, we'd made it. I slashed at two more of the things that were bold enough to come within my reach, and they danced back. Duke gave a lunge, and they scattered farther. I made a grab for his collar, keeping him from chasing after them. That's what they wanted.

The silent ring of . . . things crouched there, just out of reach, watching us with an unearthly light behind their eyes. Their skin was pale, under the grime and gore, their shapes almost human in an emaciated, hungry way. Hairless, naked, gender only visible as a seeming afterthought. The one with the missing hand was definitely female, and the sight made bile rise in the back of my throat. The creature herself seemed oblivious to the limb that ended in a jagged stub, crouching amongst her fellows. A few of them rocked from side to side, breath whistling out of their throats. Keening, I realized. Howling without voices. And they sat there. Waiting.

Waiting for what? The thought crossed my mind before I could stop it and I winced. I should know better than to ask that sort of question.

My answer came in the form of a pale man who stepped from the trees on the far side of the clearing. His suit was charcoal gray, but that was the only color about him. Everything was white, from his short hair, to his ivory skin. In the deepening dusk, he glowed, like some kind of cave-dwelling larva. Even his eyes seemed devoid of color until the moment they flared red.

Dimly, I knew that the creatures were withdrawing, skulking and cringing in the presence of this demon. I knew he was their master. I knew it because even I couldn't take my eyes off him, and all he'd done was stand there.

There was something . . . so familiar about all that whiteness . . .

He smiled at me, raised one thin hand to point at me. In that moment I knew, and in knowing, I saw through the illusion. Every part of my body went instantly numb. *No . . .*

In the space of a breath, he changed, a hulking white-furred form standing where the well-dressed man had been. On all fours, it flexed its vicious claws, tearing furrows in the forest floor. It swayed its head from side to side, flaunting the gnarled ram's horns as big around as my thigh. Its muzzle wrinkled, exposing gleaming white teeth as it smiled at me. *Nonono . . .*

It charged without warning.

I tried to move, but the signals just weren't getting through. Just like every nightmare I'd had over the last four years, my feet were rooted in place, and my mind could only conjure a litany of, "*Nonononononono-nono!*"

The Yeti galloped at me, crossing the open grass in huge leaps and I knew, even against all logic, that I was a dead man. Knew it so strongly that when someone grabbed my shoulder from behind, I couldn't even resist.

"Down!" Cameron shoved me aside like a sack of potatoes and leaped off the porch. Landing in a crouch, he slammed his palm against the ground. *"Consecro!"*

The spell went off like a bomb. I saw the ripple—like heat waves on asphalt—as it passed outward in an ever-widening ring. I almost choked on the thick scent of cloves that burst into the air, and when the blast reached the Yeti, it picked him up and hurled him into the trees, shattering branches and bringing down a few smaller saplings.

Silence reigned, the world itself stopping to gape in astonishment. Standing slowly, Cam turned to look at me, his face almost as pale as the Yeti's. "Inside." Then he pitched forward, bashing his head against the porch as he collapsed.

Suddenly, I remembered how to move.

"Will!" I grabbed Cam's jacket with one hand, feeling an absurd sense of déjà vu as I hauled him roughly up the stairs and into the cabin. "Will, I need you!"

"Busy here, Jess." Once glance told me that both Will and Cole were up to their elbows in Zane Quinn's blood. They couldn't help me.

Finally remembering to drop my sword, I flipped Cam to his back, ignoring the blood flowing down his face. The gash over his eye was the least of his problems.

The first rule of offensive magic is that it comes with a price. The bigger the boom, the worse the penalty. And that was the biggest damn boom I'd ever seen.

Before I could even assess the damage, Cameron seized, his back arching until only his head and heels touched the floor. Every muscle in his body contracted at once, drawing his face into a grotesque mockery of his usual self, knotting his hands into useless claws. His breath escaped in one long, agonized hiss, unable to even scream.

Mira had had bad reactions to spells before. Severe hypothermia, raging fevers, this one time with hives all over her body . . . But I had never seen anything like this. This was how people died, doing this.

The seizure lasted maybe fifteen seconds, but when he finally collapsed to the floor again, I knew at once he wasn't breathing. A quick listen at his chest confirmed no heartbeat either. Like every other muscle in his body, his heart had locked up. "Come on . . . don't do this . . ."

I went through the motions like I was supposed to, pinching his nose and trying to force my own breath into his lungs. Then compressions, counting in my head . . . then breathe . . . "Can't answer my questions when you're dead, asshole, come on . . ." I knew I was bruising ribs, possibly cracking them, but I had to get his heart started again. Had to.

"Will, this isn't working!"

"Try a precordial thump."

"A what?!"

"Hit him in the chest as hard as you can!"

With a grimace and a silent apology, I drew back and slammed my fist into Cam's chest with every bit of force in me. His eyes flew open, and he came back to us with a ragged gasp that ended in a fit of rough coughing. I helped him roll onto his side, where he curled into a pained little ball, and then I finally got a chance to look around the room.

Will and Cole were still working over young Zane, using whatever we had in our meager first aid supplies. Granted, thanks to Will it was better than Band-Aids and iodine, but we weren't equipped for . . . this. I couldn't tell what injuries the boy had, but there seemed to be so much blood, much more than a fifteen-year-old body could hold. The kid was conscious, sobbing. That at least was a good thing.

Oscar was huddled against the kitchen counter, watching helplessly as my brother and best friend worked over his son. The older man had a glazed look to his eyes, and I wondered where his mind had gone to flee the bizarre events he'd just witnessed.

Marty had his arms wrapped around Duke, presumably to keep him from bolting out the door again, but the big dog didn't seem inclined to leave anymore. His striped sides heaved, panting after his brief encounter with bravery.

"Are they . . . are they still out there?" Cam's voice came out hoarse and raspy, and he struggled to sit up. It was a decent question. I retrieved my sword as I stood up, moving to look out the window.

The clearing itself was empty and peaceful, and if you ignored the trail of bent and bloodied grass where I'd pulled Zane to safety, it looked like nothing had ever happened.

"I think they're—No, wait." They were there, just inside the shadows of the trees, slipping from trunk to bush like mottled ghosts. I couldn't see the Yeti, but whatever those other things were, they were still out there. Though it seemed a futile gesture, I kicked the cabin door shut and locked it. "They're still out there, but they're sticking to the tree line."

Out of habit, I retrieved my scabbard and went to sheathe my sword. Only then did I realize that there was something dark and thick dripping off the blade. I dipped my fingertips in it, and they came away sticky. I smelled it. It was definitely blood. Old blood, maybe, clotted and sickly sweet with decay, but blood. My gaze went out the window again, to those half-seen shadows in the trees.

Demons didn't bleed. What the hell was out there?

8

The mystery outside was going to have to take back-seat to the mystery inside. I wiped off my sword on the remnants of Zane's T-shirt, then sheathed it, turning to watch Cam struggle to his feet, one arm wrapped around his undoubtedly sore ribs. For a guy who al-most died, he was moving pretty good. He was also leaving a bright red trail across the floor. Head wounds bleed like a bitch.

"Dammit, you're bleeding everywhere." I moved to grab some bandage and gauze from Will's first aid pack. Cam made it to a seat at the bar and mostly fell onto it. "Hold still." Bandaging head wounds I could do.

The cut was deep, and probably should have been stitched. Hell, even superglued would have been good, but Will had used all that we had on Zane. At any rate, Cameron was going to have another scar on his fore-head. And since he couldn't exactly get away while I was taping his head shut . . .

"What did you do?" He didn't look up, but there was a faint twitch to his brows that said he was listen-ing. "That wasn't an amateur spell. What did you do, Cameron?"

Once I released him, passing him a towel to mop his face with, he leaned his elbows on the bar, mostly to prop up his head. "I consecrated the earth. We're on holy ground now."

Holy shit, pardon the pun. I moved so I could at least pretend like I was looking at his face. "You're not an *ex*-priest, are you?"

Cam shook his head. "I need a glass of water."

I fetched without really thinking about it. Instead of drinking it, he dipped a finger in it, murmuring under his breath. The scent of cloves filled the air again. I snatched his hand away from the glass, holding it firmly by the wrist. "Hey! Are you out of your mind? You're gonna kill yourself!" Magic drew from the caster's life force. Mira had drilled that much into my head. Too much magic, and the user would just drop dead, their very life given for their craft.

The possibly ex-priest shook his head again and tugged free of my hold, pushing to his feet. "Just had to bless it. Need to ward the doors and windows."

"Why? If the ground is consecrated, they can't get close."

"It won't last." He wavered on his feet, and I caught him by one arm, sloshing the now-holy water over his hand. "Takes about six priests to make a consecration permanent. The boundary is going to shrink as time goes on. I need to set up wards."

I glanced out the window. Night had fallen, hiding the clearing from view. Didn't matter. Even if I couldn't see him, I knew the Yeti hadn't gone. "How long?"

"Hmm?" Cam definitely wasn't firing on all cylinders. Understandably. We were gonna have to keep him awake tonight, watch for a concussion.

"How long until the spell breaks?"

"A day? Day and a half, maybe? I wasn't exactly prepared." With dripping fingers, he traced a symbol on the front window. *"Sepire."* The unfamiliar word prickled over my skin like static. I guess that answered the question of who had warded his apartment.

"Can you renew it?" I knew he couldn't. The first one nearly killed him. Repeating it almost certainly would. But I wanted to know if he'd tell me the truth.

"I could. But I wouldn't survive the backlash."

"Dude! You need to see this!" Will's voice reminded me that Cam and I were not alone.

I pointed a finger at him. "We're gonna finish this conversation later." Cameron just nodded and moved on to the next window.

Will and Cole were still crouched over young Zane, the boy's face gray under the smears of his own blood. Normally, the kid looked a lot like his dad, the same wiry build, the same narrow nose. Zane's hair was the same almost black that Oscar's had been in his younger days.

But now, his eyes were wide with shock. There were shadows in the hollows of his cheeks. He'd managed to choke back his sobs into tiny, tortured hiccups, but his breath was still coming in shallow little gasps of panic. Will had patched him up with what supplies we had, but even I could tell that the kid had been chewed on good. His left arm was bandaged from knuckles to elbow, and his bare shoulders showed bite marks, clear up his neck. Not cute little love bites either, but eat-you-with-fava-beans kinda bites. Human bites, I noticed sickly. Most of them were swabbed in antibiotic ointment, and seeped a little blood through the darkening bruises.

"What's up, Will?"

"Look." Will tried to lift the corner of the bandages swathing Zane's left forearm, and the kid flinched, whimpering, "Don't."

"*Shh.* Jesse can help, I promise," Cole soothed, and I gave him an odd look. What was I helping with, exactly?

Will continued to peel up the white gauze, slowly revealing the edge of a black tattoo.

"Shit." I crouched, peering under the blood-soaked cloth as best I could. The tattoo curled and wove over most of his arm between wrist and elbow. Parts of it were mangled by the nasty bite mark on his wrist— human bite, my mind pointed out again, like I'd missed it the first time—but the rest of it seemed to writhe under my gaze, sliding over itself sinuously without moving at all. I felt an ache growing behind my eyes, just looking at it. I pressed the bandage down again. "Damn, kid . . ." Zane wasn't the first kid I'd seen sell his soul, but he set a new record for being the youngest.

"It is, then?" Cole of all people would recognize the demon brand. He'd worn one himself.

"Yeah. And I think I know who it belongs to." I'd seen that particular mark before. I had the scars to prove it. Without thinking, my hand went to my rib cage, feeling the hard ridges of scar tissue even under my shirt, and I couldn't help but glance toward the door. Yeah, we were intimately acquainted.

"Jess?" I forced my eyes from the door, to find Will frowning at me. Will never frowned. I didn't think he had those muscles. "Was that him? Was that the . . . ?" He nodded toward my side. Will had been there that day, to stuff my guts back inside my chest. He knew firsthand what kind of damage the Yeti could do.

"Yeah." What else could I say? My four-year nightmare had just walked back into my life. The vocabulary for that hadn't been invented yet.

Zane's eyes were glued to the floor, and he looked so very young, sitting there all bandaged up and pale. I touched his leg to get his attention. "Hey, kid. You need to look up at me, 'kay?"

It took him a few moments, but he finally did, tears glimmering in his eyes.

"I know what you did." That made him blink a little, and the tears escaped to run down his cheeks. "What I need to know is why."

At first he gave me that shrug. Y'know, the one they give when they know they screwed up, and nothing they say is going to get them out of trouble. The one that says they know they have no right answer.

"It was your mom, wasn't it?" I looked up when Marty spoke, but I still caught Zane flinching out of the corner of my eye. Marty nodded to me. "His mother died, about two months ago. Long breast cancer battle."

That'd do it. I looked back to Zane. "Was that it? You were trying to save her?"

It took him a long time to answer. "Yeah . . . But it didn't work. It . . . went all wrong, somehow . . ."

"It usually does, kid." I sighed and rested my hand on his head for a second. I could see already where this was headed for me. I just couldn't let him stay like that.

"Will, look at his hand." Cole barely whispered, so of course, we all turned to look. My paramedic friend cursed softly, seeing the dark streaks creeping slowly up the kid's hand. Not the red of true infection, but an insidious blackness that started at his fingertips and radiated upward. You could almost watch it move.

"I've never seen gangrene set in that fast." Will looked up at me again, trying to send me a message with just his eyes. I got it. It wasn't gangrene and he knew it. He'd seen that before, too.

"What do you taste, Zane? Like . . . chemicals in the back of your throat?" The kid frowned faintly, licking his lips, then nodded, a puzzled look crossing his face. "I was afraid you were going to say that."

Less than a year ago, I'd fought for the soul of the president of this great United States. Fairly standard fight, a Scuttle demon, nothing too tricky, except where it had stabbed me through my right calf. And that's when the real fun had started. The first thing I remembered was the chemical taste in my mouth, so dry I couldn't even spit.

Will opened his mouth to say something, but Cam piped up first. "It's poisoning. Those things out there must be contaminated. It got into the wound, tainted it. It'll spread until it kills him." Apparently done with the warding of the downstairs doors and windows, he sagged against the stair railing just to stay upright. "You should get the hatchet."

"Um, for what exactly?"

"The arm has to go—there's no cure for that." The whatever-he-was shook his head. "The shock of the amputation will probably kill him anyway, but at least he'd have a chance."

"You can't cut my boy's arm off!" I'd forgotten about Oscar, who'd been watching the proceedings with a kind of mute horror. "He's only fifteen!" The man lurched to his feet, then stood there with fists clenched, like he wasn't sure what to fight, or even how to begin finding out.

"That poison will kill him if it reaches his heart. This is the only way to save him."

"No, it's not." They both looked at me, and Cameron frowned. "Will, how high can that stuff go before we *have* to cut off the arm?"

My buddy frowned thoughtfully behind his thick glasses, then drew his finger across Zane's biceps near the shoulder. " 'Bout here, I think? But I'm not a surgeon, Jess, I'm an EMT, and we don't have the stuff—"

I waved him into silence. "Find a pen, mark that spot. Until it gets there, we have time." I looked to Cameron. "It is curable. My wife can do it. If I can find out how she did it, could you duplicate her spell?"

Cameron frowned even darker. "Just who did she cure?"

"Me." I reached down and yanked my jeans up to display the shiny pink scars on either side of my calf. "Scuttle demon in January. Punched right through my leg, and the black streaks started going, just like that.

The doctors were going to take the leg, just like you said. Mira saved me."

He was shaking his head before I'd even finished. "That's not possible. We're taught, right from the beginning, that a tainted wound is fatal."

"And I'm telling you that you are *wrong*. Now." I fixed him with a look of death. At least, I hoped I looked intimidating. A little. "If Mira tells you how to do the spell, could you duplicate it?"

He thought for a few moments, then shook his head. "I don't know. It's not one of the methods I've been taught, and there really isn't any room for improvisation—"

"But if Mira can make you understand, if she can tell you what she did, can you do it?"

It took him a bit, but he finally nodded. "I can try." He turned then to head up the stairs, climbing each riser like it took real effort.

"Are you all insane?" We all turned to look at Oscar, who was wide-eyed, just this side of being a little crazy himself. "Those . . . those things were . . . escaped chimps or something. And you're babbling about magic and spells?"

I approached him slowly, like you would a spooked animal. "It sounds nuts, I know, trust me. And I don't know what those things were, but they weren't chimps; they weren't animals. Did you see the big white thing come barreling at us? That's a demon, and he's trying to get in." But why? He couldn't hurt anyone without a contract. Couldn't touch us at all. But the Yeti had come charging at us anyway, charging at me. Something wasn't right. I tried to keep my uncertainty off my face.

"A demon? You expect me to believe that bullshit?" Color flushed into Oscar's pale face. I don't think I'd ever heard the man curse, not once in all the years I'd known him.

"It doesn't matter if you believe it. Not believing it doesn't change anything." I stopped moving forward. If he was gonna snap, I didn't want to be in arm's reach.

"And just how do you know this? What makes you so fucking smart?" I didn't even get a chance to answer him before he advanced on me, fists balled at his side. "You knew about that stuff and you didn't tell anyone?! You just . . . ! You just let us all go walking around out there with those things!"

"I didn't know they were there, Oscar. And I couldn't have reached him any faster." But there would always be that little voice that asked if I could have. If I'd noticed the smell sooner, or left the porch earlier, or even run up the path faster . . . If I'd have turned back when Axel told me to, would they have come for me, instead of Zane?

"Bullshit! You didn't even try!" He shoved me, and I let him, backing up a step or two. Wasn't the man's fault his world just got turned on its ear. I couldn't say I wouldn't have done the same, in his place.

Duke, however, took offense, and a low growl rumbled through the room. "Marty, hold the mutt!" Even with his considerable strength, earned over a forge and anvil, Marty had a helluva time holding on to his two hundred pounds of pissed-off dog.

Things only got worse when Oscar came at me again, shoving me with both hands. "You just let those things . . . those . . . your fault!"

I could hear Duke setting up for that deep bass bellow of his, and I knew Marty wouldn't be able to hold him. "Oscar, you need to calm down." I promise, I used my calm grown-up voice and everything. It was when he swung at me that things got interesting. I blocked the first one easily, batting his fist aside and dropping into a defensive stance. "I mean it. You're going to get someone hurt." It was going to be him, but man, I didn't want to do it.

"Fuck you!" The second punch whiffed by my ear as I sidestepped it, and I caught his wrist, wrenching his arm back behind him and pressing up. I knew it was gonna hurt like hell, but it was the only way I could think to get through to him.

Zane was yelling too. "Dad, leave him alone! Stop!" But it didn't make a difference.

"Oscar! Chill the fuck out!" It was like he couldn't even hear me. He screamed, jerking against my hold until I was afraid he was going to dislocate his own shoulder. This was going to get out of hand if I didn't do something drastic.

"Sorry I have to do this." I released my grip on his arm, reaching around to grab him by the throat instead. From behind, I put pressure against the back of his head. He gagged as I cut off the air to his windpipe. "Just gonna take a little nap . . ."

He flailed for a few seconds, and I knew he was already seeing stars. Six seconds in, and the world would be going gray. Eight, and he slumped in my arms. With Cole's help, I lowered him to the floor and released the choke hold. Oscar gasped, blinking his way slowly back to consciousness.

I rested my hand on his chest, waiting until his eyes could focus again. "I recommend you stay down. Savvy? We've got more important things to deal with at this exact moment."

Things like saving Zane's arm. I knew that poison, knew that a raging fever and amazing pain were coming in short order. At the very least, he needed a hospital, and the nearest one was in Fort Collins.

Things like who the hell Cameron was. Not to mention how we were going to get out of this damn cabin with those things waiting out there in the woods. Yeah, it hadn't escaped my notice that them staying out meant that we had to stay in.

The dog was still growling. Even with the "danger" subdued, Duke was still reacting like there was a threat in the room. I finally looked at Marty, who gave me a strained shrug.

"Let him go. See what he does." Not my best idea, but Marty couldn't hold on to the big lummox forever.

The mastiff gave a lurch in Oscar's direction, and I tensed to head him off, but Duke did no more than pad over to sniff the downed man, hackles still bristled along his striped shoulders. I could see Oscar's eyes, wide with fright as that massive muzzle brushed against his throat in passing. Duke settled for a firm snarl, then made the rounds of the room. Zane also got a growl of disapproval, which didn't surprise me.

Dogs and the soulless just don't get along. I yanked Oscar's sleeve up, but found his arm bare. No surprise, but I had to be sure. I'd been fooled before.

"Okay, I get why he's edgy around Zane, but Oscar's down. What's bugging Duke there?" No one really answered me, but I was used to talking to myself. I looked down at Oscar, who seemed to have lost all his fire, tears leaking silently from the corners of his eyes. Taking mood swings to a bit of an extreme, wasn't he? "I wonder . . . Cole, keep an eye on Oscar please."

Above the bar hung one of those bar mirrors. You know, the ones with the gold tracing around the edges, and some beer logo from the seventies at the top. It was bigger than I was used to, but it would do what I needed.

"Cameron!"

He appeared at the head of the stairs, more sliding down them than walking. "Hmm?"

"Can you make a mirror?"

"A what?"

"A mirror." I showed him the one in question. "A mirror that lets you see across, see if anything's lurking."

He settled on the bottom step, resting his bandaged head against the railing. "I don't have the foggiest idea what you're talking about."

Dammit. This was going to get irritating. "Look. My wife does this, with these symbols here." I grabbed a napkin off the bar and started scribbling down everything I could remember. Man, I hoped I had everything right. Might be a spell to turn someone into a rabbit instead.

Cam looked over my scrawls, and shook his head. "I'm not familiar with this work. It looks . . . is this pagan?" I groaned and smacked my head against the wall. "If you know the sigils, why don't you just do it?"

"Because I don't *have* any magic. Anything I need, my wife does."

There was no mistaking the look of horror that crossed his face before he caught himself. "I . . . you . . ." He blinked at me for long, shocked moments, and I just let him. "How are you still alive??"

"I'm just that fucking good. Now answer my question. Can you do it?"

It took him another few moments of staring at me like I'd grown a second head, but finally, he gathered himself enough to address the subject at hand. "What is the mirror supposed to do? Maybe I can adapt it somehow."

"Okay . . . I need to be able to see across the veil. Then you break the mirror, and whatever's caught in it is yanked to the physical side where we can deal with it."

The possibly ex-priest thought for long moment, then nodded. "I . . . think I can come up with something like that. But why are we doing this again?"

"Because I think something got inside before you set up the wards. Maybe has been inside this whole time."

It took Cam a good hour to come up with something for the mirror trick. Occasionally, he'd ask me a question that I didn't have the answer to anyway, but for the most part he sat with his head bowed, lips moving silently as he . . . prayed, or whatever. I just checked on him from time to time, making sure he hadn't lapsed into unconsciousness instead.

In the meantime, we got Zane settled with his father. I don't think the old man had any more fight in him anyway. I kept Duke near the pair, hoping the dog's presence would ward off what I feared had gotten through. The boy looked bad. Really bad, considering that his wounds were relatively minor. There were fresh bruises blossoming every moment, it seemed, but that didn't account for the gray tinge to his face. He was scared, he was in shock, and there wasn't a whole lot we could do about it. There was only so much Will could do with a first aid kit and torn up sheets.

"Is he gonna be all right?" I asked quietly, hoping that the Quinns wouldn't hear.

Will's grim face behind his round glasses said it all. There wasn't a shred of humor left in him anywhere. He was a goofball of the first order, except when it came to doing his job. Then he was the most efficient, organized paramedic I'd ever seen. (Trust me, I've seen a lot of them.) "I remember how tore up you were, man. If that poison doesn't kill him, the shock from an amputation would. I need things we just don't have here."

I clapped a hand on his shoulder. What else could I do? "Mira would say to have faith."

"Yeah, but in what?"

My eyes went to Cam, hovering over the mirror

we'd painstakingly detached from the wall. "Right now, I'd say him."

"But, dude? Who is he?"

Damn good question. And as soon as this little magic trick was done, I was going to find out the answer.

The air in the house was almost choking on the smell of cloves. That's how I knew whatever Cam was doing was working. Funny how no one else ever seemed to notice that smell.

"So . . . how's it going?" I kept a safe distance back, just at the edge of where my skin started prickling. Never good to startle the magic man.

"I . . . think I have something that will work." Cam displayed some neat and orderly symbols scratched into the back of the mirror that looked nothing like what Mira normally used.

"That's magic?"

"No, that's prayer. Written in shorthand." We traded skeptical looks at each other.

"Will it work?"

"Only one way to find out."

With some effort, we got the mirror propped upright and one by one we paraded in front of it. Even Duke got his turn on the runway.

The mirror showed nothing, except that my little brother was starting to put on weight.

"It's all those doughnuts, little brother." He flipped me off.

"So, what are we supposed to be seeing?" Marty looked at himself in the mirror, Duke at his heel.

"Hopefully, nothing. So, either this thing's not working, or we're not infested yet."

"It's working!"

"Infested with what?!" Cameron was offended. The rest of the guys were just worried.

I motioned for Marty to help me move the cumbersome thing until we could frame the two Quinns in its reflective surface. I heard a small blasphemy from Cameron's lips, and a worse one from Will's. My own stomach twisted in a painful knot. "Infested with those."

I called them Scrap demons. They were the parasites of the demon world, giant poisonous fleas if you will. In singles and pairs, they could feed off a person, subtly sucking their will to live, nudging them toward depression, paranoia, or worse. And I had never seen so many in one place.

A veritable horde of the little bastards clung to the Quinns. Their black forms, like greasy mops, scuttled over young Zane, their spindly insectile legs exploring every inch of his body. One of them plucked at his hair with a three-toed "hand," bringing it to what I presumed was its face to sniff. Hard to tell when they didn't actually have any eyes.

"Wh-what the fuck are those things?" Oscar had found the courage to speak again. Wide-eyed and pale, he watched one of the creatures clamber up on his reflection's shoulder. To his credit, he didn't try to bat it off. Wouldn't have worked anyway.

"Those are Scrap demons. Nasty little buggers, but easily squishable." I tried to get a head count on the grubby little swarm. There were at least seven on Zane that seemed permanently attached. Another dozen or so skittered between the two, not caring if they crawled over each other, their twiggy legs catching in the oily coils of fur on their fellows. Those would be the ones to watch, the ones that would latch on to one of us just as easily.

"They don't look like much. Are they dangerous?" Will bent down to poke at the mirror, and I grabbed his hand to stop him. I didn't know if he could disrupt Cam's magic, but I wasn't willing to risk it until we were ready.

"One alone, not really. This many . . . They'll kill Zane if we don't get them off him. It's not shock, it's them, sucking on his life. They're probably what's making Oscar all pissy too. If we can scrape off the scuzzies, things will go back to some semblance of normal."

"But . . . he said this was holy ground." Oscar pointed at Cam who had finally slumped onto a bar stool again.

The possibly ex-priest looked a bit gray around the edges too. He'd way overextended himself. "The land is consecrated," he explained. "Not the cabin floor. They were inside before the wards went up, so now they're trapped here with us."

"But where'd they come from in the first place? I mean, how long have they been on us?"

If I had to guess, I'd say the Yeti sicced his little greasy minions on the Quinns when Zane sold his soul. Despair is a good motivator, and if the demon could bag the whole family, so much the better. With the kid's mom just passing, they'd have been ripe pickings. "There's no telling. With all the stress of losing your wife, you probably never noticed the behavior changes. If Zane's been a little more hostile than usual . . . If you've felt extra depressed. Mood swings, irritability, sudden bleakness. It was all explainable. Hell, if it wasn't for the big doofus, I'd have never known they were here myself." I patted Duke's head, and he leaned into me hard enough to almost knock me over. "From now on, we watch the dog. If there's something wrong, he'll know before any of us."

"All right. We know they're here. Now how do we kill them?" Cole walked over and touched Oscar's shoulder, the one that was currently hosting a Scrap demon. In the reflection, the demon scuttled away from Cole's hand, climbing down the front of Oscar's shirt, clinging to the cloth with its three-toed claws. Interesting.

"First, we need weapons." Cole reached for his holstered handgun—when had he found time to put that on?—and I shook my head. "Bit of overkill there, little brother. Besides, we might need the bullets. Just . . . find stuff that will stab or smash. They're crunchy inside. Think of them like really big, really hairy cockroaches. With huge mouths full of shark teeth. And oh yeah, they're venomous."

The look from the group as a whole said, "Are you out of your freaking mind?!"

9

The first thing we did was light every lantern we could find. The sun was well and truly down by now, and the last place I wanted to be hunting demons, even little ones, was in the dark. Every shadow was a potential hiding place, and we positioned the lights to eliminate as many as possible.

"Count them. We have to get them all. There aren't any other mirrors in the house, so this is the one shot we'll get at them." The troops were lined up, hanging on my every word. Sort of.

We'd managed to wrangle weapons easy enough. My sword, some fireplace implements, a hatchet. Duke. It had been decided that Oscar and Zane weren't up for helping, nor was Cameron. So it would be just me and my buddies on bug-squishing duty. The trick was going to be getting all the little buggers before they got over their fright and faded back across the veil.

"They're going to scatter the moment the glass breaks. They'll know they're visible, and they'll try to hide until they can gather their wits and slip back across. So we gotta move quick. If one gets away from you, watch Duke. He should be able to keep up with them if we can't." Man, I hoped I was right. Duke was more known for his cowardice than anything else. It remained to be seen if his sudden bravado would hold.

"Whatever you do, don't get bit."

"What happens if we get bit?"

"I . . . don't actually know. Just know you're not supposed to get bit." I nodded toward Zane and his blackening fingers. "It's not like that. It's a different poison. If it gets on your skin, it's gonna feel like battery acid, and it'll eat through your clothes just the same too." I was trying to cram as much information into one briefing as I could, but I just knew I was going to forget something. "When they die, they're gonna just mist away. Try not to get too much of the black stuff on you. It won't do any damage in small doses, but it'll make you numb and cold temporarily. Any questions?" No one spoke up.

Somewhere deep inside, I was proud of them. Cole had dealt with demons before, but never in combat mode. Will had glued the pieces of me back together often enough after a fight, but had never seen one. Marty . . . well, there was a large leap between "knowing" and "seeing" and he'd just made it in the last couple of hours. And none of them seemed fazed.

It took us another fifteen minutes to get a head count on the little demons that we could all agree on. Each of us took up a position more or less surrounding the Quinns, and Cam stood ready next to the mirror.

Unfortunately, the skuzzy little vermin were not being cooperative. We had to have them all within the confines of the mirror to get them all yanked across. One of them, maybe sensing its imminent demise, crept around just at the edges of its fellows, pausing to comb through its greasy mat of fur about every third step.

"Dammit, come on . . . scoot over . . ." It would scurry almost into frame, then hesitate, backing up a few steps. It seemed reluctant to stray too far from Zane and Oscar, but at the same time it was afraid to get too close.

"Here, maybe if I . . ." Watching himself in the large mirror, Zane held out his hand to the creature, palm up. Though there was nothing visible in the room with us, in the reflection we could watch the parasite sniff the kid's hand, swaying on its three-toed feet in indecision.

Finally, it seemed to come to some conclusion, and clambered its way on to Zane's hand, spindly legs scrabbling for purchase on his narrow arm.

The kid frowned a little. "I . . . can't feel anything. Just cold. My fingers are cold." Slowly, he retracted his hand until he was holding the little Scrap demon in his lap, and then it scuttled off to join its brethren in their constant exploration of the Quinns.

"Let's get this show on the road before any more of them get adventurous." I found a place above one of the demons, holding my sword just above the greasy little mop. I nodded to Cam. "Do it."

With a good hard swing of a hammer, the glass shattered, falling out of the frame to fragment all over the floor. What followed looked like the greased pig chase from Hell. Literally. All we were lacking was the Benny Hill music.

The Scrap demons screamed as they were yanked

into the physical world. Now, one of them is bad enough, but eleventeen of them screeching in unison was enough to almost deafen us. Even as they sprinted in every direction, I drove my sword down with both hands, feeling the crunch as it cracked the hard carapace and stuck in the wood floor. My first victim wriggled spastically for a heartbeat, then poofed into a small black cloud that dissipated almost immediately. I wrenched the blade free and went after another.

"Get 'em, boy!" Marty called encouragement to his dog even as his hatchet split one of the parasites in two. Duke didn't need the urging, bellowing as he barreled into the knot of them. Scrap demons went flying everywhere as the big mutt whipped his head from side to side.

One of them made a scuttle for the kitchen cabinets, and I dove after it. "Get back here, you little—" It turned to hiss at me, toothy maw gaping. The venomous mouth took up almost the entirety of its greasy little body, the mop opening up to reveal rows upon rows of sharp, serrated teeth. One good sword thrust between the dentures, and it was so much blight, drifting back to where it came from.

I could hear the sickening cracks as one by one, the Scraps were reduced to their base essence, wafting away to darker realms. Will pinned one to the wall with the fireplace poker, and another attempted to clamber up his back, fleeing in blind panic. "Don't move, Will!" Good man, he froze and I batted the thing off with my sword, in Cole's direction. "Get it, little brother!"

"There's one under the coatrack!" Oscar pointed,

but Duke got there first, and there was a screech as the scruffy thing met its demise in the dog's massive jaws. The coatrack itself . . . well, we could use it for kindling later.

A twitch in the curtains behind Marty caught my eye. "Marty, the curtains!"

The hatchet made a solid thunk as it buried itself in the wall, thrown with deadly accuracy, and the demon gave a sad little twitch as it died. I blinked at Marty, and he shrugged. "Blacksmiths do that."

"Little help here!" Will had one on the run, but it was making a beeline for the fireplace. If it got up the chimney, we'd lose it. My buddy launched his poker at the creature, and it clanged against the hearth, sending brick chips flying. The demon reversed course and scurried toward Marty.

Unarmed, Marty stomped down with one heavy boot, and the greasy thing went splat, its legs flailing until they disintegrated into blight.

It took us all a moment to realize we had no more targets in sight.

"Was that . . . was that all of them?" We turned in slow circles, eyeing the shadowy corners of the room.

"I think so." My eyes were on Duke, though. The mastiff prowled the room, sniffing under things until he was satisfied. Only once did he hesitate, at the foot of the stairs, a faint growl rumbling through his chest, but whatever was up there wasn't worth pursuing because he let it go. I made a mental note to check out the second floor later. If the dog wasn't worried, it would wait. "I think we're good."

"How soon will we know if it's gonna help Zane and Oscar?" Will was already eyeing his patient critically.

"Dad? Dad, you okay?" We turned to see Zane peering at his father as the older man blinked in confusion.

Oscar took a few deep, experimental breaths. "Yeah, I think so. I just . . . I can breathe again. Like there's a weight gone." The older man rolled his shoulders hesitantly, and breathed deeply.

"'Bout that quick. See how Zane's doing. I'll get this glass cleaned up." Mirror shards crunched under my boots, scattered all over the floor in the chaos.

Cameron was on his feet, albeit wobbly, when I took the mirror frame away from him, leaning it on the bar. "I should go sit with the Quinns. Maybe I can offer them some comfort . . ."

I grabbed his shoulder, squeezing harder than was strictly necessary. "I don't think so. You owe me a talk." Now that the immediate threat was over, and I had time to really think about it, I was getting pissed. Cameron was so much more than he'd pretended, which meant he'd lied to me, my friends, my wife, and most importantly, to a woman I greatly respected and cared for. Dr. Bridget was my wife's best friend, yes, but she was one of mine too. And if you think protective dads are bad, just wait 'til you get a load of me.

He glanced around the room, and I knew we were both thinking the same thing. *Civilians.* "Not here. Upstairs."

I nodded, and went about cleaning up the mess first. There was glass to sweep, and blood to mop, and that was just the start of things. It was going to take him a bit to get up the stairs anyway, in the condition he was in. I was honestly amazed that he hadn't collapsed already.

By the time I got the glass in the trash, the possibly ex-priest was out of sight. I headed for the stairs with one of the lanterns. This wasn't a night to be in the dark.

I picked up my sword, too, on the way up. Duke was wary of the second floor for some reason, and I wasn't taking any chances. In the white light of the Coleman lantern, there seemed to be nothing amiss, however. The sleeping bags were all still laid out where we'd left them, and there really wasn't anywhere for anything to hide. Just the darkest shadows, gathering in the eaves of the roof. I raised the light higher to banish them, proving to myself that there was nothing there. Nope, just me and the hiss of the kerosene lantern. And Cam of course.

He eyed my bared blade from his seat on his own sleeping bag. "Thinking of using it?"

"I guess that's going to depend on what you say. Jesse's a very grumpy fellow at this exact moment." I set the lantern on the floor.

"Does Jesse often refer to himself in the third person?" When I just gave him a flat look, he sighed wearily. "You've got every right to be angry. And suspicious." Instead of offering more, though, he just sat and looked at me.

"Look, I'm not going to play twenty questions with you. Spill it. Now." I'd never turned my sword on another human being in my life—*What* were *those things outside? Shut up, Jesse.*—but at that moment I wanted to.

"All right, but you're not going to like most of what I'm going to say."

I settled for perching on Will's sleeping bag, still rolled into its little ball. "You don't get to presume to know me that well. Talk." The lantern left us in a small bubble of light, with the night pressing in all around. I felt like we were two kids, telling ghost stories in the dark. Only there really were ghosts in the dark, and they were trying to eat my face.

"I wasn't honest with you. With any of you. About who I am."

"Y'think? Is Cameron even your name?"

He nodded. "Brother Cameron, to be more precise."

"Oh God, you're a monk?!"

He was trying for patience, and I knew I was sorely testing it. Couldn't help myself, it's my nature. "It's a title. Just a title. I'm part of the Ordo Sancti Silvii, the Order of Saint Silvius. I don't know if you've heard of us . . ."

"I usually call you all the Knights Stuck-up-idus."

A faint smirk crossed his face. "I've heard that before. That was you?"

Demon hunters, champions like me, only run by the Catholic Church. Five men, never fewer than five, operating under the name of a saint who didn't exist. They had as little to do with us, Ivan's champions, as possible. Mocked and reviled us, even. So why the sudden interest in fraternization?

"So that makes you a holy roller?"

"Yes, I am an ordained priest. Technically."

"And what are you doing here?"

He sighed, raking fingers through his short hair. "We were . . . afraid something like this might happen. I was supposed to stay near you, keep an eye out."

"Something like *what* exactly? You knew we'd be ambushed and trapped inside a cabin in godforsaken nowhere?"

"No." Weariness just oozed from his pores. I'd seen Mira after some big magic, and it knocked her on her butt for days. I was surprised Cam was still upright, much less speaking coherently. "No, if I'd have known about this, I'd have come ready. Me being *here* on *this* day was just . . ."

"If you say divine intervention, I'm going to kick you in the face." Okay, there was a small flicker of guilt at the thought that I was threatening an actual priest, but it was a really *tiny* flicker.

"Let's say happy coincidence."

"So what do you know? *Brother* Cameron." I leaned forward, keeping the sword between us. Y'know, just to remind him it was there.

"Surprisingly little. I'm one of the frontline soldiers, not someone who calls the shots." He blinked slowly as the tip of my sword came to rest on his hand, pinning it ever so lightly to the floor.

"Look at me, Cameron." I waited for him to raise his eyes. "I don't trust you, and I don't believe you. If I have to keep prying things out of you, one secret at a time, things are going to get ugly. In your current condition, you might want to think twice about trying to take me on." See, in my world, where the code of the *bushido* ruled, Cam had already marked himself as a dishonorable man by lying to me. Punishing him for it was therefore just and right. Guess it was a good thing for him that I was a nicer guy than that.

He looked me in the eyes for long moments, weighing his options, I guess. Finally, carefully, he picked the blade up with two fingers and moved it away from his hand. "We had heard . . . rumors. Rumors of a hit going out on champions, us, anyone who makes a name for themselves fighting against the demons."

"Rumors from where?"

He hesitated for long moments until I tapped the back of his hand with my blade again. "I'm not . . . There are things that aren't known outside the order. I shouldn't speak of them."

"But you will." I saw it in his eyes. He'd follow whatever orders he'd been given, but they didn't set easily on him. He wanted to tell me; he just needed a little encouragement. "We're all in danger here, Cam. We have a right to know why."

"There's a book. An ancient text, older even than the oldest known printed Bible. It predates . . . everything, as nearly as we can tell. Written in three languages, left as an instruction manual of sorts. The order is based around it."

"Go on." Ghost stories. In the dark. That's all.

Cameron rubbed the uninjured side of his head, and I could see him weighing his words carefully. "The book details a time of great strife. A time when the residents of Hell would rise up and war with each other. The war will spill over into the human world, causing complete and total destruction."

Like riots, droughts, wildfires. Revolutions and famine. Everything we'd been seeing on the news for months now. And this was just the beginning. "Chaos, mass hysteria, dogs and cats living together . . ." He didn't get the reference and just gave me a puzzled look. "*Ghostbusters?* No?"

He gave me a flat look. "I got hit in the head today, forgive me. Anyway, like any prophecy, the clues and portents are open to interpretation. But our cardinal believes that the time is now, and that Hell's first order of business will be to remove us. All of us."

I could tell Cameron believed it. I mean, *really* believed it. His order thought the end was near, probably in all capital letters. Normally, I'd have laughed in his face.

Normally, that is, except for a few stray comments from Axel that I just couldn't get out of my head. *"They don't follow the rules, Jesse." "Think of it like a family food fight."* There was trouble brewing Down There. Axel was trying to make light of it, but there was some kind of internal discord. I promised myself that the next time Axel showed up, I was getting some kind of information out of him one way or another.

"But they can't hurt us. We have to allow it, we have to bargain for the fight, or they can't touch us." Ironclad rule. Except Axel's words from last spring were marching double time around inside my head now. *They don't follow the rules, Jesse.* Over and over again, like an alarm blaring. And more recently, *We always come back*.

That one single fact was banging around in the back of my skull, part of me screaming in hysterical terror. The Yeti was back, but if I stopped to think about it right now, I'd cease to function. I'd think about it later. Hopefully.

"Those things out there bled, didn't they? You wiped it off your sword." He nodded toward my blade. "Then they're not demons. And they're not subject to the edicts."

He was right. Whatever those things were . . . they weren't demon, and all bets were off. Christ, I had to get to a phone, I had to call Ivan and warn him, send out an alert through Grapevine. Something. Anything. *Oh Jesus . . . Estéban . . .* The kid was with my wife and daughter. If they went after him . . .

"We were watching all of you. All that we knew about. They sent me to Kansas City to . . . try and mitigate damage, I guess."

"And then you followed me up here. What about Estéban? Who's watching him?"

"The boy?" Cam blinked a little, obviously puzzled. "He's just a kid. He wasn't considered a priority, I guess. They didn't think about putting someone with him—" He choked, possibly because I had him by the shirt collar, hauling him into my personal space.

"That *boy* has killed a demon. And now he's alone, with my wife and daughter. If anything happens to any of them, because *you* didn't consider him worth saving . . ."

His hands were strong—much stronger than I'd thought—as he gripped my wrist, trying to loosen my hold. Cam was a creature of surprises. "They said . . . no homes . . . Too hard to hit the homes, too much . . . protection . . ." He gasped when I let go, gulping air.

Someone moved at the bottom of the stairs, a shadow sprawling across the ceiling above us. "Jesse? You guys okay up there?" Cole. And calling me by name was code. If I answered with anything other than "little brother," he'd be up the stairs in a heartbeat, guns blazing. Figuratively. I think.

"We're fine, little brother. We'll be down in a little bit."

"A'ight."

Cameron was still rubbing his throat when I looked back at him. "*Who* said, Cam? You keep saying 'they said.' Who is 'they'?"

"There was . . . an interrogation. I wasn't there. I told you I'm just a foot soldier. Information was obtained."

"They interrogated . . . what? A demon? How did . . . ?" The concept was alien to me. How do you hold something that can disappear at will, let alone interrogate it with any semblance of credibility? "How do you interrogate a demon?"

"Trust me when I tell you that you don't want to know."

"Even better than that, how did you find one? One just happened to fall for the box-and-stick trap?" Cam looked down, away, and a chill settled over my skin.

"You summoned a demon, didn't you? Summoned it, bound it somehow."

He still wouldn't meet my eyes. "Not me personally, no."

"Doesn't matter." Something like that, you can't just sit still for. I stood up to pace the confines of our small circle of light. "Christ on a freaking cracker, Cam. You're supposed to be the good guys, and you're *summoning* demons? You don't summon demons! Not for anything, or anyone. That's how they get in, just that little bit of acceptance. And after that, maybe a small deal, something harmless. Then a little more. Then more. Then they have you by your short and curlies and there isn't crap you can do about it, unless you come to someone like me. You simply do *not* summon demons!"

"It was necessary. We knew something was coming—we needed details. It was the only—"

"Oh screw your details. I notice you didn't impart any of this great wisdom on the rest of us. What if we hadn't brought you on this trip, Cam? How many of your other 'brothers' weren't anywhere near the people they were supposed to be watching? I mean hell, there's only five of you to begin with!" Again, he refused to meet my eyes. "More than five. Probably lots more. Any other lies you'd like to clear up, while we're up here?"

"None of these things were my decision, Jesse. You have to know that."

"I don't care whose decision it was. You just better hope the rest of your 'brothers' are as good at their job as you are. 'Cause if your secrets got anyone hurt, I will personally turn you over to Ivan Zelenko for an ass-whupping." Ivan was one person that I never *ever* wanted mad at me, and if the knights had endangered his people . . . Mad wasn't even adequate to describe the old man's reaction. I don't think they'd invented a word yet for how pissed he was going to be. "And then I'm gonna kick the crap out of the pieces of you that are left."

He nodded, and I could see the exhaustion weighing down his shoulders. There were circles forming under his eyes already.

"You need to rest as much as you can. We can't let you sleep, in case you have a concussion, so you'll have to make do." I headed for the stairs, leaving the lantern behind. "We'll continue the conversation in the morning, when you're coherent."

I was halfway down the stairs before he spoke again. "Jesse." I stopped, looking back with my eyes just level with the floor. "It may not have been the best idea. But they did what they had to do for the information. And it probably saved your life today."

"Yeah? Tell that to the Quinns. Let me know how safe they feel."

10

There really wasn't much else to do. Wisely, no one wanted to venture out into the darkness with those things, and so we were left with nothing to do but bed down for the night and wait for the sun to rise.

I was never any good at waiting. As the guys hauled their sleeping bags downstairs (opting to sleep in front of the fireplace instead of up in the loft), I did a walk-through of the cabin, checking defenses. Cam's spell may be holding the nasty-bads back for now, but by his own admission, it wasn't going to last forever.

I started in the main room, and while it may have looked like I was merely watching the night outside the windows, I was actually passing my hand over the glass, feeling for Cam's wards. At each one, I found the telltale prickle of magic in place, and I was careful not to touch it and disrupt the protections. With those in place, I might be able to doze a little, at least.

On my way through the kitchen, I gave the faucets a twist, just to see the clear cold water come running out. The water was actually piped in from a spring just behind the cabin. A spring that, I hoped, was still on consecrated ground. "Hey, Marty? If you guys have any buckets, start filling them with water." Siege strategy said that you first cut off water and food from those penned in. I didn't know if the Yeti was versed in siege warfare, but why take the chance?

Outside the back door, the night was cool and silent. To the west, the mountain peaks still had a faintly lavender glow, but otherwise night had fallen. Was dark always so black? In a few hours, the moon would be rising somewhere behind me, but right now all I had was the faint gleam from the cabin windows.

The ward tingled a little when I passed through it, and I stood on the back porch for a few moments, listening to the world around me. Nothing moved. No birds, no animals, hell, I don't think there were even any insects buzzing around. Everything sane had cleared out hours ago. Even if I couldn't see the Yeti and his pets, I knew they were there.

I flexed my fingers on the hilt of my sword and stepped off the porch. Funny, holy ground didn't feel any different from regular ground, except for the very faint tingle across my skin. Magic. Cam could call it prayer if he wanted, but it all smelled and felt the same to me. I paid special attention to that tingle as I walked across the clearing, ready to jump back if I crossed the barrier between consecrated and not.

Things were moving in the trees now, rustling softly. The only reason I could even hear it was that everything else was so freakin' quiet. Whatever they were, they knew I'd left the cabin, and they were tracking right along the edge of holy ground. That wasn't encouraging.

The spring itself was the only natural sound for yards and yards. The water burbled quietly, trickling from a small spill of smooth rocks into a man-made pond. It was still within the boundary by about three feet, and I had to wonder how long it would take for the spell to fade, to open this up for attack. Once we lost our water, we'd be out of time to make decisions.

How soon? I dipped my fingers into the pond, letting the pure water trickle over them while I had a good think. *How long do we have?* How long did Mira and Anna have, if those things were after Estéban? How long for Ivan, and Sveta, and Avery, and all the others I'd never even met?

Barely a yard in front of me, the bushes parted and a bald head appeared, nose wrinkling to sniff the air. I stood slowly and brought my sword up, dropping into a defensive stance. The creature leaned forward, testing the invisible barrier between us, then hissed in silent displeasure. Whatever it was, it wasn't willing to cross Cam's threshold. "That's a good boy. You stay right there."

It cocked its head to one side, a very human gesture of curiosity, almost like it understood what I was saying. Its eyes were solid black, but glowed somehow, and I got the impression that something larger was looking out at me from the inside. Goose bumps ran laps up and down my back.

Another one slipped through the brush, roughly shouldering the first aside, and they bared their teeth at each other before turning to look at me again. I took the opportunity to get a good look at them, despite the darkness.

Both male, that much was evident, their bodies were

almost skeletal, stained and dirty skin stretched tight over a framework of bone. Their teeth were rotted black, and the odor of decay slowly permeated the area. They breathed, but made no other sound that I could hear, and they crouched on all fours like a hound rather than moving on two legs. Their movements would have been fluid on another animal, but on them they were strange and alien, like their bodies just didn't fit what their brains were telling them to do. *Or what their master is telling them to do.*

Their bare feet weren't clawed, per se. More, it looked like their toenails had simply overgrown. The same with their fingers. Still, there was no mistaking the dexterity of their hands. I'd seen them grab and shred.

Briefly, I wondered what would happen if I stood at the very edge of the marked boundary and cut their heads off. Something told me that would be a bad idea. I mean, shedding blood on holy ground? Just didn't seem to be a good thing.

A third joined them as I watched, the handless female I'd taken a bite out of earlier. If she noticed her missing appendage, it didn't show. She shuffled around on the stump just as easily as on her remaining hand. The wound itself wasn't bleeding, but I could see smears of something black and thick left on the foliage as she passed. I swallowed hard and tried not to think about what that was. Just looking at her was making me a bit queasy. I could have handled something more . . . animal, I think. They were just human enough to be grotesque. The wrongness of it all turned my stomach.

The female silently snarled at the two males, and they slunk back, giving her space. Her gaze fixed on me, and there was something in there, something more than that otherly blackness the males had. I felt like she actually *saw* me. "And just who are you in there?"

There was more movement in the bushes to my left as even more of them gathered, drawn by some unheard signal. It was time to go. Slowly, I backed toward the cabin, not willing to turn my back to the eerie creatures who had massed to my presence. I was never so glad to feel my heels hit wood as I was that night, stepping back up onto the small porch.

"Darling, aren't they?"

Either I was getting slow, or Axel was really freakin' fast. My sword missed his head by a fraction of an inch. I may have sliced hair. "Jesus freakin' Christ!"

"*Shh* . . . No reason to get *him* involved." The blond demon hooked his thumbs in his belt loops and leaned against the wall, shushing me with a grin. "And we wouldn't want your buddies to come investigate the ruckus, would we?"

"How the hell did you get here? The ground is—"

"Consecrated? Yes, I know." He made a face and spit. "Nasty business that. Hadn't counted on that."

"Counted on wh- . . ." It made sense, suddenly. "You were inside already. Upstairs. That's what Duke was growling about."

"Stupid mutt. At least he's smart enough not to take me on."

"But how'd you get out here? The wards . . ."

Axel snorted. "Your little priest friend should learn his limits. There's barely enough power here to make me itch." With a smirk, he demonstrated, hopping back and forth over the threshold of the open door. "I'm on the east side, I'm on the west side. I'm on the inside, I'm on the outside."

"Wonderful. So the wards aren't any good." Just what we needed.

"Au contraire. They'll work perfectly fine against anything that isn't me." He grinned, and it occurred to me that his injuries from earlier were gone. Only the faintest hint of a shadow showed where the worst of the bruising had been. Damn, demons healed fast. "I'm just that good."

"What about the ones at my house?"

"Ah, now *those* are good wards. Your little priest could take some lessons from your wife." Somehow, that made me feel better. If Mira's wards would keep Axel out, surely they could keep out anything else Hell sent at her. Just until I could get home.

"So you're . . . what? Lurking around here so you can offer to clue me in for . . . dun dun dun . . . a price?" I wasn't up for playing games tonight.

The demon frowned at me. "Now there's no need to get snarky. I am what I am."

"Boy, don't I know it." I tried to move past him, and he barred the door with one arm.

"Jesse, in all seriousness. You need to talk to me." Sometimes, when he got all serious in my voice like that, I could almost believe him. Almost.

"In exchange for what? I think I'm gonna be needing my soul soon, so I really can't offer that up at the moment."

He nodded. "Yes, you're going to need it. Even if I tell you not to, you'll do it. Maybe *because* I tell you not to. But that's because *you* are what *you* are. Rather static creatures, aren't we?"

"Same shit, different day." Dammit. I needed information, and at this moment, I trusted the demon on the porch more than the priest upstairs. "All right. What info do you think I need, and what do you want for it?" There was this little voice in the back of my head screeching *"Warning, warning!"* but I ignored it.

He pursed his lips a bit, moving to gaze out into the darkening night. "Aren't you even going to ask me what they are?"

"Would you tell me?"

"I might." He grinned without looking at me, but I could hear it in his—my—voice. "If you ask the right question."

"Can they be killed?" 'Cause really, that's what it came down to. Whatever they were, wherever they came from, if I could kill them, I had options.

"Decent question. The answer is yes." He looked at me, waiting.

I gritted my teeth. "*How* can they be killed?"

"Ah, now that was a good question." He nodded. "Destroy the neural pathways, and the body will cease to function."

"So . . . boom, headshot."

"If you like. They do feel pain, and they know fear, but . . . they aren't allowed to react to it. For the controlling force, they are tools, nothing more. Expendable. Don't expect mercy from them. Don't expect to reason with them."

They were still there, sitting silently in the bushes. It seemed, without my proximity to react to, they were simply left, waiting. I was reminded eerily of empty dolls, abandoned by some careless child. I shivered. "He's the controlling force. The Yeti. Yes?"

"The Yeti?" That got a laugh from him. "That's priceless. I'm going to have to call him that from now on. Yes, they're his. They only respond to him, because he made them."

"Made them how? What are they?" I honestly expected him to dodge that one. I mean, how to kill them was a pretty valuable piece of information and he'd just handed it over. Asking for more was just being greedy.

You can understand my surprise when he kept talking. "You all look alike to us. Did you know that? If you and your brother stood silently side by side, I don't know that I could honestly pick you out." He gave me a small, sly smile. "It's the voices that tell you apart. The voice is what calls us out of the darkness. That is what we follow into the light. Your voice is the doorway to your soul."

"That's real poetic, Axel. You should write that shit down."

He rolled his eyes at me and pointed out into the night. "They make no sound. They have no voices of their own. Think about why."

"Am I going to be quizzed on this later?"

"Maybe." Dropping his arm to his side, he sighed heavily. "Nasty business, those things. Not done very often. It's one of those things I wish we could un-learn."

I caught a hint of disgust in his voice, and I wondered at it. "Do you have any? Your own little army of creepy spider-monkey people?"

"No." The answer was short, clipped. "Whatever you think of me, there are things that even I won't do, Jesse. And that is one of them."

Well, holy crap. Who knew Axel had morals? "So what do you want in return for all this? You don't ever give me anything for free. And I'm fresh out of sticks."

He turned to face me again, his eyes flaring red for just a moment. "Never think this is a selfless act on my part, Jesse. These events work toward my agenda. All I ask from you at this time is to do what is true to your nature. And I'll do what is true to mine."

"That's not exactly comforting."

"It wasn't intended to be. Unfortunately for you, you're caught up in something you don't understand. You're the piece of straw being whipped around by the tornado."

I winced. "You had to say tornado?" After my close call with one last spring, I was more than a bit para-noid about even uttering the word. "So Cam was tell-ing the truth? About a war in Hell?"

Axel smirked again. Or still. Really, it was kinda his permanent expression. "You should get back inside be-fore they come looking for you."

Ah, there it was. His limit. "And what about you?"

"Me?" He shrugged his lanky shoulders. "I'll be around if you think of any more good questions."

Great. My personal demon was gonna be playing Peeping Tom. There was one more thing that I really needed to know, if he'd tell me. "Cam says it's a hit. That you're all out to get us."

In the doorway, Axel stopped, glancing back at me. "Don't trust the priest. He's carrying around more secrets than you can possibly imagine." Between one step and the next, he vanished. There was no scent of sulfur, proving that he wasn't truly gone, just unseen.

I gave it a moment longer, then went back inside myself. I suppose someone might have laughed at my dilemma. Should I trust the priest, who had already lied to everyone I knew, or the demon who fully admitted to having his own agenda? Yup, that was a corker.

The guys had managed to draw up a couple of buckets of water, and Cole was looking over our food supplies when I passed through the kitchen. "How are we set, little brother?"

"We were planning on a week, so we've got food. Water. Our real issue is going to be Zane." We both glanced toward the big living room. I could see the Quinns sitting quietly with Cameron, three hands clasped together. Praying, maybe?

Cam had his glass of water with him and I watched with interest as he dipped his fingers into it, tracing invisible symbols on Zane's injured arm, paying special attention to the darkening flesh of his hand. The boy grimaced a little, as if it hurt, and the priest asked him something, to which he nodded. I lost whatever they were saying in Cole's next comment. "At least those things can't get close."

I didn't have the heart to tell him it was only a temporary reprieve. Hopefully, we'd be long gone before Cam's spell broke.

After a bit of discussion, it was decided that sleep was the first order of business for everyone but Cameron. We'd each take a turn at watch, and take a turn at keeping him awake too. I, of course, intended to stay up and keep watch (I can sleep when I'm dead) whether they agreed to it or not. Marty opted to go first, and stood in front of the window, watching the clearing in front of the cabin. I elbowed him lightly as I passed. "You can sleep if you want, man. I got this." He grunted in response, but really didn't move.

Duke's massive form lay sprawled at the foot of the stairs, and he opened one eye when I bent down to scratch his ears. "Good boy, Duke. Very good boy." Poor dog. I could only wonder what he thought of this whole situation.

The big mastiff enjoyed the scratching for a few moments, his doggy sigh coming in somewhere between a moan and a growl. I knew how he felt.

I settled near the dog, propping myself up against the stair rail, and we turned the lanterns down as low as we were comfortable with. Total darkness was not a happy thought.

I lost track of time. Maybe even dozed a little. But when Duke moved, I came alert. The big dog raised his head, ears pricked, and whined softly in the back of his throat.

At almost the same moment, Marty said, "Do you hear that?"

I couldn't hear a thing at first. Duke whined again and heaved himself up to his massive feet, padding to the door. He cocked his head and raised his paw like he might want out, then dropped it. His tail was tucked firmly between his legs, and his hackles rippled up across his muscled shoulders.

Cole and Marty both got up, moving to the window again. "It sounds like . . . voices?" Once he said that, I could hear it.

"Don't . . . don't go outside . . ." Cameron's voice was faint, distant. Drowned out by the plaintive call from the darkness.

Outside, someone was calling. It sounded like a man. I grabbed my sword—I wasn't letting that out of arm's reach again—and stood up, moving to take hold of the dog's collar. Together, we opened the front door and stepped out on the porch, despite Cam's continued protests. Duke seemed content to press tightly against my leg, torn between whining and growling.

"Is someone out there?" Marty and Cole joined me, both looking to me like I should have all the answers. I was getting a bit tired of that look.

The strange man's voice called out of the night. "Order now before time runs out!"

We all exchanged looks, and the call came again. "Just jump, I'll catch you!"

"What the hell *is* that?"

The man's voice was joined by another, and then a third, both calling out nonsensical phrases. "The rain looks like it should hold off the evening." "Honey, what's for dinner?"

Soon, a woman was calling out from the distant forest, too, and I just knew it was her, the handless one. "If you don't clean your room, you're both grounded!"

Cole snorted a small laugh at that one, but it was mostly to drive off the growing sense of unease we were all feeling. It was gibberish, nonsense phrases taken out of context, but it made my stomach churn.

"Has anyone seen my hammer?"

"Dad, your phone is ringing."

"Ninety-nine cent burgers after four o'clock!"

There was . . . a pull to it. Something under the voices . . .

Some of the calls came from farther away, and the words were impossible to understand, but the tone of entreaty was clear. Underneath the words was a message, wheedling at the edges of my mind. *Join us*, they said. *Help us, save us.* I felt like, if I could just get a little closer, I could make out what they were saying. *We're cold, we're frightened, it's so dark . . . Help us . . .*

I could help them. I could save them. I could bring them back here, where it was warm and safe . . .

Cole grabbed my shoulder, pinching a nerve cluster hard enough to make my entire arm go numb, and only then did I realize I was halfway across the clearing. Pain in my wrist made me look down, and I found my arm encased in Duke's huge maw, the dog holding me with enough pressure to stop me, but not enough to draw blood. I had no memory of having crossed the distance. "Whoa, big brother."

The moment I heard Cole's voice, fog around my brain seemed to clear. "That is . . . so not cool."

"Tell me about it." Cole showed me his own left hand, the clear mark of the dog's teeth visible. Duke hadn't broken skin, but it was going to bruise bad. "Mutt bit me."

"Thank him." Duke, deciding that he had done his duty by me, released my wrist, and I patted him on the head. "Good boy."

"How are they doing that? I hear them say things, but it's like they're tugging at me." Cole frowned at the hidden serenade. "It sounds like . . . like a bunch of TVs left on, y'know? All on different channels."

That was exactly what it sounded like. In fact, once he pointed it out, I recognized a few of the phrases from commercials. One of them called out, "It cleans up in the dishwasher" and I finished the sentence under my breath, "And breaks down for easy storage." Hey, I watch a lot of late-night info-mercials.

"I don't know what it is, but I think we should get back inside." Standing only a few feet from where Cameron's consecration spell ended was making me twitchy. What if Cole hadn't grabbed me in time? "Maybe keep watch in pairs."

"Hey . . . where's Marty?" At Cole's puzzled question, I turned to look back at the cabin, at the now empty front porch.

The creatures called from the night, mocking. "Being a good neighbor." "What a fashion faux pas!"

"He was right there . . . maybe he went back inside?" Nausea curled in my guts. "Marty? Hey, man, you there?"

At some unspoken signal, my brother and I bolted back toward the house, thundering up on the porch and through the door to find exactly what we dreaded. No Marty. I was back outside in a heartbeat.

"Marty!" My own voice bounced off the mountain and back to me. The insidious calls were my only answer. "Martin Shane Wallace! Answer me!"

Cole stood beside me, both of us holding our breaths, so scared we'd miss a telltale sound, a rustle in the brush, a cracking twig. Even Duke was tense and silent; his shoulders bristled as he scanned the tree line.

And then it came, the sounds of breaking limbs. "There!" Duke beat me off the porch, but only barely, and the pair of us had left Cole behind by the time we hit the edge of Cam's magic barrier. Both of us barreled through without a thought, crashing into the forest at full speed.

11

You don't think. You react, you move, you run. But you don't stop to think, "Hey, I just ran into the deep dark woods full of man-eating whatsits and gorilla yeti demons." Because that's your friend out there. Your best friend.

I lost Duke almost immediately, the mammoth mutt outdistancing me in huge bounds, but I kept running, trying to follow the crashing ahead despite the fact that I could barely see the trees in front of me.

The branches and bushes lashed out almost like they had minds of their own, catching me across the face, and I could spare only one arm to protect my eyes. My other hand held my sword, and if running into the woods was stupid, then losing my weapon would be insane.

The cabin and its light and safety were long out of sight when I jerked to a halt, straining to hear anything that wasn't my own heaving breath. The voices had stopped, and the freight train that was Duke had fallen silent.

The night rendered all things in shades of gray. Shapes were meaningless. That tree over there could have been one of the creatures, standing still. That reaching, grasping arm in front of me could be the limb of an old oak, knocked loose by simple age and weather, or it could have been a filthy, grimy claw, just waiting for me to walk within reach.

I relaxed my vision, let my senses search for movement instead of shape. There was nothing. Not even a night breeze coming down off the mountain. The only thing living out here was me and my heartbeat, thundering too loudly in my ears.

That wasn't true. Duke was out here, and Marty. If I could just find them.

The screams, when they started, sent ice stabbing through my heart, and I was off again before I truly registered what they meant. That was Marty out there, screaming, and over that, the big mastiff's bellow rang out. Duke had him, and I thanked whatever deity might be listening.

I dodged trees more by sense than sight, hurtled deadfalls without thought for what might be waiting on the other side. I know I ran a hundred yards over rough terrain before I was forced to stop again. Forced, because the screams had stopped, and silence reigned again.

Dammit, Marty, don't do this . . . I couldn't go back. Even if I knew where the hell the cabin was and how to turn my ass around to get there, I couldn't go back without him. I couldn't leave him out here if there was any chance at all.

"Marty, answer me!" That was Cole, tracking somewhere off to my left. "Jesse!" Through the trees, I could see a white circle of light bobbing as Cole searched with his flashlight. He'd gone back for it, genius that he was.

Marty wasn't answering us for whatever reason, but Duke . . . maybe Duke would. "Duke! Here, boy! Duke, come!"

Immediately, there was a whine to my right. Cole heard it too, because the flashlight came bobbing in my direction. Ten yards through the trees, and we found them.

Marty was sprawled on the ground, Duke planted firmly on his legs, and for a gut-churning moment, I thought they'd gotten to him. Then he moved, shoving vainly at his dog with one hand. "Gah, get off, you big dork."

I'd never admit it to the guys, but I actually felt a bit weak in the knees for a second. Relief, I guess. "Good boy, Duke." The mastiff grumbled and finally got up.

Cole arrived with his flashlight, playing the beam across our friend's face. My blacksmith looked pale and sweaty under his beard. "You all right, Marty?"

"Yeah, just messed up my ankle. Tripped over a goddamn tree branch in the dark, trying to get away from this big doofus." He roughed Duke's short fur to show he wasn't angry with the dog. "Thought he was a bear." Only then did Marty glance around with a frown. "How the hell did I get out here?"

"Still working on that." They were out there. I knew they were. Why hadn't they pounced on Marty the second he crossed that barrier? The way they'd gone after Zane, the way they'd massed to my presence earlier, I figured fresh meat would be too much to resist. But there wasn't a peep, not a rustle. Nothing to betray their location. "Where are you?" I muttered.

"Come on, we'll get you to Will. He can patch you up." Cole reached for him when the voices came again.

"Mom, have you seen my sneakers?" It was right behind me, and I whirled, sword at the ready. Nothing. Not even a twitch of movement. Cole's light shone over the brush without revealing anything.

Duke growled softly. "Cole, grab him before he runs off. Get Marty on his feet." There was motion behind me as they followed my orders. I kept my attention on the trees around us, waiting for whatever came next.

"Hey, take the trash out when you go!"

My head snapped around hard enough that I saw spots for a second. The voice, a woman's, came from my left, only a few yards away. And for a heartbeat, one second of eternity, it sounded like Mira.

It wasn't. I knew it wasn't. After a moment to think about it, I could hear the differences, the slight change in tone and pitch that said it was some other woman, some nameless, faceless voice in the night. But there for a second . . . for a second, my world was over, and I realized belatedly that I'd shifted my weight, ready to run into the trees like a madman. Not good.

Cole's voice was uneasy when he spoke. "We have to get out of here before they get us surrounded."

"Pretty sure we're already too late for that, little brother. Marty, you ready to make a run for it?"

"Yeah. I'm good."

Mockingly, the random phrases echoed around us. "And it's fourth and goal!"

"So I said she could just stuff it, if that's how she was gonna be."

"Daaaaadeeeeeee! I'm scared!"

Cole cursed softly under his breath. "Christ . . . that's a child." Even Marty winced, and I don't think it was his ankle. It was the father in all of us, that place that responded to a frightened child even if it wasn't ours.

"No. No, it's not. It's them, somehow." Somehow, those things that weren't supposed to have voices were having quite a nice chat out there. I couldn't even count them all and if I listened too hard, my head started swimming again, my senses drifting. "Marty, take Duke. Cole, take Marty. Let's get this circus on the road." I wanted my hands free, my sword free.

"You wanna take point?"

I snorted. "Are you kidding? I have no freakin' clue where we are. It's all you, little brother." I couldn't be sure in the darkness, but I think Cole rolled his eyes at me.

Making our way back to the cabin was easier said than done, even with Cole's uncanny directional sense to guide us. Marty was limping worse than I'd realized, and face it, the guy was short but he sure wasn't light. It was a struggle for him to hold on to Duke and lean heavily on my brother at the same time. Cole kept his flashlight trained ahead of us, and I brought up the rear, watching for the ambush I just knew had to come.

Why haven't they attacked yet? The eerie, nonsensical calls came from all around us, and every one of them tugged at some place just in front of my spine, a place in my gut that churned with nausea. The worst ones were the children's voices, and one of them kept wail-

ing out "I'm a little teapot" over and over and over
again. It might have been funny, in another time, another place, but here in the near pitch darkness, there
was a wheedle to it that was simply horrifying. It was
a tiny urge, a subtle entreaty to go galloping off into
the wilderness, just like Marty had. I bit my lip as hard
as I could without drawing blood and kept moving.

Now, I was no navigational expert, but it seemed to
me that we were drifting conspicuously uphill in our
path, and I didn't recall coming that way on my blind
rush into the trees. The more I thought about it, the less
certain I was that Cole was leading us in the right direction. Before I could comment on it, I nearly stumbled into the trio when they stopped abruptly. "What's
up, guys?"

Since I'd been walking pretty much backward, I
dared a glance back to see Cole shaking his head, trying to clear it. "It's like they're in there, in my head. I'm
getting a little muzzy."

"How muzzy, little brother?" Face it, I was never a
Boy Scout. If Cole couldn't find our way back, we were
well and truly humped.

He hesitated a moment, then said, "I think we're
good."

About ten yards and an eternity later as we worked
our way around deadfalls and thorny vines, Cole
brought them to a stop again. "No, no, we're not good.
Shit, I have no idea which way we're headed. My
head's reeling."

Oh hell no. I was *not* gonna die out here, probably
within yelling distance of safety. More importantly, I

wasn't going to let either of those two idiots die either. I couldn't.

I moved to grab a handful of Cole's short hair and yanked his head up to make him look me in the eyes. The flashlight beam cast his face in dark shadows, hollowing out his eyes and cheeks into a skeletal mockery of his actual face. My face, too, we looked that much alike.

Up close like that, he reeked of fear sweat, that particularly pungent aroma brought on by massive doses of adrenaline. We all did. Except maybe Duke. He just smelled like dog. "Listen, little brother. You are gonna get your shit together, and you're gonna get us out of here. And you're gonna do it with a smile on your face and a spring in your step, you got me?" It took him a moment, but he finally swallowed and nodded. "That's my boy." I butted our foreheads together lightly, just enough to give us both a good thump.

Only then did I realize the voices had fallen silent, and I had approximately two seconds to wonder why. That was the moment they chose to spring, of course, with all of us sufficiently distracted. And they took out the most dangerous of us first.

The thing must have been just above our heads the whole time, waiting in the branches like some kind of gruesome spider, and it dropped down onto Duke's back like one of those monkeys at the rodeo. The dog whirled with a savage snarl, trying to get at the tormentor clinging to his shoulders, and nearly knocked Marty sprawling in the process. Mastiff and minion went brawling into the brush and out of sight.

"Duke!" Marty lunged to go after his pet, and Cole and I both grabbed for his shoulders to stop him.

"Duke can take care of himself. We have to get out of here." Even as Cole said it, another of the creatures darted out of the bushes, slamming into my brother's right arm. The flashlight strobed as it went spinning into the darkness, and the creature vanished into the night again. The third one clipped Marty in the back of the knees, but the solid bastard was just too stubborn to fall. The minion bounced off those tree trunk legs and into the bushes again in a crackle of brush. Somewhere a few yards distant, Duke was still going at it with his new special friend. From the sounds of the snarling , the dog was winning.

"Shit . . . Backs together, boys." The three of us took up positions, shoulders pressed together as we waited to see where they'd come from next. But really, what were we going to do? I was the only one armed, and Marty was half gimped.

One darted forward, almost at Cole's feet, then retreated when my brother lashed out with a vicious kick. "What they hell are they doing? Why aren't they just attacking?"

The next one dropped out of the branches above us again, and only the snapping of twigs warned us in time for Marty to lurch to the side. The thing landed on all fours on the forest floor and paused to hiss at us before leaping back into the brush. Damn, it was fast. I couldn't even get a decent swipe at it with my katana.

"Pack tactics." Marty got back into position, closing

the gap in our circle. "Like a wolf pack harrying an elk. They're trying to wear us down."

"They're smarter . . . unh! . . . than they look!" Cole paused in midsentence to kick at another one that darted in and out of the trees in front of him, taunting.

"They're not. It's him." The Yeti was dancing his little puppets on their strings, trying to scare us into recklessness, trying to tire us out. And it wasn't lost on me that the nasty things hadn't made a single lunge toward me. That pretty much told me all I needed to know. The Yeti didn't want me dead. He wanted something much worse.

What he wanted, I could use against him.

"Hey! Hey, ugly!" My voice bounced up and down the hillside, echoing. *Ugly! Ugly! Ugly!* The forest fell silent, even Duke's unseen battle dying down. After a moment, the mastiff's big square head poked out of the bushes, and he limped back to Marty, favoring his right hind leg but otherwise all right. "C'mon, stinky! Show yourself!"

"Jess, what are you doing?" I shushed Cole with a wave of my hand. Believe it or not, I knew what I was doing. Pretty sure. Maybe.

After a long moment of waiting, a branch above us creaked, and we looked up to find one of the minions hanging upside down from it, like a wingless bat. It was the female, the one with the missing hand. Her clawed toes and remaining fingers sunk into the bark to give her purchase, and her head twisted at a bizarre angle to look at us right side up, the blackness of her eyes glowing from within. Tendons in her neck creaked audibly in protest at the unnatural position.

"Hey there, ugly. You in there?" He was. I could feel him watching.

The thing's mouth opened, but her lips didn't move. Instead, the voice emerged from her throat, like through a loudspeaker. "I see you." It was his voice, the Yeti's voice. I would never forget that guttural rumble, coated with oil-slick taint.

"I just bet you do." I stepped forward, separating myself from the guys, ignoring Cole and Marty's whispered protests. "Shame on you, skirting around the rules like this. You'll never get what you want this way."

The minion's head twisted almost full circle the other direction, still focusing those eerie black eyes on me. "And what do I want?"

"You're too big and ugly to be coy. Let us go. Or you'll never have it."

Behind me, Cole whispered, "Never have what?" and I swatted at him without looking.

The Yeti chuckled, but his speaker never moved. "And just how do you propose to stop me?"

"Because if you don't let all of us go, right now, when I get back to that cabin, I'll blow my own fucking brains out, and that'll be the end of that."

"Jesse!"

"Shut *up*, Cole!" I smacked at him again, and kept my eyes on the Yeti's little pet. "You know me. You know the samurai believed in ritual suicide. Don't push me." I wouldn't, of course. The samurai may have believed in ritual suicide, but I believed very strongly in me-not-being-dead. But I was hoping the Yeti wouldn't call my bluff. Really, really hoping.

Suddenly, the Yeti was no longer amused. The handless female's claws shifted on her branch, unsettled in her master's anger. "You will not. I will devour them all."

"Then it seems we're at an impasse, aren't we?" And this was the tricky part. How to deal with a demon, without really dealing with a demon. Take lessons, kiddies. "How about we talk this out, once everyone's back on safe ground? Say, tomorrow?"

She scuttled closer, the branch dipping under even her slight weight until her gaunt and filthy face was level with mine. "You will swear this. To willingly present yourself."

"*If* you let us go now. All four of us. Let us get back to the cabin untouched, and without any of your choir boys singing out."

A low growl uttered from the skeletal creature's chest, but in the end the Yeti agreed. "I will see you on the morrow, champion." The light in the minion's eyes went out like a snuffed candle, but she didn't move. Her head slowly rotated back the other direction, keeping us in her hungry black gaze.

"Guys . . . start walking. Slowly." I didn't know if those things were like most predators, but I didn't want to take the chance that running would trigger them into pouncing. I didn't believe the Yeti's promise of safe passage for a moment. I just hoped it would buy us a bit of time.

"Jess . . . what have you done?"

"Just walk, little brother. Keep walking, and don't stop for anything."

Cole got us pointed in the right direction—I'd been right, they'd been luring us the wrong way—and we started picking our way through the thick underbrush.

The creatures shadowed us all the way back. Duke's constant rumbling growl was indicator enough, even if we hadn't been able to see them slipping through the branches like demonic spider monkeys. Every once in a while, we'd round a fallen tree or a pile of dead limbs to catch one of them leaping silently out of our path. They kept their distance, and there were no more eerie calls to scramble our brains.

It was hard, once we could see the clearing through the trees, not to just bolt for safe ground, but I had Cole's shirt knotted in my fist, and he held Marty's, and the three of us calmly and slowly crossed those last few yards. "Walk," I kept murmuring to them. "Just walk."

The tingle of Cam's consecration spell never felt so good, as we crossed that invisible line of safety.

I could breathe again.

12

Will was waiting for us on the porch, with Cole's handgun. My brother made a big show of taking it back from him and unloading it, glaring at me all the while. I glared back. If he didn't know me well enough to know I'd been bluffing, that was his problem.

And of course, the damn voices started up again the moment we were inside. "Ain't he a dandy!" "I'm bored, are we there yet?" "I'm a little teapot!"

"I swear, if I never hear 'I'm a little teapot' again," Cole growled, and I was inclined to agree with him. The song was forever ruined. "We're never gonna get any sleep if that keeps going on."

We tried, at first. Those who weren't on watch tried muffling the calls with their sleeping bags pressed tightly against their ears, but nothing seemed to drown out the wheedling, entreating pleas. I could feel it like a mosquito whining in my ear, and any time I started to let my guard down, to try to sleep, it was there, trying to lure me out the door. So long as they were calling out there, we were all in danger of dashing off to our deaths, and I had the feeling they intended to call all freakin' night.

I briefly entertained the idea of trying to negotiate better terms with Big Ugly, but deep down, I knew the Yeti wasn't going to bargain twice in one night. Besides, he was well on the way to getting what he wanted from me already. I had nothing left to offer.

Zane had a bad night too, but it seemed to be more from the pain in his arm than the eerie voices in the dark. He tossed and turned, whimpering quietly in his sleep, but as I watched him closer, it didn't coincide with the calls from outside. Even Cameron, who was borderline unconscious, twitched and flinched in time with every pleading voice in the darkness. But Zane *was* definitely sleeping, even if it was unsettled.

"Hey, little brother?" Cole was propped up in the corner, half dozing, but he opened his eyes when I called to him. "Watch the kid."

"He's not hearing them," Cole concluded after a few minutes. "Why is he not hearing them?"

"The poison, maybe? The brand? Protecting Ugly's property?" Or maybe . . . Cameron had prayed over the kid. He'd anointed Zane with the blessed water. And while I still wasn't sold on this whole "god" thing, I did believe in the power of will. "Look at his arm." There, where Cameron had traced his mysterious symbols, the creeping blackness had hardly advanced at all. It wasn't healing the damage, but it was at least slowing it. If it could stop the poison, maybe it was stopping the magic in those voices, too.

Cam's glass was still sitting on the mantel, half full, and when I dipped my fingers in, they tingled. *Hmm.* "Cole, c'mere." I gestured at his forehead with my wet fingers. "Cross or pentacle?"

"What?"

"Cross or pentacle, they're the only ones I know."

Hey, just because I didn't have any magic of my own didn't mean I was above using other people's.

"Um . . . cross, I guess." I drew an invisible cross on Cole's forehead with the blessed water, while my brother raised a skeptical brow at me. We both stared at each other for a few seconds, and then Cole finally nodded. "I think . . . that helps. It's still there, but . . . not as bad."

"Not as bad is good enough for me." I went through the house anointing everyone else, including the dog. Out of sheer perversity, I painted a pentacle on the sleeping priest's forehead. Almost immediately, the tension started to fade from the room.

Luckily, once we'd broken out of the lure, it seemed easier to resist. We bedded down as best we could, still taking turns at watch, and tried to salvage what was left of the night.

There was one nasty tussle with Will around two a.m., trying to keep him from walking out the door. It never occurred to me before how much heavier he is, and he packs quite a wallop when he puts his mind to it. It took Cole and me both to put him down, and then Marty dumped the last of Cam's blessed water over his head. He came out of it spluttering, soaked, and embarrassed as hell. I came out of it with a healthy new respect for my buddy's strength, and a bruise across my right cheek that was gonna be a shiner by morning.

Marty was up most of the night too, watching out the window. They say there's nothing so dangerous as a man with nothing to lose, but I don't think that's true. Men with nothing to lose go out in a blaze of glory—big, but quick. When you have everything to lose, when you know what you're fighting for, that's when you're a truly dangerous man. That's when you take out every single motherfucker in your path, calmly and cleanly. That's what I saw in Marty's eyes. All he wanted was to get back to his wife and his unborn child. They almost got him once, and nothing out there in the dark was going to stop him now.

Close to morning, Zane started running a fever. I remembered that fever, so bad I'd hallucinated in full Technicolor and surround sound. Even thinking about it made my mouth dry and parched, and I drank sparingly of our small water supply. Poor kid was in for worse.

Oscar tried to stay up and care for his son, but in the end even he drifted off. I felt for the guy, really I did. If that had been Anna there, gnawed on like that . . . I understood the need a father has to protect his child, even if he had no idea how to go about it. Oscar was doing all he could, and hating himself every moment because it wasn't more. I knew.

Thankfully, the voices vanished at dawn, though it would be a couple of hours before the sun would be high enough to peek over the treetops. I didn't believe for a moment that those things were gone, but if the light was going to chase them away for a bit, I'd take it and be happy.

Besides, I had stuff I needed to do, and a promise to keep no matter how badly I didn't want to.

I picked a moment when the guys were all mostly

dozing. Only Duke raised his head to watch me slip quietly out of the cabin with my sword belted on.

Palm out, I followed the brown, crusty trail of Zane's blood toward the trees, feeling for the edges of Cameron's consecration spell. I found it about halfway across the cleared area, the point where the tingling on my skin ceased, like a switch turned off. The holy ground was shrinking fast. I dug a line in the dirt with my scabbard at that point, and took two big steps back.

For a moment, I eyed the forest around me, too quiet by far. Nothing was stirring, no birds were singing. As if I needed more proof that I wasn't alone.

"Hey! Ugly!" My shout echoed off the mountain, bouncing back to me mockingly. I winced a little, knowing that it was going to rouse the guys, and I so didn't want them to interfere with this.

Almost instantly, one of the creatures appeared at the edge of the forest, clinging to a tree trunk about eight feet off the ground. This one didn't even have a nose, something black and gooey trickling down its face from the gaping hole. "Not you. Other Ugly. Go get your master." The Yeti was watching through those black eyes. I could feel his gaze on me, even by proxy, but I was done dealing with lackeys.

The minion never moved from its spot on the tree, but there was a rustling farther back. Three more of the little pets clambered spiderlike through the tree branches above us, but they found places to settle and moved no more. Not like the white-furred behemoth shouldering his way into view. He didn't even bother with the human illusion, this time, smashing saplings flat as he passed like they were so many blades of grass.

I called his kind Skin demons, the animalistic Abrams tanks of Hell, and the Yeti was the biggest I'd ever seen or heard of. Though he moved along on all fours, it was more of an apelike walk, leaning on the front limbs only as a convenience. Fully upright, he'd top me by a good four feet, and his forelegs were as long as I was tall. Christ, was he this big last time? Or was my own remembered agony coloring my perceptions?

He'd changed, that was for sure. He'd been a four-legged death machine when I'd faced him last, but more like a polar bear than a gorilla. He'd grown strong enough in just four years to come back across the veil into the real world, and he was closer to humanoid this time. He was evolving.

"Jesse James Dawson." Oh yeah, he remembered me. His oil-slick voice oozed into my head, and I fought the urge to hunch my shoulders against the intangible taint. He came to the edge of the clearing, his muzzle wrinkling as he sniffed the air. "You reek of fear."

"You try staying cooped up in a cabin with six other guys and no shower for a couple days. You'd reek too." I rested my hand loosely on my sword, mostly because it would stop the shaking. He was right, I was freaking terrified. He was standing yards away, but in my mind I could feel that hot breath on my face, feel those claws digging their way into my rib cage. *You beat him once. You can do it again.* That was getting me nowhere. I tried again. *A samurai does not fear death, only a bad death.*

Yeah, that didn't help much either. Not in the face of *that*.

"What do you want, little man?" As if he was thoroughly bored with me already, he rubbed his curved horns against a nearby tree, stripping bark in wide swathes and gouging deep into the heartwood.

"I think it's more about what you want. You're here for me, right?" He smiled, exposing great white fangs as big as my palm, and didn't answer. He didn't have to. "So let's deal."

The chuckle was more of a growl. "What makes you think you have anything I want?"

I got to answer with a chuckle of my own. "Oh come on. I handed you your ass four years ago. I spanked you all the way back down to Hell, and that was *after* you got a look at my insides. You know you want a piece of me again." That wasn't *entirely* accurate, but it got the job done.

The Yeti swung his massive head in my direction, claws raking lines in the forest floor. I could smell the sulfur of his breath as he snarled. "You got lucky, sack of meat. And this time, I will finish the meal I began." He snapped his teeth on empty air, and I was insanely proud of myself for not flinching.

"Then this is the part where we start discussing boundaries and whether or not we can see other people." I moved my scabbard and dropped down into a crouch I could hold for hours. I'd need to, if this negotiation went like normal. "You wanna start, or should I?"

"Stakes!" he barked. Of course. Always know the

reward for your toils. "I will return the soul of Zane David Quinn."

Oh that was just pathetic. "Nice try, and no dice. I will, however, take the soul of Zane *Christopher* Quinn." I shook my finger at him admonishingly, and I was secretly proud that I'd thought to ask the kid's full name the night before. Sometimes, Jesse is smart. Not often, but sometimes. "*Tsk-tsk*, you can do better than that. And just for that, I want his soul, *and* I want a promise of safety for everyone inside that cabin."

He growled, something I could feel vibrating through the earth where I sat. "And what do you offer?"

"I offer the soul of Jesse James Dawson." I hoped he'd accept it. It was all I had, after all.

He actually paused to think about it, the bastard. His head swayed back and forth, rattling twigs out of the lower tree branches. Finally, his eyes flared red, and he snarled, "Done!"

A black slash seared across the back of my hand, from the first knuckle almost to my wrist, and the smell of burning flesh filled the air around me. The mark had delicate little hooks at each end, the beginnings of a more elaborate design.

Shit, that always hurt. The pain would pass in a moment, but that first burn was always startling, always the worst. Even more startling was the fact that he'd accepted my terms. Safety for the guys had come way too easy. I'd screwed up already, somehow, even if I couldn't see it yet. If I could figure it out before this was over, maybe I could compensate.

"Weapons." We'd trade off like that, one of us making a demand, the other agreeing or vetoing. And every single word was so very important.

"I will fight with what I am given." He flexed his claws at me, waiting for me to make assumptions about his weapon choices. Assumptions are bad, m'kay?

"No. Declare it." I watched him closely. His efforts at deception were amateur at best. He was playing me, somehow. A demon didn't get to be that strong by being bad at his job.

My demand was followed by another growl, but he conceded. "Claw, and fang, and horn."

"I will fight with a melee weapon of my choice."

"NO!" Something in my insides went to jelly at that roar, and I heard it bounce off the mountain, echoing back at us. "Declare it!"

Damn, he called me out on that one. "I will fight with this sword." I drew my katana from its scabbard, holding it up for display. "The sword that ripped your throat out and sent you back to Hell once before."

I hate being pinned to one weapon. If my sword broke, or mysteriously disappeared sometime before the big fight, I'd be screwed.

"Done." Another acceptance, another flash of pain as the terms seared into my very skin. This time, my grimace was more of a smile. I'd won that round, though an onlooker might not realize it. In agreeing to only his physical weapons, the Yeti had forfeited any use of his magic. Sadly, so had I, but since I didn't *have* any magic, it was a small loss.

"Your call, fuzz ball."

His head swayed a bit, muzzle wrinkling as he sniffed the air, pretending to be deep in thought. "Aid."

Oh, that was a laugh. Like I was going to even dream of going up against him *and* his pets. "A one-on-one fight, just you and me."

The mammoth creature blew out a breath, the reek of sulfur hanging heavy in the air, before nodding his horned head. "These will not aid me." He gestured to the trees above, and I looked up to realize that there were at least five of the gaunt minions up there, all watching me with the same black eyes. "And the ones in the cabin will not aid you."

This one was tricky. "These" was such a mutable term. Did he mean "these five here," or "these types of creatures," or ...? And what did he define as aid? Marty couldn't reinforce my armor? Cam couldn't say a prayer for me (not that I'd ask him to, but just as an example)?

Still, he'd left me a loophole too. Only those in the cabin were banned from helping me. If they *left* the cabin, however ... Or even better, if I could call in Ivan and the cavalry ... It was all about the letter of the contract. There was no spirit to it.

Did I call him on it, force a better deal, or recognize the danger and take the loophole? I pondered that for a few moments, before nodding. "Done." Zap, another streak of black wound itself through my flesh.

It was a weak term. He knew it, I knew it, and we both moved on. I personally thought I had the best of that deal. I knew what he'd throw at me. He had no idea what those brilliant lunatics in that cabin might come up with.

We addressed armor. I wanted some, and just because I didn't have mine on me at this moment didn't mean that I couldn't come up with some later. It took some flattery on my part ("You have that thick pelt— it's only fair. Do you think your claws can't open me up through a thin layer of metal?") but he accepted.

We couldn't agree on a "where." My answers were too vague for him, and his were obviously designed to put me at a disadvantage. We argued that one point for forty-five minutes, while the sun crept westward and the light shifted in my favor. There was something comforting about basking in that warm glow while the big fur ball cringed farther and farther into the trees. Even so, I wanted this done. The sun would pass beyond me soon, and then the trees' shadows would creep back in my direction. I didn't want to be out here when that happened.

"A clear area, at least forty feet in diameter, with no innocent lives to endanger."

"I did not ask about dimensions or populations, I said WHERE?" His white-furred fist hit the ground, causing a minor explosion of soft forest soil. He really wasn't going to let this one go. "Will these mountains suffice for you? You have the whole range to choose from, to find your 'clear area.'"

It'd have to do. Pissing him off any further wasn't going to get me anywhere. Besides, the "where" was easily manipulated by the "when?" I agreed, and he growled at me, indicating that it was my turn to name the next term.

"When I call your name."

That brought him up short, and he shuffled back and forth on his huge paws for a bit. I knew what he was thinking. On the one hand (paw?), it allowed me to completely control my environment. I could make sure we were somewhere without collateral damage; I could make sure I was armed and armored. Hell, I could wait a year and never call the fight due, if I wanted.

On the other hand, calling him by name meant he could get to this plane, fully formed and ready to brawl. He could ride my voice (if Axel was to be believed) across the veil on that one word, without any drain on himself. Just mentioning his name made it swim to the surface of my mind, and my mouth went dry. I'd never spoken a demon name, had sworn I never would. But desperate times called for desperate measures.

Yes, I knew what advantage I was giving him. But if I was going to have any chance at all in fighting him, I had to delay this as long as possible.

The word "done" wisped through the air, and my forearm burned in response. The design stretched from my knuckles almost all the way to my elbow in sharp angles and impossible swirls. Like Zane's brand, it writhed if I looked at it too long, and made my head ache.

The minions in the trees shifted a bit, the first sound

they'd made since they perched themselves above us, and I glanced upward. They were all looking at me now. Well, they'd been looking at me all along, but now, their gaze held some kind of hungry anticipation, and two of them slid a few feet down the trunk they were clinging to, getting closer. What in the world had drawn their attention?

That's when I felt the barest caress across the back of my knuckles where they rested on my knees. It was the feeling of a soap bubble, opening slowly around an intrusion.

Cam's spell had reached me.

I stood up, dropping my sword into my hand again as I stepped back away from the ever-shrinking barrier, and the Yeti chuckled deep in his barrel chest. "I think we are finished here, champion. I will listen for your call." He stepped backward, fading into the safety of the shadows.

"Wait. I'm not done! You will let us leave here!" Dammit, I wasn't ready to let him go.

The darkness itself seemed to laugh. "I think not."

"Motherfu- . . ." Wasn't going to do any good. He was gone, and his pets faded back into the canopy. I expected a demon to try to screw me in a deal. Didn't expect him to just walk out on one. Every time, a new trick.

Hours spent in a crouch left me stiff, and I hobbled the few yards back to the cabin. Maybe Dr. Bridget was right. Maybe I was getting too old for this crap.

The walk to the cabin was shorter than I would have liked, proving just how small our consecrated area had

become. The spring would be exposed by now. I hoped
we had enough water to last. Last for how long? Shit, I
didn't know. I had to find a way to get them all out of
here, to get help for Zane. If the spelled area kept
shrinking at this pace, we had one more day, tops.

Cole opened the door for me as I stepped up on the
porch, and I got the impression that he'd been standing
vigil for me for the last few hours. The smell of food hit
me like a ton of bricks, and I suddenly realized how
very hungry I was.

"I don't know what it is, but it smells good."

My little brother grabbed my arm as I tried to slip
past him. "What's the deal, Jess?"

I looked down at his hand on my arm, then back up
with a raised brow. "The deal is I'm hungry. Who
cooked?"

He ignored me. "When are you fighting?"

"When I choose. I have to call his name." I lowered
my voice to answer him. "Then I intend to take my
sword and lop off his furry head. Any more questions?" Honestly, it was no one's business, except
maybe Zane, and I didn't feel like discussing it in an
open forum. All I really wanted was breakfast. Well,
lunch by now. I stared at Cole until he released my
arm, and went to fill up my plate.

Lunch was a silent affair. We huddled over our
plates of nondescript slabs of venison and some canned
baked beans. Nobody talked, really, but I could feel
their eyes on me. Mostly on my newly tattooed arm.
By now, they all knew what it meant.

Nobody really had the guts to ask me about it, and I

didn't feel like offering up any information. That's the thing about demon slaying. Ultimately, it's a very solitary activity. They couldn't help me. I was on my own.

I spent a lot of time thinking about what the hell I was going to do, but quite honestly, I wasn't having a lot of luck with it. Calling the fight due now, when I had no armor, was just suicidal. I'd faced the Yeti like that once. I had no illusions about surviving it a second time. But I had no idea how to get the guys out of here safely. The Yeti wasn't just going to let us wander down the trail whistling "Dixie." Every scenario I ran through in my head ended badly. Very badly.

There was some small discussion among the others about trying to get the hell out, but about the time they started that, the shade from the tall trees was creeping up on the front porch. The minions weren't openly prowling the clearing, but we could see them slipping in and out of the brush, testing the boundaries of the light and Cam's spell. None of the guys were crazy or desperate enough to want to brave the night with those things out there. Yet.

By morning, the consecrated ground would be gone. And since Axel had proven that Cam's wards were strained at best, I knew we'd have to move then. Seemed like everyone else knew it, too. They started packing up their gear in somber silence, and we ate dinner without saying a word.

We knew the moment the sun set, because that was when the voices starting howling from the woods again. They were closer this time, sounding like they were right under the damn windows. There were more kids' voices this time, like they'd figured out the perfect way to rattle us.

Standing at the front window, I could see the dark shapes moving against the forest. In the dark, in the trees, it was impossible to count them. They clambered through the trees, dangled from branches, scurried over each other without regard to any law of physics. Occasionally, one would stop, raise its head, and we would hear a voice calling out of the dark, pleading, enticing.

Even knowing the lure was there, protected against it, I could feel the pull, somewhere below my ribs, just in front of my spine. That was the part of me that would feel better, feel calm, if I could just put one foot in front of the other, just walk out the door to the waiting calls. It wasn't overwhelming, and knowing it was there made it easier to resist, but it was enough to make everyone unsettled, almost queasy. Either that, or the venison had turned. Same sensation.

The guys bunked down to try to get what sleep they could, but no one really expected to be well rested come dawn.

Marty found me by the window after a while and stood with me in silence, the both of us watching the night grow darker. Finally, he cleared his throat a little, his voice coming out hoarse. "One of them sounds like Mel." When I looked down, there was anguish in his eyes, a strain in his face that he was trying very hard not to let me see.

I tilted my head, trying to listen for that particular voice without success. If he said one of them sounded like his wife Melanie, I would have to take him at his word. No one would know her voice better than he. "She's fine, Marty. She's at home, or out with Mira, probably shopping or baking or whatever it is they do when we're not around."

"Then why do I hear her out there? Calling for help, calling my name . . ." He pressed his hand against the windowpane and it fogged up immediately, leaving a ghostly palm on the glass. The temperature had dropped during the day. Autumn had arrived in the Rockies while we were busy with other things.

"Because you miss her, man. Because right now, there's nowhere else you'd rather be." Okay, I made that up, but it was as good an answer as any. "You think I don't want to be home right now, with Mira and the kids? It's just your mind playing tricks on you."

I had to wonder, though . . . Axel's earlier comment about the voices niggled at the back of my brain. They had no voices, he said. Voices, which were our doorways to our souls. They had no souls, then? They mimicked others, aping something they could no longer do on their own. I had to wonder, did they have souls at one time? If so, what were they before? As human as they looked, the thought unsettled me to my core.

"But what if it's really her? What if they found her, took her?" His eyes searched the clearing out front, looking for the source of his wife's voice. With night fully fallen now, he'd never be able to see the minions creeping around out there. "The baby . . ."

"Marty, she's fine. I promise you, she is not out there." *Oh please don't let me have just lied to him.* Marty hadn't signed up for this shit. This wasn't his fight, wasn't his fault. But he was stuck in it, just like the rest of us, because of me. How do you apologize for something like that? Can you, even?

He gave me a bleak look. "Easy enough for you to say. It's not Mira calling for help out there." He wandered over to where Cam and the others had started bedding down by the fire, and burritoed up in his bedroll, trying to muffle the sounds with the down sleeping bag.

I knew it was my job to get the guys out of here and home safe. That was a given. But right then and there I swore it to myself, swore on whatever I could think of and to whatever higher power was listening. I had to get them home. I couldn't let Mel be a widow, when she wouldn't even be able to understand why.

Duke and I, we decided to keep first watch. Sleep was for wussies.

Sleep was also for those who didn't have a demonic poison coursing through their veins. Zane whimpered and tossed for a long time, and I couldn't count the times Will was up to check on the kid and Oscar right with him. Finally, I shooed them both away, promising to sit with the boy for at least a while. Reluctantly, Will curled up in his sleeping bag, but if he got any rest at all it would be a miracle. Oscar hesitated, eyeing me warily, but weariness finally won out. Maybe I was the lesser of the evils, in his mind.

Duke and I found an open space near the ailing teenager and settled with my sword across my knees. With one hand, I idly rubbed the big dog's ears.

"Jesse?" Zane's voice drew me out of a near doze, and I looked down to find the boy's eyes glassy, but lucid. "Could I have some water?"

"Sure, kid." I fetched him a cup, waiting while he struggled into a sitting position before I handed it off. His eyes followed my newly tattooed hand as it passed through his field of vision. "You doing okay?"

He barely drank enough to wet his lips and lay back down. "My arm hurts. And I'm hot."

A quick examination showed that his fever was high, but steady. It wasn't bad enough yet to make him delirious. "You want me to wake Will up, see if he has something he can give you?"

"No. I'm okay." There was a deep pause there, the kind that fills the silence with all sorts of unsaid things. I waited. "Jesse? Can I ask you a question?"

"Sure."

"Cameron explained to me about the deal. For my soul. Why did you do it?" He kept his eyes fixed on the ceiling, unwilling to look at me. The soulless do that a lot, I'd noticed, out of shame maybe.

"This?" I rubbed at the black marks seared into my arm. It didn't even hurt anymore. "Why wouldn't I?"

"But I'm nobody, to you. Not family or anything." His eyes flickered my way once, then went back to studying the wooden beams above us. "That thing is going to try to kill you, and you agreed to it and I don't understand why."

I shrugged a little, leaning my head against the brick hearth. "Kid . . . There's only one thing I've ever been good at, and that's tearing stuff into tiny bits. I guess

I'm just trying to turn that skill into something useful. So I help people, when I can."

"But why?" His brow creased. He was really trying to understand.

It was hard to find the words for it. I mean, I could have rattled on for hours about *bushido* and honor and all of the things that I use to govern my life. But really, it boiled down to four words. "Because someone has to."

I don't think that answered his question, but a few moments later as he pondered on it, his eyes drifted closed. I'm not sure he slept, really. I don't think any of us did. But we were at least still for a while.

13

We took turns dozing, off and on. Duke sacked out somewhere around two a.m., his doggy snores rumbling through the cabin like a miniature eighteen-wheeler. It was soothing. It drowned out the voices.

I think it was the silence that woke me first. My internal clock couldn't decide what time it was, but the windows were still dark, so that made it sometime not-morning. Propped up against the brick fireplace, I examined the last few moments, trying to decide why I wasn't asleep anymore. The voices had stopped. No more wailing from outside, and the sun wasn't even up yet.

I realized Duke wasn't snoring anymore when the massive mutt padded over and shoved his head under my now-tattooed hand. "Good boy, Duke." I tried to scratch his ears, but he dodged it, stepping back a few paces.

I let my hand drop and struggled out of my sleeping bag to stand, but the dog came back, pushing under my hand again. The moment I tried to touch him of my own volition, he stepped back again.

"Duke? You okay, buddy?" I reached for him again, and he let me rest my hand on his back briefly. I could feel the vibrations of silent growls through his muscled flanks. He tolerated it only for a moment before retreating again, taking another step away from me. His golden eyes fixed on me intently, almost like he was thinking about making a lunge for my throat. But that wasn't the kind of dog Duke was. Believe it or not, I decided he was trying to tell me something.

"Whaddya got, big guy?" We danced for a few moments, me moving toward him, him retreating until we got to the bottom of the stairs. Then he gave a massive bark and bounded up into the dark loft above.

I grabbed my sword—I'm not stupid—and said, "Cole, bring a light." I heard the thrash of a sleeping bag, and knew my little brother would be right behind me.

The loft was mostly empty. We'd moved all the sleeping stuff downstairs, leaving only our pile of half-packed bags.

In the light from below, I could see Duke pacing beneath the eaves at the far end, pausing on every pass to sniff at the shuttered ventilation window. It wasn't big enough to even really be called a window. Round like a porthole, the metal shutters had been fastened tightly and latched from the inside. The mastiff stopped to paw at them, and I could see the ridge rise along his back at whatever he sensed on the outside.

My shadow grew longer on the floor in front of me, and for one heartbeat I was really freaked out until I realized it was only my brother with the requested light source. Cole came to stand beside me, but his eyes weren't on the dog. Instead, he eyed the ceiling, dark above us despite our warm circle of light.

"What the hell is that?" He raised both hands, and I

realized he had his gun, trained along the beam of the flashlight.

It took a moment to hear what he heard, the softest of sounds, easily missed before in the heavy breathing of sleeping men and the snoring dog.

"That's . . . scratching against the shingles. Almost like digging . . ." Our eyes met, coming to the same conclusion. "They're on the roof."

The how wasn't really important, but even as my eyes flew back to our suddenly breached defenses, I knew. In my mind's eye, I could picture the south side of the cabin where the trees were the closest. Trees that had, in the last few hours, been bared of Cam's consecration spell. Trees whose thinnest branches drooped over the tall cabin. I'd seen those creatures scamper up and down the spindliest trees like it was nothing. Climbing those trunks would have been child's play, once the spell on the ground wore off, and while those branches were too spare for any human to risk crossing, for the Yeti's little pets it would be like walking down a four-lane highway right onto the roof over our heads.

Before we could even formulate a plan, the metal-shuttered window exploded inward. Duke was the fastest to react, grabbing the filthy arm that reached through the portal and ripping it off with a wrench of his great head. Black gore spattered over the floor.

It didn't stop the creature crawling its way through the window, however. In fact, I think it made it easier, the lack of an arm making for less body to stuff through the tiny aperture. Its shoulders contorted in an unnatural way, almost folding in half to wedge itself into the circular opening. Its remaining arm braced against the wall and it slithered through up to its rib cage, where the unyielding bone caught it up for a moment.

"Duke, heel!" He came to me, thank God, carrying his grisly trophy with him. "Head shot, little brother." Without a word, Cole leveled his gun at the bald head. The thing hissed at him once before its skull exploded in a rain of rotten brain matter, splattering all of us. The rest of it hung in the window, twitching spasmodically.

The sound of the gunshot in close quarters brought everyone awake, with a chorus of "What the hell is going on?" from downstairs.

"Where the fuck are Cam's wards?" I growled to myself, but Axel had already proven that they were shaky at best. If the Yeti's little friends were getting inside, I think we'd now passed into the realm of "completely useless."

First order of business was to get those nasty bastards off our roof, before they succeeded in digging through to the loft. Even as skinny as I was, going out a window of that size was out of the question, so we left Marty and the dog up there with the hatchet to make sure no more made it inside from that entry point.

Will and Oscar armed themselves with a fireplace poker and a hammer, prepared to defend the first floor if it came to it, and Cameron plopped himself near Zane, eyes closed and mumbling to himself. There was no scent of cloves, so I assumed he was praying, for whatever good it was going to do us. Either that, or he was totally tapped out, and trying to do something stupid anyway. I just hoped the idiot didn't kill himself. He was out of mojo even if he didn't want everyone else to know it.

Lacking a ladder, our only choice was to clamber up the support posts on the porch, and then up onto the roof proper. I belted my sword on and hoisted myself up, holding my breath at every scrape and scuff I made. Cole waited on the ground, covering me with his gun, but we couldn't see any of the demonic spider monkeys from that side and nothing came over the crest. I hoped maybe the gunshot had scared them off. The other option was that they were simply too stupid to protect their flank.

I stood guard on the roof of the porch until Cole joined me. He motioned me forward with a whispered, "After you, big brother."

The moment I put my hand on the main roof, I knew they weren't gone. I could feel the vibrations as something on the other side of the peak scuttled and rasped at the shingles. Crouching low, I started for the top.

The chimney bricks were warm when I pressed my back against them, and part of me just wanted to stay there, clinging to that slightest bit of heat. The nights had gotten cold, suddenly. But I had work to do. Cole stayed crouched below me, and I peeked my head around the edge to see what could be seen.

There were four of them on the other side of the roof's peak, three scratching and prying at the shingles while the fourth would raise its head from time to time as if keeping watch. One of them was the one-handed female, and her lack of clawing fingers didn't keep her from digging at the edges of the shingles with the jagged bone at the stump of her wrist.

Four here, and one dead in the window. Was this all he had left? The five I'd seen in the trees before? I showed four fingers to Cole, then pointed to the trees with a questioning look.

He tilted his head, listening for a moment, then shrugged. They'd fallen silent, so there was no telling if the Yeti had more waiting out there for us.

Through some very crude and highly improvised sign language, we decided that Cole would pop over the ridge and take the first shot, which would mean facing three in rather precarious close-quarter combat. In order to do that, Cole had to take my place against the chimney.

I should have remembered that some higher power somewhere hated me.

As I tried to maneuver back down the steeply sloped roof, my heel managed to find the one loose shingle in the entire structure. It slipped out from under my foot to skid down and off the edge, and sent me sliding after it with a clatter. One flailing hand found Cole's boot, and I jerked to a halt with my legs dangling out over empty space.

Cole, quick thinker that he was, managed to brace himself to keep us both from going over, and reached his free hand down to offer me help back up.

As I looked up, reaching for the outstretched arm, I saw the first minion crest the ridge. Thanks to my less than graceful descent, they'd finally noticed us.

"Cole!" He didn't need my warning. My brother's shot took off the top of the thing's head. The half-headed body took a swipe at empty air anyway, too stubborn to admit it was dead, before toppling down the slope, crashing into me on its way. The other three barreled over the top before Cole could take aim again.

With a heave, Cole hauled me up onto the roof until my feet could find purchase, and then he was forced to let go, clubbing at the vicious things with the butt of his gun. I couldn't figure out why he wasn't shooting, until I realized he didn't know where I was. He wouldn't risk hitting me.

I ducked one of Cole's wilder swings and grabbed the first thing I could lay a hand on, a filthy, skeletal ankle. It was a start. I yanked my sword from its scabbard with no finesse at all, reversed it, and stabbed down. The blade bit through the putrid flesh, shattered the joint, and went on through into the shingles. The foot fell away, twitching.

Now, losing a foot wasn't going to stop one of those things, but I by God had its attention. It came boiling out of the pile on Cole, oblivious to the appendage that was no longer attached. I backed my way across the roof, leading it away from the brawl and giving myself room to swing my katana.

"I'm clear, Cole!"

My footing wasn't ideal, and with my luck I fully expected to wind up back on the ground with a few broken bones, but I was going to take this nasty bastard with me.

It was more than happy to oblige, and no more than

three feet away, it sprang at me, clawed fingers out-stretched. Maybe the missing foot threw it off. Maybe it simply didn't understand how fucking good I was. But when my sword entered under its chin and scraped against the top if its skull, there was no mistaking the flicker of surprise in those black eyes before they dimmed and died.

The body jerked and spasmed until I kicked it off my sword, sending it pirouetting off the porch roof below. Two down, two to go.

Only, when I looked back to Cole, he was still struggling to hold off three. And up over the ridge, another gaunt head poked, rotted teeth bared in a snarl.

"Oh that's just not fair!" Numbers unknown, they were coming across the branches, reinforcing their comrades.

Another body went sailing out into the darkness, and I heard a sick crunch as every bone it had shattered. Cole got his gun up under another chin and fired, blowing putrid brains all over the place again.

My little brother's face was frozen in a gleeful snarl, and I realized he was actually enjoying himself. Okay, have at it. I had to stop the reinforcements.

With a war cry (the situation just seemed to call for it, okay?) I launched myself over the roof's peak, and barreled into two more minions feetfirst. One went tumbling over the edge, ending in a sick crack and the explosive smell of burst innards. The other latched claws into my pant leg and fastened teeth into my boot, gnawing like there was no tomorrow.

With my free foot, I kicked it in the face until I felt

bone crack, but it still refused to let go. Our combined weight was dragging me down the sloping roof, and though my sword thrusts were finding flesh, I couldn't manage to get a killing strike in. Just when I thought my ticket was punched, Cole's gun sounded, and half the thing's skull vanished.

I kicked the half-decapitated skull off my boot and watched it go bouncing down the roof and off into the night, then looked up to nod my thanks to my brother. His eyes went wide, and his mouth opened, but he didn't have time to call the warning.

There was that split second when I knew that bad shit was coming and I couldn't stop it, and then the thing hit me from the far side of the roof. Somehow, it had gotten behind us, or past Cole, or maybe it had been there all along. But it was on me in two inhuman bounds, and the only reason I knew I was fucked was the brief sensation of flying as we were launched off the roof.

I landed in a pile of reeking muck (what was left of one the creatures, I realized later), and it was probably all that saved me from broken bones. All the same, the air was crushed from my lungs, and I could only gasp like a fish staring up at my brother's face so far above me. He was shouting at me, my name by the shape of his lips, but he was pointing past me, toward the trees.

Dazed, I managed to flip over to find myself staring into the minion's eyes. It was on all fours, shaking its head like the fall had knocked it loopy too, but it was definitely recovering faster than I. It realized that at the same time I did. I was barely able to get to my knees when the thing sprang.

I couldn't bring my katana up fast enough, and the sword got pinned between us. Blunt, rotten teeth fastened on my shoulder, bruising like hell through my shirt, but not enough to break skin or tear muscle. Twiggy arms scrabbled to entangle me, fingers raking at my arms, my shoulders. I ducked my head to protect my eyes and shoved as best I could with my arms all bound up. My sword got tangled in the chaos, and I hoped like I hell I wasn't about to cut my own fingers off with it.

And just as suddenly, the thing released me, an inhuman scream rising from the gaunt throat. In comparison, the Scrap demons' screeching sounded like a five-part harmony. I could feel something in my ears vibrating on a frequency not meant for humans, and it was all I could do to clap both hands over my ears, curling up to protect my sensitive hearing against the unholy sound. Something warm and sticky trickled against my cold palms, and I realized my ears were bleeding.

The Yeti's minion was no longer interested in me at all. It thrashed and flailed in the grass, clawing its own filthy skin off in long, jagged strips. Its body performed contortions with enough force to crack its own bones, like it was trying to turn itself inside out to escape whatever was plaguing it. It slammed itself repeatedly into the side of the cabin, fleeing blindly in panic and too disoriented to realize it was running the wrong way. The screaming seemed to go on forever, no small feat considering they weren't supposed to even have voices.

The strident sound eventually died down to a pathetic moan as the thing's throes subsided, and eventually, there was silence. The thing smoldered a bit, the dirty skin blackened and curling around the torn edges. The reek of putrid meat roasting assaulted my nose, and I swallowed the bile at the back of my throat with grim determination.

Only then did I realize that there were no more creatures poised to rip my throat out. I stood cautiously, sword at ready, but there was nothing there. They'd retreated.

When I realized that I could see the trees around me distinctly, I knew the sun was rising. The dawn had driven them off. Is that what happened to this one? I toed at the steaming remains. Didn't seem like a barely risen sun should cause this kind of reaction.

Once I got my bearings, I realized that somewhere in our mad tumble off the roof, we'd crossed what little was left of Cam's holy ground barrier. The consecration had literally eaten the creature alive. As I watched it, it dissolved into a puddle of black goo, the thicker parts taking longer to disintegrate. At least I wouldn't have to bash its head in. The last thing to go was the skeleton, and whatever they looked like on the outside, the bones were distinctly human. The skull's dark eye sockets watched me, grinning, until it oozed into the grass.

Movement at the corner of my vision made me flinch, and I barely pulled my strike in time to avoid taking off my brother's head. He raised his hand defensively until he realized I wasn't going to remove important body parts, then mouthed something at me. It took me a moment to realize that he was shouting. All I could make out was a faint hum.

My lipreading skills were rusty, but I think he said, "Are you all right?"

Was I all right? I couldn't hear jack shit, and my hands were gummy with whatever that gunk was. My left shoulder ached like a mother. I was pretty sure I wouldn't be able to move by morning. Yeah, on average, I was all right. I nodded, and pointed at my ears. "All broke." I could hear my own voice rattling around inside my skull, but it was like listening through a bale of wet cotton.

Cole popped the clip out of his gun and frowned at the remaining bullets. "We can't last here much longer." At least, that's what I thought he said, through the ringing in my ears.

I knew he was right. This was the last sunrise we'd see at this cabin, one way or another.

14

Will tried to look me over as I came back inside, but I brushed him off with a grumpy snarl. Wasn't anything he could do about damaged eardrums anyway. I could only hope that it was temporary. I didn't relish the idea of trying to fight demons without all of my senses up and functional.

Marty took my katana away from me, cleaning the blade with loving care while I washed the goop off my hands at the kitchen sink. There was no way I could salvage my blue jeans, however. The thick black gunk had soaked through to the skin and dried to a thick black crust, and we weren't even going to talk about the smell. Even Duke pawed at his nose when I passed by. "Hey, you tangled with a skunk once and you didn't smell like a daisy either." My voice sounded like the teacher out of Charlie Brown, all "wah wah wah."

I had to dig through the backpacks to find mine, and stripped down as quickly as I could to shuck into clean jeans. The adrenaline rush was fading, and I was quickly getting cold.

"Somehow, I figured you for a briefs kinda guy."

I was unarmed, half naked, and I had already ducked to one side before I remembered that I shouldn't have been able to hear that statement. Standing in the shadows under the eaves, Axel smirked at me. "You're getting jumpy in your old age."

"I don't think immortal supernatural creatures get to make age jokes." I kept my voice down (at least, I thought I did), not wanting to draw anyone else upstairs. It was hard to judge, with my own skull acting as an echo chamber. I finished pulling my jeans on, buttoning them quickly. I didn't really want to stand around talking to a demon in my underwear.

The demon walked over to poke through my extra clothes, wrinkling his nose at my collection of snarky T-shirts. "My Indian Name is Runs-with-Beer? Really?"

"It was a gift." Axel's voice—my voice—was coming through loud and clear to me, but the sounds from downstairs were still little better than a low thrum in the back of my senses. "Why can I hear you when my ears are all messed up?"

"Can you hear yourself when you speak?"

"A little, yeah."

He shrugged and stood. "There you go. It's your voice, Jesse. I'm just . . . borrowing it."

That sent a small chill down my spine, which seemed a bit unfair considering how cold I already was. I'd always rather hoped that Axel's voice was coincidence, or even my imagination. It was creepier, knowing that he'd deliberately chosen to mimic me. "Why?"

"I like your voice. It has a rather mellow timbre to it. Makes me all warm and fuzzy." He grinned and his eyes flared red for the space of a breath. Man, I hate it when he does that.

"You lied to me," I pointed out.

He gave me a look of shocked indignation. "I never!"

"You said they didn't have voices."

"I said they didn't have voices of their *own*." He continued to pick through my shirts, either nodding his approval or frowning in distaste at my collection. "Word choice, Jesse. Learn to listen."

"Is there something you wanted?" I grabbed a T-shirt out of his hand and yanked it on over my head, then added two more on top of it. Warmth was at a premium, and layers would act as armor. Sort of.

"Have you figured it out yet?"

"Figured what out?"

"What they are. His little pets." There was a gleam in his eye, not the usual demon red, but a more mundane "I'm dying to show what a know-it-all I am" kinda shine.

I'd had a lot of time to think about that, so yeah, I had my suspicions. They ranged everywhere from aliens to sock puppets, but deep down I knew, and it gave me the heebie-jeebies. "They're . . . human, somehow. Or were."

"Yes! I knew you'd get it." He beamed like a proud papa. It was . . . disturbing to say the least.

"But what has he done to them? Why are they like that?" He was so anxious to spill his secrets that he forgot to negotiate a price for the answers, and I found that interesting. I'd never seen a demon pass up a chance for a deal. I didn't think they could. Stuff was going on with Axel, and it remained to be seen if it was going to work for or against me.

The demon motioned me to step closer as if we were coconspirators. I don't think he noticed when I stayed where I was. "Have you ever seen someone bargain away their soul, Jesse? Not like what you do, but the others. The weak ones who get pulled in by temptation."

I shook my head and bit my tongue. I wasn't going to distract him by arguing about how he viewed his victims.

"Do you know what they never *ever* bargain for? I mean, maybe one in a thousand does. One in ten thousand." Again, I shook my head. "They never say when we can take their soul. They just assume we'll wait 'til they're dead, and lay claim."

He was waiting for me to say something. "So . . . ?"

"So . . . What happens if the soul is claimed from a living body? Just yanked right out. Whoosh." He mimed the movement with his hands.

I frowned, the idea creeping me out on several levels. "You can't live without a soul, so . . . So, what? They're like . . . zombies?" I hate zombies. Hate hate hate them. Every inch of skin on my back tried to crawl off and go hide. I mean sure, I'd suspected that's what they were, but confirming it . . . That was worse somehow.

"Close enough. You humans have called them many things over the centuries. Zombies, vampires . . . Not the angsty, poetry-spouting vampires, but the original nasty ones. In Hindu, they're called a *vetala*." He frowned thoughtfully. "The lore surrounding that one isn't quite right, but I suppose I shouldn't expect you apes to get everything correct.

"In place of the soul, he puts a bit of himself, enough to give them a kind of intelligence. But the body rots, mostly because he forgets to take care of them. They eat, when he remembers to tell them to, but it's never enough to sustain them. Especially as many as he's created now. He's stretched so thin."

"Well, he's quite a few less now." I had the proof caked all over what used to be a perfectly good pair of jeans. "So what's up with the voices? I didn't think they could talk, but last night they were calling, and that one just now . . . it screamed. If they have no souls, how is that possible?" I had to get as much out of him as I could, before he clammed up again.

The demon leaned against the wall, lounging in his own superiority. "Think of them like . . . echo chambers. They're empty. All that space craves filling. They ape back things they've heard, memories of conversations that rattle around in all that empty until it rattles its way out the open mouth. With their master directing them, they'll take on voices of people you know, care about, if they've been near them. Psychological warfare." He chuckled. "Face it, you people really are so suggestible. You simply hear what you want to hear. Not every tempting siren is a blonde with double-Ds."

"And the screaming?"

"There are . . . some kinds of agony that even being soulless can't silence."

I suppose being dumped on holy ground would qualify as that kind of agony for one of Hell's children. Even one that started out human. "So . . . he just yanks their souls out. Leaves the body an empty shell, yes?"

"Yes."

"And he can do it to anyone, if he owns their soul."

"Yes."

"So . . . what about Zane? Could he just . . . yoink?" That was a disturbing thought. If the Yeti could just rip Zane apart like that, turn him into one of those things . . .

"He must touch them." He glanced down the stairs, and I got the feeling that he could see Zane right through the floorboards. "I would be very careful with your young friend, down there. I'd hate to see any-thing . . . tragic happen."

He pushed off the wall, and I thought he was going to do his little disappearing act again, but he stopped. "Have you figured out why he came after the boy, of all people?"

Yeah, I'd had the chance to think about that too. Long hours spent not sleeping lent themselves well to in-depth pondering of all the universe's injustice. I didn't like my conclusions. "Because he knew I'd be here. He knew I'd find the kid, and I'd fight for him."

"Your fatal flaw, Jesse. That damned honor you hold around you like a warm blanket." The demon sounded downright disappointed in me. "You would live a lot longer if you'd learn to be a bit more self-absorbed."

"Hold your breath 'til that happens."

He chuckled softly. "And do you know why he

came for *you*? I mean, specifically why him, why you, why this?"

"Because he hates me?"

"That's a given, but do you know why?" I shrugged, and Axel grinned. He was enjoying this. "Think about it, Jesse. Voices call us forth, but simple words won't do it. What do you know that no other *living* champion does?"

His name. Because I'd faced the Yeti before, I knew his name. And names have power. In all honesty, I'm not sure what *kind* of power. Mystical Shit 101 was full last time I tried to sign up. Whatever it was, it meant something to the demons. Somehow, me possessing that name was a threat. A big enough threat to kill for.

I only nodded, showing him that I understood. Even thinking of it, the demon's name swam dangerously close to the surface of my mind, fluttering like a moth with razor-blade wings, and I bit my tongue to keep it from somehow slipping out by accident. I'd have to say it, call him out when the time came. I wondered if, deep down, that made me any better than Cam and his little cadre of demon-summoning priests.

"What use is it? What can I do to him, with his name?"

Axel looked at his bare wrist. "My my, look at the time. I think our session is up for the day."

"You're a dick, Axel."

"I've had a long time to perfect it, thank you."

"What about the other champions? Are they all facing ghosts from their pasts, names they know?"

The blond demon shrugged. "Dunno. I don't have a vested interest in the rest of your little playmates."

I eyed him suspiciously. "You're being awful liberal with your information."

"Like I said, I just want you to be you. It works in my favor at the moment." His eyes looked past me, over my shoulder, and he grinned with demon red eyes. "Oh this is about to get interesting."

I turned to find Cameron at the top of the stairs, staring wide-eyed at Axel. His gaze darted from the demon to me and back, and I saw a grim resolve settle into his eyes. The smell of cloves sprang up strong—stronger than I thought him capable of really—and he opened his mouth to do . . . something.

"No!" I jumped, clamping my hand down tight over the possibly ex-priest's mouth. "Don't even try it. You don't have enough juice to bless a sneeze anyway."

He struggled halfheartedly (I think a true fight between us would be a lot messier), but finally settled for trying to pry my hand away from his face. I looked back at Axel. "You've caused enough trouble. Go on, get."

Cameron's eyes got wider, and though I couldn't hear him, I could feel the movement of his protest against my hand. "Look, he's . . . He's a friend." *Sort of.* "He's not the thing that's out there."

"Aw, Jesse . . . I'm touched. Tears in my eyes, really." I glared at the demon, and he just chuckled. "Wanna bet he'd wet himself it I walked over and touched him?" Axel wiggled his fingers with a leer.

"Would you quit? This isn't helping."

"Oh I'm sorry. When exactly did I offer to help?" He smirked.

Cameron said something else behind my palm, and I gave him a look. "Can I let you go without you . . . doing some hocus-pocus or whatever?" He nodded, his eyes promising to behave. I removed my hand and stepped back.

"That's a demon!" His voice was distant, tinny, but I could make out the words so long as I was looking at him. Cameron pointed an accusing figure at Axel, who just laughed.

"Give the little priest a big cigar!" The smile Axel gave him was nothing short of predatory and the demon advanced on Cameron. "Now what are you going to do about it?"

"Nothing. He's going to do nothing." Will someone please explain to me later how I wound up protecting a demon from a priest? I put a hand on each chest and pushed, noting that yet again, Axel's touch didn't trigger Mira's protection spells. In fact, he felt all too human. It was . . . yes, creepy, okay? I didn't have a better word for it. "Both of you go to your separate corners and cool off."

Cameron ignored my well-meant advice, of course. "What's it doing here?"

"*It* got stuck inside when *that* set off that rather poorly constructed consecration spell," Axel spat. "*It* had no intention of hanging around this little ape colony any longer than absolutely necessary, up until that point."

"Axel . . ."

"What? He can be rude but I can't? Demon, hello . . ." Whatever tirade he was going to go off on next was interrupted by a booming voice from outside, so loud that even I could hear it.

"ARCHITECT!"

Axel cursed, too soft for me to even tell what language he was speaking. My stomach gave a small lurch, so I was guessing it was demonic.

"ARCHITECT! Come out!" It had to be the Yeti because the mere sound of the voice made my skin crawl and I tasted oil at the back of my tongue.

I looked at Axel. "Architect?"

He ignored me. "I believe, gentlemen, that that is my cue to depart." Axel sketched us a small two-fingered salute and headed for the stairs. Cameron scrambled to get out of his path.

I know the guys downstairs had to be saying, "What the hell?" (again) when Axel calmly walked down the stairs and headed for the front door, Cameron and I thudding after him.

I think we'd all forgotten about Duke. The mammoth mutt took one look at Axel and made a lunge for him, bellowing to high heaven. Without breaking stride, Axel snarled—literally snarled, with bared teeth and glowing eyes—at him, and the dog nearly did a backflip trying to come to a halt on the hardwood floor. Axel barked, "Sit!" and the big lummox cowered, making a puddle on the floor. So much for our valiant defender.

I snapped a quick, "Stay inside" at the guys, trying

not to sound like I was telling them to sit as well, then followed Axel out onto the front porch. Cameron trotted after us pretty quick, and everyone else pressed against the windows to watch.

The Yeti was standing just inside the tree line, carefully out of range of the morning sun. He'd assumed his human guise again, the albino in the charcoal gray suit. Knowing what he really was, I could see both forms, flickering over each other like a bad film clip, managing to fill both the hulking space that was the Yeti and squash itself into the slender man's form at the same time. It was going to give me a headache before too long. Dark shadows swirled around him, wisps of blight coalescing where he stood like fog seeking low ground.

Axel leaned against the porch rail nonchalantly. "You rang?"

"We must speak, Architect. Come here to me." The suit-clad figure was still, but the other, superimposed over the first, swayed side to side, shifting from clawed foot to clawed foot. Almost like he was nervous.

I strained to hear the Yeti's words. The voice part of it was still muffled in my damaged ears, but the demon side, the sickly oil-slick side was getting through loud and clear. Ugh.

Axel snorted. "No, you come here." It was a moot point. Neither demon was going to cross the last strip of consecrated ground. The Yeti did inch out of cover though, fidgeting until he found a place safely shaded from the light. The furry form snarled its reluctance, almost like it was pulled forward against its will, while the man in the suit merely stood with his hands folded together in front of him.

"We must speak," he said again, his colorless lips barely moving at all. "Of many things."

"Of cabbages and kings?" Axel examined his fingernails idly, apparently finding them infinitely more interesting that the creature across the clearing.

"Of your transgressions." I had a feeling that not only did the Yeti not have a sense of humor, but he had never read Lewis Carroll.

Axel laughed, and part of me cringed to hear myself laughing at the Yeti. I was really going to have to talk to Axel about using someone else's voice. "You and I might have all the time in the world, but our friends here do not. Perhaps you should pick just one great sin to harp on?" At some point, I realized, Axel's language had changed. He'd become all stuffy or something. More formal. I started to understand that, whatever this was, it wasn't just a regular old chat between buddies.

Furry Yeti's head tossed in agitation while Human Yeti's image remained calm, cool, and collected. "You should not be here. You violate your own laws."

The blond demon snorted again, and I swear I saw the real Yeti flinch. "There is no law that says I cannot try to collect a soul, especially one I've had a claim on for years. Check the ledgers, you'll see my mark."

I gave Axel a "what the fuck?" look, but he refused to take his eyes off the other demon.

"Yes . . . the Architect's little pet." The Yeti was not happy. The man in the gray suit frowned, jaw clenching, and overlaid on that image, the big hairball's muzzle wrinkled, his claws digging furrows into the forest floor. "A mark unclaimed is a mark unclaimed. Your presence here exerts undue influence—"

"YOU DARE?!" That hurt, and out of the corner of my eye I caught Cam clamping his hands down over his own ears too. Damn, Axel had some lungs on him. "You DARE question ME?"

And it wasn't just us. I swear, the Yeti about wet himself. He looked just like Duke making a puddle on the floor. It's kinda hard to be scared of something that looks like a spanked puppy. "The laws . . ."

"I know the laws! Did I not write them? Shall we really start tallying up just who has violated what?" Axel moved down to the very last step, as far as he could go without touching the ground. "Do you really want that eye focused on you?"

I've heard of the power of personality, but I don't think that I truly appreciated what that meant until I watched Axel back the Yeti down with nothing more than a stern glare and a few cold words. Even without his gaze fixed on me, part of me wanted to go slinking back inside too, and I'd taken two steps before I caught myself.

"You are sworn to be neutral." Even cringing and all but melting under Axel's gaze, the Yeti had enough spine to try to resist. "Remove yourself."

"YOU WILL NOT COMMAND ME!" Leaves fell

from the trees; rocks clattered down the hillside behind us. Axel's voice reverberated for what seemed like forever. "MY WILL IS LAW!"

I don't know what he did. He flung his hand out, a casual gesture, and there was a flash of light, brighter than the sun. When I finished blinking the after images out of my eyes, the Yeti was gone. After a few moments Axel's shoulders relaxed, and he dropped his hand to his side. "Well. That's that, then." He shook his head, frowning at something, and finally said, "Well, shit."

There wasn't enough time in the world to formulate all the questions I wanted to ask. Geez, where would I even start? Architect? Laws? What? I finally settled for, "What the hell is going on, Axel?"

He looked at me like he'd just remembered my existence, and shook his head, the sun glinting off his piercings. His injuries were gone, I noticed in a distracted way. Too tough to keep him down for long, apparently. "There's no time, not today. He won't stay gone forever; he's grown too strong for that. You need to listen to me, because I can only say these things once, and then . . . I most likely won't be back for a while."

When he put it that way . . . I just nodded.

"The creatures out there aren't gone. They're his. I don't have the power to command them. Without him here to direct them, they'll be feral, rabid. He's starved them, so they'll be very hungry." Axel spoke quickly, an urgency in his (my) voice that I hadn't heard before. "Your Yeti will be back as soon as he can marshal his strength. You need to go *now*, or you won't leave here alive. I can't protect you anymore."

So many things to ask, "Why?" being only the first in a very long list. And there was no time.

"I feel weird saying this, but . . . be careful, okay?" He'd helped, okay? For his own reasons, yes, but he'd helped. A little. Don't judge me.

Axel paused a moment, then smiled, and I could almost believe it was sincere. "Thanks." A whiff of sulfur and he was gone. I knew he wouldn't be back. Not until this was over.

I shook my head when Cameron tried to speak. "No time. Grab your shit. We're outta here."

Somehow, now that Axel was gone, I felt like a real little worm on a big damn hook.

15

"I think there better *be* time, Jess." I'd fully expected the guys to jump when I said jump, but instead they faced me in a semicircle, Marty's dark brows drawn together in the deepest frown I'd ever seen on him. "Who the hell was that? Don't give us shit about him being a coworker. I think that ship has sailed."

Oh yeah. I'd been hoping they'd miss that part. "I don't know his name. I call him Axel. He's a demon."

"You knew that. You knew that, and you let him around our families. Our kids."

"He's . . ." Harmless? Not dangerous? Like Marty had said, I thought that ship had sailed. "Can we do this later? We need to get the hell out of here."

"Why are we leaving at all? Isn't his magic protecting us?" Oscar pointed at Cameron, and the priest shook his head.

"It isn't magic, it's faith. God has chosen us to—"

"Look! We seriously don't have time for a lesson in semantics!" Even Duke flinched when I raised my voice. "First, Cam, you can call it whatever the hell you want, but my wife can do all that you just did, and she doesn't even believe in your god. In fact, I'm pretty sure your god and her goddess aren't even on speaking terms. So chew on that before you start spouting off about being the 'chosen of God.'

"Second! The wards here are blown. The consecration is gone, and Cam can't even keep Axel out, so we need to go and we need to go *now*. If anyone wants to further discuss this, submit it to the committee and I will have an answer for you in six to eight weeks. *Provided* that we live! Now move your asses!"

I didn't have to tell them twice. Well, technically, yeah, I did, but there wasn't a third time. We grabbed everything that remotely resembled a weapon, shrugged into our backpacks, and were out the door in five minutes.

I gotta say, I was impressed with every single person there. I mean, we were voluntarily leaving a semi-secured position, to take a stroll through woods teeming with pseudozombies. I guess bravery is really just the ability to shout louder than the little voice in your head that screams, "Run, stupid!"

Marty, ankle wrapped so he could walk on it, tied Duke's lead around his waist to keep his hands free, and we walked in tight formation, keeping Zane in the middle. I'll give the kid credit. As sick as he was getting, he kept up, marching out of the clearing in grim silence. I hoped he'd make it at least to the truck, 'cause there was no way in hell we'd be able to carry him and fight at the same time.

Cole took point with what few bullets he had left. Being right-handed, I stayed on the right side, scanning the trees as we walked. Marty and Duke had our left flank, and Cam stumbled along at the rear (more to keep an eye on me than anything, I suspected). Oscar was armed with the one and only hatchet we had, and he and Will walked on either side of Zane.

Without Duke, we'd have been toast in the first rush.

Barely ten yards into the trees, they dropped down on us from the branches above, and the only reason we had any warning was Duke's raging bellow. In fact, the big dog yanked Marty right off his feet, lunging at the nearest threat.

The creature on that side—the handless female, I realized, which meant she'd fled the roof last night instead of being slaughtered with the rest of her kind—hit the ground on all fours and immediately sprang back into the brush, vanishing from sight. Duke, roaring like a grizzly bear, did his damnedest to drag Marty with him, chasing after it.

And while we were all looking that way, three more hit us from the other side. Even as I turned belatedly, cussing at myself for falling for the ruse, one of them leaped at Will and I knew I couldn't get there in time. I shouldn't have doubted my buddy. For all that he pretends to be a bumbling doofus, his mind is sharp and his reflexes were even better. The creature skewered itself on Will's fireplace poker, then went flying into a tree as Will gave a huge heave and flung it off. It wasn't a killing wound, though, and the thing went scurrying off into the trees again before we could go after it.

Cole did manage to take out one with a clean shot to the head, but the other was into us too fast, and he couldn't risk the shot. I saw Oscar brace himself for the oncoming charge, and knew he just didn't have the skill to take the thing down in close quarters. "Oscar! Down!"

I couldn't use my sword without hitting someone friendly, so I just lowered my head and met the thing in a full-out body block. I felt its ribs crack against my shoulder, the decaying bones fracturing wetly. I also felt it sink its long fingernails into my many layers of T-shirts and hang on for the ride. Did *not* count on that.

We went down in a heap of raking nails and clacking teeth as the thing tried to take a bite out of me and only got my pack. There was more shouting, dimly heard through my damaged ears, but with my face pressed into the muddy grass, I wasn't exactly in the best position to see what was happening.

The minion wasn't heavy by any means, and I got myself up to my hands and knees at least by the time it reversed itself to make a lunge at my neck. I jerked my head back and smashed its face, feeling the sticky goo creep down the back of my neck.

"Don't move!" It was Cole's voice, and I froze immediately. The heavy metal clang that followed reverberated in my teeth. The creature fell off my back, and the gunshot after made my head throb. I raised my head to find my little brother standing over me, gun in one hand and one of the CO_2 tanks in the other. Let's hear it for improvisational weapons.

Unfortunately, two dead wasn't even going to stop them. In and out they darted, testing our flanks, moving too fast for us to even get a count. It didn't help that, aside from the handless female, it was hard as hell to tell the nasty things apart. They moved in unison like the first time, coordinating to snap and harry us on all sides.

We couldn't move like this. Marty was fighting Duke more than anything, struggling to keep the dog from barreling off into the trees, and it was impossible for us to hold a tight defensive formation while in motion. Face it, we weren't trained soldiers.

"Cam, if you know any tricks that won't kill you, this might be the time to use them."

He said something that I couldn't quite hear, not looking at him as I was, but it sounded affirmative. The next time the beasties made a try for us, he raised one hand in the air, opening his fist as he shouted, *"Prima luce!"*

Light burst all around us, lighting up the underbrush like high noon. There was a crash in the trees as the things retreated in a panic, and then all was silence. Cameron sank slowly to the ground, panting. Fresh blood stained the bandage on his head.

I did a quick glance around, but no one else seemed to be hurt. A few bumps and bruises maybe, and Zane of course was looking more like death warmed over the farther we went, but we were upright. Mostly.

And what the hell was up with the Yeti's pets? I thought they were supposed to be animalistic, wild, but they were obviously thinking, planning. They weren't supposed to be able to do that, without the Yeti to guide them. Which meant . . . they had another leader?

The handless female had left the roof last night, rather than face Cole and me. She'd left the others to fight and die, but she'd retreated. She was smarter. Cunning. Their tactics were just like Marty'd said, like a pack of wolves. A pack could bring down something the size of a moose, just by constantly darting in and out and wearing it to exhaustion. I didn't think my little group stood any better chance in the condition we were in.

Cole popped his clip, shaking his head at his dwindling ammo. When he caught me looking, he frowned. "We can't keep fighting these things hand to hand, and I've got half a clip left."

"Yeah, well, I don't think paintball guns are going to take them down. If anyone has a better idea, let's hear it." He was right, though. In close quarters, we were more hazardous to ourselves than anything, and if we spread out too much, we'd be easier targets. And if the Yeti came back and entered the fray, we were all screwed.

Marty fished his possibly illegal slingshot out of his pack and fastened it to his arm. "If we can find some rocks, I can try this out." No one really had any inclination to go rock hunting off the trail, however.

"Will it shoot paintballs?"

Marty shrugged. "For whatever good it would do, yeah, I suppose. Not gonna hurt much, but damn they'll be pretty while they eat our faces off."

My gaze happened to fall on Cameron, still crumpled on the ground. "Cam . . . ? How much juice you have left?"

He raised his eyes, and I instantly regretted asking. His face was gray, drawn, and his pupils were dilated oddly. He wasn't doing well. "I can't do the light again. Only works once, and it didn't hurt them, just scared them. It's a novice's trick . . ."

He was done in. Drained, nothing left. I could see that. And I asked anyway. "Could you put a blessing on something? Just a little?" Defensive magic took less than the big attack spells. Maybe, it would be enough less.

He took a long time to answer, so long that I wondered if he could even hear me. Wasn't I supposed to be the deaf one? Finally, he nodded. "Nothing big, like a patch of ground. But something small, yes. I think so."

"Guys, get your markers out. Have Cam magic the paintballs." They all looked at me like I was crazy. "Come on, we don't have much time!"

It took a few minutes to get the guns assembled, and another few for Cameron to gather up the willpower to actually cast the blessing. At the last second, Marty stuck a pocketful of change in the pile too, and we wound up with holy quarters and nickels. Hey, if he thought he could shoot those with a slingshot, more power to him.

I could smell the cloves on the air as Cameron passed his hands over the colorful jumble of ammunition, but the scent was so faint. The priest was just plain out of mojo, and I honestly wasn't sure if he'd make it down the trail. If we couldn't carry Zane, we damn sure couldn't carry Zane *and* Cam.

I gave Zane my marker, hoping he could at least fire off a few shots with his good arm, and slipped my now free left hand under Cameron's arms as he stood up. "All right, folks, hobble like your lives depend on it."

It took a bit for the nasties to rally and come at us again. It was possible that they were afraid of Cam's light, but I didn't believe that. Handless was figuring out a better way to kill us. We got about fifteen minutes of peace and a good chunk of distance behind us without incident.

Then the howls started up, the voices all around, echoes of other people's lives.

"I'm a little teapot!"

"Pow, right in the kisser!"

"Hey, does this smell funny to you?" The tiny bit of protection from Cameron's blessed water still held, but that didn't make it any less nerve-racking, marching through this gauntlet of macabre commercial slogans and sitcom theme songs.

It did occur to me, sometime during my stint as Cameron's crutch, that we were leading the creatures down into a populated area. Sure, Ericson's store wasn't exactly a teeming metropolis, but there were innocents there. Somewhere along the way, we'd have to make a stand, get rid of as many of them as possible, or subject everyone there to the seductive lure of the stolen voices.

At the next dark patch in the trail, a place where the trees overhung enough to block out a good portion of the late-morning sun, we found out why they'd taken so long to attack us again. The bitch and her pack had set up an ambush for us. I was seriously going to have to talk to Axel about his definition of "feral," 'cause these things were doing too much thinking for my comfort level.

The voices cut off abruptly at the same instant that Cameron threw a shoulder into my ribs, flattening me. A split second later, an enormous dead tree crashed down across the path, sending wickedly sharp pine needles flying like shrapnel. While the trunk missed us, we were both caught in the skeletal branches, and I couldn't even struggle free before something dark and reeking landed on top of us. Only luck put my sword across my own chest, enough that I could use it to fend off my new best friend.

This one had tangled with something before. Something I rather suspected was Duke. There were gashes across what was left of its face, gray, decayed tendons visible through its hole-riddled cheeks as it gnashed its rotting teeth inches from my nose. Its breath—if you could even call it that—reeked of busted guts and bile. Only the thought that I'd choke to death kept me from vomiting, and even then it was a near miss.

And the worst part (yes, that other stuff wasn't even the worst) was that I could almost see the human it had been in that ravaged visage. There was a strong jaw there, under the gore, high cheekbones. Once, this had been someone's son, or father. Husband. Brother.

Of course, at this exact moment, it was trying to eat me, so my sympathetic horror had to take a backseat to survival.

For all that it had very little body mass, and its bones were made of balsa wood, the damn thing was strong! We fought over my katana's blade, both of us gouging ourselves on the entangling tree branches. It wasn't smart enough to let go of the sword to claw at my eyes, thank God and Buddha both, but the sharp side of the blade was slowly working its way through the filthy palms, and soon it would cut the hands right in half, leaving the thing free to collapse down on top of me.

Whatever I was lying on was wriggling, and I remembered Cameron about the same time his hand shot past my face, delicate gold chain dangling between his fingers. Whatever he had, he slapped it against the minion's forehead with force, and a breath later it reeled back, abandoning its attack with an ear-splitting shriek. Or, it would be if my hearing wasn't already fried. Beneath me, Cam cried out in pain and writhed as he tried to protect his own ears.

No sooner did the creature stand fully upright than bone chips exploded out the left side of its skull. Something shiny and silver dropped out of the open mouth, and the scream was cut off abruptly. It dropped like a puppet with the strings cut.

Nothing else immediately tried to rearrange my bodily organs, and I sagged a bit, only then noticing how Cam's knee was digging into the small of my back. He squirmed uncomfortably too, and with some effort, we managed to thrash our way clear of the dead branches.

The silver object from the now dead creature (I know it was dead, 'cause I stomped the skull to gooey bits, just to be sure) turned out to be a quarter. I fished it out of the tall grass and stuffed it in my pocket. Guess

I really wouldn't be able to give Marty any crap about his slingshot now.

The other gleam I retrieved from the foliage was Cam's delicate gold chain, sporting a very plain gold cross. I handed it back to him, and he nodded his thanks.

We won that one, mostly. Aside from some nasty cuts and scratches—mostly mine and Cam's—the tree had done little damage to us other than scattering our forces. There were four dead creatures, three of them splattered with colorful neon paint. I could see where the blessed paintballs had blistered the skin beneath, no doubt distracting them long enough for my brother to deliver the coup de grace with his gun.

One of the corpses was in several pieces, and Duke refused to relinquish the severed foot he was proudly carrying in his massive jaws. His brindle fur was as colorful as the things we'd just killed, and his muzzle was almost entirely neon pink.

I grimaced and swallowed hard. "Take that away from him."

Marty looked at the big dog—who outweighed me by a good fifty pounds—and back at me. "You go ahead and try." I didn't.

None of the bodies was female. I checked twice. Handless was still out there, and we had no way of knowing where, or how many friends she had with her. *It. Think of it as an it.* If I started thinking of it as a person, even a former person, I was afraid I might go completely bonkers.

As we gathered ourselves to move on again, I cornered Marty. "How far do you think we still have to go?"

He glanced up and down the trail like he could chart our position just from looking. I don't know, maybe he could. "Another half an hour, if we don't get stopped. We should be in sight of Ericson's by then."

Our departure was delayed further when Will had to check Zane over. The black streaks were almost to his elbow by now, and even from a few yards away, I could see how fever bright his eyes were. Will had him dry swallow some painkillers, but it was just over-the-counter stuff. It wasn't going to do much. He didn't make a peep about how much pain he had to be in, but believe me, I knew, and my heart went out to the kid.

When we finally got moving, Oscar was supporting his son with one arm, but at least Cameron was managing on his own again. Somehow, our ragtag and wounded bunch managed to make it down the mountain.

I swear, I have never been so happy to see asphalt in my life, and only dignity kept me from dropping down and kissing the parking lot as we stepped out of the trees.

I'd had visions of the Suburban sitting there with four slashed tires, but luckily it seemed intact. While Will and Cole got the walking wounded loaded into the big truck, Marty went to retrieve the keys from the clerk. Me? I stood nervous guard on the side of the truck not visible to the store. Didn't think I wanted to explain to the customers why I was running around the parking lot with a bared blade.

It was hard getting everyone into the truck when we had two more people than we started with. I don't know why it didn't occur to us to have Oscar get his own vehicle, but no one thought of that until hours later. Jackasses (me included).

Once we were all wedged in (and sadly, the sword had to be stowed for safety's sake), Will started passing out cell phones from the glove compartment. Mine, of course, was dead. "Fuck!" I had Ivan's number. I had Viljo's. Neither of which could I get to in a dead phone. If someone was making a move on the rest of the champions, I had to warn them, and the stupid battery was fucking dead!

"Don't you know the numbers?" Cole asked.

"No, I don't know the numbers! I put them in the phone so I wouldn't *have* to know the numbers!" I thumped my now useless piece of plastic and circuitry against his forehead.

Thankfully, Cole's phone was still just fine, and he started trying to track down my wife to get her miracle poisoning cure for Zane. Not so thankfully, Mira seemed to have dropped off the face of the planet. She wasn't answering the home phone or her cell and though Cole was set on going through his entire contact list, no one else seemed to know where she was either.

Please . . . please let her be okay . . . She was at the movies. Or . . . getting her hair done, or . . . I pressed my head to the back of Marty's seat and forced a few deep breaths. There were a couple of dozen explanations for her not answering the phone, all of them perfectly mundane and safe.

Focus, Jesse. One thing at a time. First, Zane had to get to a hospital.

Marty didn't exactly squall tires getting out of the parking lot, but only because I'm not sure the Suburban was capable of such a feat. Next to me, Oscar was turned around in his seat, keeping an eye on Cameron and Zane, stuffed into the back with Duke. The big mutt had curled up next to the injured boy, as if his mere massive presence could make things all right.

Turned around as I was, also checking on the invalids, the first sign I had that something was wrong was the enormous "THUMP" and Marty spewing out more curse words than I even knew. The vehicle swerved hard, throwing me against the door, and something heavy dented in the roof, almost smacking Oscar in the back of the head.

"It's on the roof!" Well, no shit, Will. Before any of us could do anything, the window next to Cole shattered inward, and a skeletal arm reached in, snagging his shirt with filthy, grasping fingers.

A grotesque head hung upside down in the window, and through the shouting and the broken glass and the careening truck, I recognized it as Handless. I couldn't even imagine how she was hanging on with her stub of an arm, grappling my brother with the only hand she still possessed.

Cole had the heel of one palm jammed against her chin, trying to keep her snapping, snarling mouth away from his face, while the other pried at her fingers, her rotten skin coming away under his nails. "Somebody get this bitch off of me!"

I snatched Oscar by the belt and pitched him over the back of the seat, not caring if he landed on Cameron. There wasn't a lot of room to maneuver in the cramped backseat, but I managed to swing my legs around and aimed a few vicious kicks at Handless. Bone crunched under the first, and the second caused her to lose her grip. The filthy thing didn't fall, though, using her hold on Cole to flip right side up, her clawed feet scratching loudly down the door as she looked for purchase.

Cole couldn't get to his gun, and my sword was useless. But the truck was still moving, and I braced myself against my own door. "Cole! Door! Marty, tree!"

The Suburban swerved, and tree branches whipped through the broken window, spattering us with shredded leaves. Cole let go of Handless long enough to grab the door handle, and I kicked outward with all my might. The door went flying open, taking Handless with it, then slammed back shut with a crunch as it impacted the next tree we passed. Black goo splattered over Cole, and Handless's now severed arm (the one *with* the hand) flopped into his lap, twitching feebly for a moment. And Handless was gone.

With a disgusted exclamation, Cole flung the arm out of the window, trying to scrub his hands off on his gore-splattered jeans.

"Did it kill her?" I crawled across Cole despite his protests, sticking my head as far out the window as I dared. I couldn't find her.

"Sweet cartwheeling Jesus," Cameron breathed, and I was inclined to agree with him despite the blasphemy. Only he wasn't worried about Handless and her missing appendages. "Look." He yanked on my shirt until I turned to look out the front window.

The road, about a hundred yards in front of the truck, was full of Yeti. Okay, there was just one Yeti, but damn he was huge. And very obviously pissed off.

"Jess, what do I do?" Marty asked, the truck slowing as he took his foot off the gas.

I leaned over the front seat to get a good look, locking eyes with the white-furred demon. "Punch it."

"You mean it?"

"Hit him."

Without hesitation, Marty put his foot in it, and the Suburban lurched forward, diesel engine roaring as we barreled toward the massive creature. The Yeti bellowed back, standing his ground as we came on, and I started to wonder if maybe I'd made a huge mistake.

Just as I tensed for impact, and Will braced his arms against the dash, muttering, "Oh shit," the demon vanished, and we passed harmlessly through a cloud of quickly dispersing blight. When I turned to look out our back window, the road was empty.

I think every person in that truck deflated, letting out the breaths we'd collectively been holding. I clapped Marty on the shoulder, noting that only now was he flexing his white-knuckled hands on his steering wheel. "To Fort Collins, Jeeves. And don't spare the horses."

I collapsed into my seat, feeling broken glass grind against my legs, and I just couldn't bring myself to care.

16

The nearest hospital was in Fort Collins, more than an hour away, but through some miracle we made it there in record time and unmolested.

There was no way the ER staff was ready for us. We came in like a herd of drunk buffalo, so many of us covered in blood and unidentifiable goo that they finally just herded us all into the back to let the actual docs sort us out. Even Duke managed to slip by, and he made camp next to Zane's bed, doing a pretty damn good disappearing act for something the size of a small horse.

I tried to disappear. My injuries were superficial at worst, and after spending so much time in them, hospitals in general give me the heebie-jeebies. I found an out-of-the-way corner and pretended that I was invisible, lost in the scent of bleach and the monotonous beep of a dozen different monitors. Maybe if I held really still, no one would notice me.

I know you're not supposed to use phones in hospitals, but I was desperate to get word to Mira, Ivan, anybody. I filched Cole's phone while he was having some glass shards removed from his neck, and kept trying to get my wife on the phone. Nothing. Nada. Bubkes.

A passing nurse paused briefly, thinking to chastise me over the phone I'm sure, but she took one look at my face and thought better of it. Instead, she grabbed some antiseptic swabs and started working at the cuts and scrapes, holding my chin in an iron grip no matter how I tried to pull away. We took turns glaring at each other as I dialed and redialed the phone, but by the end, I think we'd found some kind of happy truce. Neither of us liked the other, and we were okay with that.

Cameron, despite the fact that he looked like the walking dead himself, was trying to explain Zane's condition to the doctors. "I'm telling you, he was attacked by an animal, and the wound went all nasty like this in just a day. We got him here as fast as we could." They obviously didn't believe him, which was logical since he was lying out his ass. I wondered if he'd have to mention that in confession later. "No, we don't know what kind of animal."

The bite on Zane's hand was fairly obscured by his demon mark and the insidious infection. The others, however, over his arms and shoulders . . . well, those couldn't be anything but human. Even I could see that, and I wasn't a medical professional. Cameron was going to have to work on his song and dance skills if he wanted to explain that away.

Will could have backed him up, but my buddy hung back, his normally chattering self uncharacteristically quiet. He didn't like lying about medical stuff. It went against his own personal code of helping people. But when you can't exactly run around telling people that a zombie bit your friend, you either lie, or you shut the hell up. He was doing the only thing he could, and still live with himself.

Oscar could have backed Cam up too, or at least nodded along or something, but I think he'd finally spent the last of the energy that had sustained him throughout his introduction to this terrifying new world. He took up a chair next to Zane's bed, holding his son's good hand while the staff rushed to get IVs and other medical paraphernalia in place. Already, I could see the powerful painkillers taking effect, and the tension in the teenager's face easing. The best they could do for him was let him sleep through this. Their medicine wasn't going to do a damn thing beyond that.

"Any luck?" A bandaged Cole found me pacing through the ER. It looked like he'd gotten away without any stitches. "I see that Nurse Ratched got her hands on you too." He nodded toward my own lovely collection of gauze and tape.

"Mmph." Cole's wife wasn't answering either. Oddly, that made me feel better. Steph and Mira were probably out together, doing some girl-bonding thing now that the kids were all in school during the day. They were . . . getting their hair done. Or . . . maybe catching a movie. What do women do when we're gone? Hell, they could be having an orgy with oiled-up cabana boys, and I don't think I'd care so long as they were safe.

All I was doing was running Cole's battery down too, and I finally forced myself to give up, flopping in the nearest chair. I yanked the hair tie out of my ponytail in sheer frustration, and grimaced when I realized how much foulness I had in my formerly blond hair. This vacation had most definitely not gone as planned.

"So. Wanna bet this is the last official Colorado paintball trip?" My little brother flopped beside me, the pair of us looking like matching bookends.

I snorted. "Ya think? I'll be lucky if anyone on this trip speaks to me at all after we get home."

"It's not that bad, big brother." I gave him a look, and he shrugged. "Nobody died."

"Day's not over yet." Even if we could get Mira on the phone, I had to wonder if Cam would survive casting the spell to save Zane. This still had the potential to turn out all kinds of bad.

"Listen." Cole leaned forward, resting his elbows on his knees. "None of this is your fault."

"Um . . . every single bit of this is my fault. If it weren't for me, none of this would have happened." I gestured to the entire ER, more than half the beds currently occupied by people who arrived with me. "Zane wouldn't have been targeted. Cam wouldn't be hurt. Marty . . . Christ, he didn't sign up for any of this. Will either."

My brother blew a long breath out his nose and shook his head. "Jess . . . Why did you tell Will and Marty about all this in the first place? Way back when, what made you confide in them, when you've hidden it from almost everyone else?"

What the hell kind of question was that? I blinked at him, perplexed.

"Humor me. Why'd you bring them into this?"

"Um . . . I guess, because I needed their help. I couldn't do it alone."

"Yeah, but you could have found someone else. You

could have found armor and weapons somewhere, especially after Ivan surfaced. You could have found another doctor type. So why them?"

I had to really think about it. I didn't recall consciously making the decision to tell my two best friends about my new calling in life. It just . . . happened. It never occurred to me not to. "I guess because they're my friends. My best friends. Why wouldn't I tell them?"

Cole nodded with a satisfied smirk. "Exactly. They're your best friends. They're not gonna ditch you over this."

I just shrugged. Only time would tell, and honestly, I wouldn't think ill of Marty and Will if they ran the other way screaming. If they were smart, they would.

"So what do we do now?" My brother leaned back in his chair again, stretching out his long legs.

"I don't know. We need Mira to help Zane. Until then, there isn't a lot we *can* do." And I needed to get to the numbers in my phone. Viljo had to get the word out, warn people if it wasn't already too late.

Viljo . . .

"Oh holy fuck." I scrambled up out of the hard plastic chair, sending it across the sterile tile floor with an obnoxious screech. "Marty, I need your keys! Cole, can I steal your phone? I need the GPS."

Marty handed over his keys, but not without looking to my brother for confirmation first. That hurt a bit. Hurt even more when Cole held his phone just out of my reach. "Where are you going?"

"Can't tell you, but I'll be back in like five hours."

Hopefully. "If you guys manage to get Mira on the phone, have her call me on yours."

"Why the hell can't you tell me?" Unspoken in Cole's question was the fact that, after all of *this*, I was keeping even more secrets? Really?

But what I'd managed to remember, slow study that I was, was that Viljo, dear, geeky Viljo, lived near Pikes Peak. Pikes Peak, which was barely two hours from where I stood at that very moment. And at all costs, no one else could know where the über-dork was, 'cause if they found him, they'd find Grapevine. And then they'd find all of Ivan's champions, if they didn't already know.

"Because anything I tell you, someone can take from you, probably involving horrific torture and a lovely vacation somewhere very hot. Glare at me all you want, little brother, but I'm not budging on this one." The whole champion game had changed in the last year. I felt this to the core of my being. We—all of us champions—had tried to pretend like it hadn't, tried to go on with business as usual. But it was the thing we never talked about, the demonic elephant in the room. Somehow, we puny humans had stumbled into something much bigger, and even if I didn't know what it was yet, I could feel it looming near, like a rabbit in a hawk's shadow. We had to take precautions, things we'd never dreamed of before. We had to cover our asses, which meant first and foremost protecting Grapevine.

Finally, Cole handed over his phone, but he wasn't happy about it. I figured I was in for a lecture later.

I delayed my trip long enough that my buddies could grab their packs for anything essential. Pulling Cole aside one last time, I told him, "If anything goes wrong, do *not* let that big furry son of a bitch touch Zane. If he touches the kid, he'll turn him into one of those things. At all costs, he can't take the kid." Cole nodded like he understood, and I took off, paintball marker in the seat beside me, aired up and loaded with holy ammo.

Driving Marty's Suburban was like maneuvering a garbage barge after driving my little Mazda pickup, but I'd manage. I knew Viljo's address, since we'd mailed him Mira's dead computer earlier this summer, and I plugged that into Cole's phone and pointed myself south.

The problem with long drives is that it gives the mind too much time to wander. Mine, of course, kept going back to the Yeti, and I scratched at the black marks on my skin a few times. It didn't itch, really. It burned like hell, sinking in, but that passed quickly. Mostly, it was just the knowledge that it was *there*, y'know?

I made myself look straight ahead, trying to be a conscientious driver and all, but there was that insidious voice in the back of my head, the one that was whispering all the horrible crap that was going to happen to me. Pretty sure that going into a battle fully expecting to lose was a bad thing.

But I knew damn well that the last time I'd faced him, I'd been only lucky.

That wasn't entirely true. I mean, I had skill, even

back then. No brains, that's for damn sure, but I could swing a blade. If I hadn't been good, he'd have ripped me in half before I'd taken two steps.

The kicker was, that thing that cornered us up at the cabin, that wasn't what I'd fought, last time. He was . . . bigger. Stronger. Just . . . more. He couldn't have handled his little zombie army, back then. Couldn't have stood up to Axel, even if I had no idea who and what Axel really was. The Yeti was a thug, then, not a master.

Still, I'd been lucky.

It was my second challenge, ever. A local television reporter that Cole had known. Sold his soul for his fifteen minutes in the TV spotlight, I guess. He was dying, when Cole brought him to me. He actually passed away a few months after the fight.

At that point, I hadn't asked Marty to make my armor yet, so it was just me and my sword, and balls the size of boulders. I really thought I was hot shit.

Will had been there, the first time I ever asked him for help. I didn't expect to need it. My first challenge had gone so smoothly. My second one . . . did not. If he hadn't been there afterward to duct tape my guts in, I'd have bled out on the spot. Lucky, see?

I guess it could have been worse. I mean, I held my own for about half an hour before I realized the Yeti was just toying with me. Like a cat batting a mouse around. I imagine I had amused him greatly. Scrawny little human darting around with his big flashy sword. I'd scored a couple of hits on him, blight trickling out, but nothing big enough to take him down, nothing crippling enough to finish it. I figure he'd let me have those strikes, just to see what I was made of.

The moment he decided he was bored, it was all over. Even as huge as he was, he moved faster than anything I'd ever dreamed of. This vicious flurry of claws, flying at my face, at anything I couldn't defend with a single blade. I clearly remembered the last feint, flowing into a block for a strike that wasn't coming, and knowing, *knowing*, I'd been had.

He picked me up like a bowling ball, sinking his claws into my ribs. Some act of divine providence kept my sword in my hand, and I forced myself to open my eyes when I felt his fetid breath on my face. He sniffed at me, and obviously found me wanting. Those jaws, bristling with fangs the length of my head, opened up, and that's when I opened his throat. I let him hold me up, feeling my own weight fracturing my ribs on his claws, and slashed the big furry neck almost to the spine.

I was covered in blight, freezing and numb, and I remembered hitting the ground. At that point, I didn't really care. It was warm there, lying in a pool of my own blood, and the stars were very bright that night. I remembered being vaguely annoyed at Will for blocking my view at one point. And then I didn't know anything until weeks later, when I woke up in some ICU with more tubes and monitors than NASA.

You can understand why I wasn't anxious to use that particular strategy again. Not like it was an option. The Yeti would never let me get that close again, never pause to gloat. He was going to rip me into tiny Jesse kibbles and that would be the end of that.

The scars down my ribs itched too, again more a product of my mind than any actual physical cause. There were details about that long-ago fight I was pretty sure I had wrong, things I'd blocked out, or forgotten or whatever. But what my waking mind couldn't remember, my sleeping mind did. I'd dreamt of the Yeti ever since, and every single time, he killed me with little to no effort.

Contemplation of my own impending doom got me as far as Denver, where I was forced to stop for fuel and something that vaguely resembled a cheeseburger. By the time I got the big truck full, I'd promised myself that I'd find something else to think about for the remainder of the trip, even if I had to resort to singing show tunes. Luckily, I found a radio station that played classic rock, turned it up to a level even I could hear with my damaged eardrums, and I was on the road again.

Another hour saw me in Manitou Springs, ready to crush Cole's phone into tiny electron particles. Yes, I understand that GPS systems are only as good as the data that's been entered into them, but when it kept telling me that Viljo lived in a Taco Shack, I was pretty sure it was wrong. I mean, it would be brilliant, not having to leave the house for food and such (if Taco Shack counted as food, which was debatable), but I didn't think even Viljo was that much of a shut-in.

Finally, in frustration, I rolled the window down and asked the next person I saw walking along.

"Oh, you want *Old* Backlick Road. That's up toward the Peak." The man pointed in the direction of the looming mountain in question. "You go up the highway a piece, take a left at the Git-n-Go, go a couple a miles. You'll see a blinking yellow light—keep going straight. Then you'll come to a T in the road. Hang a right, go about five miles, and you'll see the sign. If it hasn't fallen down again."

Of course. *Old* Backlick Road. How silly of me. Lives were at stake, and the GPS wanted to quibble about the age of the freakin' road.

What my very helpful guide neglected to tell me was that the blacktop ran out shortly after the isolated, possibly abandoned gas station. Keep in mind that I was no stranger to gravel roads—Missouri has plenty, and not far from my house—but I was driving a monster of a strange vehicle, and these particular roads had ruts that made the Grand Canyon envious. Five minutes in, and I was sure that every vertebra in my back was pulverized, and my teeth clacked together as I jounced over the road so hard that I saw stars.

Luckily, the sign for "Old" Backlick Road—which still said just BACKLICK ROAD, I might add. And what the hell kind of name is that??—had not fallen down, and with some deductive reasoning (I guessed), I took a right and headed out into what is officially known as "the boonies."

It took me another half an hour to find what I hoped was Viljo's place. The double-wide trailer sat off the main road (and I use the word "main" loosely) quite a ways, and the path that passed for a driveway was so overgrown, it might as well have been nonexistent. The only reason I even realized it was there was the mailbox at the corner, and the pile of FedEx boxes sitting under it. Surely, they'd be delivering out here only if someone was around to pick up the packages.

The Suburban rattled down the treelined trail until I found a very large, very angry-looking plywood penguin pointing an intimidating flipper at me. The sign around its neck said TRESPASSERS WILL BE REFORMATTED. Okay, I admit, I have no idea what the penguin had to do with anything other than being flat-out bizarre, but the menacing sign was definitely a computer reference, so I assumed I had the right place.

The double-wide trailer I found at the end of the trail could have been anyone's trailer, really, except for the numerous phone and power lines running in through the top of it. Lines that I really should have noticed, coming off the road. Proof that humans, as a species, seldom think to look up.

I turned the diesel engine off and sat in silence for a few moments, waiting to see if anyone was going to come investigate. Truthfully, despite my rural upbringing, overly rustic places like this always make me listen warily for banjo music on the wind. The last thing I needed was to get out and find myself looking down the barrel of a shotgun.

There had been a halfhearted attempt to mow what passed for a lawn, maybe two months ago. The lawnmower sat where it had been abandoned, tiny tendrils of vines climbing their way up the handle in slow-acting revenge.

The trailer itself was some nondescript shade of weatherworn gray. Could have been blue, in a previous life. The windows on one end of the house trailer were boarded over. The rest were heavily curtained. I watched them, to see the telltale twitch of someone watching me, but there was nothing.

I eased out of the truck, holy paintball marker in one hand, and shut the door softly behind me. In the trees around, I could hear birds chirping, and the breeze was a decidedly chilly but perfectly mundane source of my goose bumps. It took me a few moments to realize that the low throb I heard wasn't my heartbeat, but the deep bass of some loud music, emanating from within. A piercing wail, muffled but audible, escaped through the insulated windows. *Björk. Gotta be.*

I had to smirk to myself. Definitely the right place.

17

"Viljo! Open the goddamned door!" I pounded on the door for the third time, well aware that the flimsy structure would totally cave if I decided to just kick it in. Before I could truly talk myself into that, the pounding music silenced, and I heard the sounds of someone moving around inside. "C'mon, Viljo, it's cold out here!"

There was no peephole in the door, but someone—Viljo, I assume—had cut a small square out of the wood and positioned some kind of flap over it. That flap lifted, but there was nothing on the other side but a glass lens, staring blankly at me. I glared at the tiny technological spy. "I don't have time for this, Vil. It's a freakin' emergency."

After a moment—during which I seriously considered painting that little lens neon pink with paintballs—the flap dropped shut, and I could hear multiple locks rattling on the inside of the door. Judging from the sound of it, the door was solid metal behind the wooden exterior. Okay, maybe I *wouldn't* have been able to kick it in. I was vaguely glad I hadn't tried, 'cause that would have just been embarrassing.

The door finally swung inward, and I peered into the darkened trailer . . . and then I looked down. "I . . . thought you'd be taller."

The man who looked up at me was five feet tall, if he was lucky. His stringy hair was dyed matte black, and pulled back into a ragged ponytail. The sparse attempt at a mustache looked like it had been painted on with mascara, and he blinked at me behind his heavily smudged glasses. "Jesse?"

I shrugged. "Surprise."

Viljo stepped back to allow me in, and I caught him slipping something back behind the door. A quick glance revealed a baseball bat. "Who did you think was knocking, Vil?" I felt no magic tingle as I crossed his threshold, and it made me pause for a heartbeat. Viljo's trailer wasn't warded. Oddly, I realized that I'd expected it to be.

"Never can be too sure. Immigration could come calling at any time." And he was gonna take a bat to them? Remind me not to spook the little geek.

Viljo glanced around his dimly lit abode, and frowned. "Please excuse the mess. I do not get visitors, often." It went without saying that he preferred it that way.

The place really was a disaster. The one trash can I could see was overflowing with empty energy drinks, and there was a stack of pizza boxes as high as the kitchen counter. I think there was a couch against the far wall, but it was covered in what looked to be a pile of black T-shirts. The single lamp in the corner was smothered by yet another black T-shirt thrown carelessly across the shade, and I moved to whip it off, thinking "fire hazard!"

Of course, a fire might have been appreciated. It was

freezing ass cold in the trailer. I mean, it was colder inside than out, and my breath frosted in front of me. "Air conditioner works."

"The cold is good for the servers." He spent a few moments locking the door securely behind me. "You said this is an emergency? What kind of emer—?" His eyes lit on the tattoo on my arm. "Oh. That kind. I thought you were on vacation."

"So did I." I looked for a place to sit, then decided it was more sanitary to stand. I did set my paintball marker down, fully expecting it to be swallowed by the T-shirt monster breeding on the sofa. "Have you heard anything weird over Grapevine? Anyone missed checking in or anything?"

He snorted. "Over the last three days? No. Though I have been unable to contact Father Gregory, as you asked me to."

That didn't surprise me. The knights knew what was going down already, they didn't feel the need to keep in touch. "We need to send out an alert, get everyone on the phone or the computer or whatever. Everyone needs to check in."

"Why?"

"Because they really are out to get us." I put a hand on his thin shoulder and turned him toward the back of the trailer (where I presumed his computers were) before he could ask any more questions. I wasn't sure I had answers anyway.

The rear half of the double-wide was taken up entirely with servers and computers and monitors and wires and . . . I counted ten screens before I gave up, and made it only halfway around the room. There were no lights beyond the flickering of multiple monitors and the glow from at least seven computer towers, each in its own violently bright color.

The temperature was noticeably warmer in there, due to all the active machines, I guess, and I came to appreciate Viljo's cranked up AC.

The geek planted himself in a chair and rattled something off on a few different keyboards. Instantly, the monitors went from their swirling idle phases to windows that seemed to open up into different locations in cyberspace. Viljo didn't think I saw him shut down the porn windows, and I smirked to myself.

"So, should I tell everyone why I am blowing up their phones, or is it to be a surprise?" Once he focused on that monitor, his eyes never wavered from it. I was left talking to the back of his head.

"It's possible that the demons have put a hit out on us." I scratched at the black marks on my arm absently. "One had a trap waiting for me up at the cabin." A trap that he'd had to have put in place months ago. Chilling, really, when you think about it. I suppose immortal creatures really aren't constrained by things like "time."

Viljo's fingers paused on the keys. "That is . . . not possible. The contracts . . ."

"They've found a way around it." I finally spotted a footstool, buried under a stack of gaming magazines. Shoving the pile off onto the floor, I dragged the stool over so I could have a seat next to Viljo. "We have to warn everyone to watch their backs."

In a few keyboard taps and a half dozen clicks of the mouse, Viljo had the message winging across the ether. "Should we warn the Order, also?"

"No." And if the bastards had warned us in the first place, God knows how much of the last few days could have been prevented. I added that to my mental list of "things to punch Cam in the face for."

"Okay then. Alert sent. When Ivan calls, you get to talk to him." Viljo rocked his chair back, folding his hands over his stomach. Images and screens kept flickering up and down over his monitors, almost like the network had a mind of its own.

One Web site caught my eye, and I leaned forward to see better. "What's that?"

Even in the darkened room, I caught his blush. "Just . . . something I have been working on."

"So you've sold your soul, now what?" I read off the screen. "You made . . . a self-help Web site. For people who've sold their souls."

"It just started out as a way to tweak my Web design skills. Practice, you know?" His hand twitched at the mouse, obviously dying to minimize the window to keep me from looking at it. "Then I started getting hits, and . . . well, most people treat it as a joke. Something funny. I added a contact address, though. In case anyone really wants to contact a champion."

"Any takers?"

"Not yet." Finally, he clicked the window closed, to keep me from prying. "But I am getting over two hundred thousand hits a day. Word-of-mouth traffic has been huge." He brought something else up on the screen, some kind of log detailing who viewed the site and from where. "Ivan thinks it is a brilliant idea."

Of course he would. I suppose I could see the value. For every thousand people who thought it was a joke, there was that one person, alone and scared, who might reach out. It could be helpful. "Keep me posted on how it goes."

We kind of ran out of things to talk about, then. Outside of demon slaying, we really didn't have a lot in common. After a few moments of awkward silence, Viljo looked at me. "Want to wager on who calls in first?"

"Hm. Sveta will be last." Time zones would dictate who called in first, and I had no idea who was where at the moment. But Sveta, the one and only female champion and poster girl for rebellion and authority issues, would most certainly drag it out as long as possible.

Viljo snorted and gave me a sly grin. "I think she will be first."

"What do you know that I don't, Viljo?" I was still giving him a suspicious look when the phone beside his keyboard broke into the opening riff of Santana's "Black Magic Woman."

Viljo made a big show of picking it up to answer it and setting it to speakerphone. "Why, hello, Svetlana."

I could hear her even with my ears half functional, swearing in her heavily accented English. "Viljo, I swear by all that is holy, if this is another of your 'system tests' to get me to call you, I will come there and stuff that phone up your scrawny little ass!"

The geek put his hand over the phone, giving me a

grin and a shrug. "She loves me," he mouthed. "No, my sweet Ukrainian blossom, this is actually an alert requested by one Jesse Dawson, currently occupying my ottoman. Would you like to speak to him?"

Though she didn't say yes, he pushed the phone in my direction. I rolled my eyes and flipped the speaker off. Raising it to my ear, I caught the tail end of a mutter that sounded like, "I don't have enough vodka to be awake this early."

"Sveta?"

There was a bit of startled silence at the other end of the line. Then she said, "Oh! You really are there. I thought Viljo was making lines at me again." Her accent, so similar to Ivan's thick Ukrainian, made me smile. Man, I hoped we'd gotten to everyone in time. Ivan was getting on in years, and if a demon managed to ambush him somehow . . .

"No, it's really me. Are you all right? Have you noticed anything strange?"

"Mmph." That was the sound of someone struggling with a pillow. I made that same noise often. "Stranger than Viljo?"

"You haven't been contacted for a contract? No strange creatures lurking?" What else might they do, what else? "No strange men following you?"

She was quiet for a moment. "You know . . . there was a man yesterday. I saw him several times throughout the day, but he seemed to be traveling with a tourist group and I thought on it no more."

"What did he look like?"

Her patience was getting thin. I had to wonder what

time it was, wherever she was. "I don't know. Like a man. He had dark hair and nice buttocks."

Ew. "Could he have been a priest?"

"How am I supposed to know this? He had no collar, no . . . what is the word? . . . cassock."

She had a point. I felt stupid. "All right. Well, if you see him again today, go up and talk to him. Find out if he is one of the Order, and if he is, stick close to him. I don't think he'll object."

Sveta yawned hugely, right in my ear. "As entertaining as seducing a priest might sound, is there a particular reason?" She was already drifting back to sleep, I could tell.

So I explained things to her. In graphic, smelly, oozy, Catholic-y intrigue-y detail. By the end, she was listening intently, and Viljo looked like he might puke. "If they're coming for you too, you have to be ready."

"*Tak.* You are right. Thank you for the warning, Jesse Dawson."

"Take care, Sveta."

Viljo was already back on the computers, fingers flying over multiple keyboards, so I just set his phone down beside him. It rang almost immediately (a normal ring, I noted, not the special one he obviously had for Sveta), and he snatched it up without looking. "Chen."

What followed was a rapid exchange in Chinese that totally flew over my head. Who knew the little geek spoke Chinese? I should have known, though. I mean, Viljo *was* GMontag, who took down the Great Firewall of China for three months, once.

I guessed Viljo was talking to Chen Li Zhao, a Chinese-born champion who typically worked his own large corner of the world. Whatever they were saying, the hyperactive geek was dead serious this time, relaying information back and forth with brisk efficiency.

As he spoke on the phone, several windows popped up on his screen, other champions logging in to Grapevine in response to his urgent text messages. Window after window after window, and Viljo's phone kept ringing. God, how many were there? Way more than the ten or so I thought we had left. There were people on those screens I'd never seen before, faces that were totally foreign to me. Viljo knew them all, though, and I made a mental note to ask him what the hell was up with that later.

Twice, I caught a glimpse of people I recognized. Avery on one screen, in San Francisco, and another man I thought might have been Colin somebody from London.

Part of me hoped that I'd see Estéban's face pop up, that I could find out where Mira was, make sure my family was safe. It didn't, and even when I went out to the Suburban to get Cole's phone, I had no luck locating anyone. As far as I knew, Kansas City had dropped off the face of the planet.

I found Cameron's phone number on Cole's contact list, too (because that's how anal my little brother is), but I got nowhere with it, either. Figured. The Goody Two-shoes actually turned his phone off in the hospital.

As more and more people checked in (And why didn't I know about this? Were we all kept in the dark this way?), Viljo became more and more absorbed in his duties, alternating between his phone and a dozen different Webcam windows on his many screens.

About the time I heard Ivan's booming voice come through Viljo's cell phone, I ducked out of the room, taking a short walk through the trailer to stretch my stiff muscles. Twitching one of the heavy curtains open a bit, I realized that it was getting dark outside already. I'd blown the five-hour time limit I'd given Cole, and he was going to be fretting. I'd done all I could here. I needed to get back to the guys.

"Hey, Viljo? I'm gonna take off, okay? Come lock up behind me."

The geek emerged from his fortress of nerditude, nodding his agreement. "Ivan says you are 'to beink careful.'" He mimicked the accent almost perfectly, if not the deep gravelly voice, and I chuckled.

"I'll do my best." I picked up my holy-loaded paintball gun, then had second thoughts and handed it to Viljo. He gave me a questioning look. "Blessed ammo. Just . . . in case. I noticed you don't have wards on your doors."

He blinked at me in nerd horror. "Do you know what that kind of spell does to sensitive server equipment?"

"Vil, I just watched you whack one with a wrench."

"It was a highly specialized wrench."

I showed him how to take the safety off the marker, and gave him a quick how-to in case a ball broke in the barrel. "It won't kill most things, but it'll make them think twice. I'll be back to get this later, so don't break it."

He snorted, obviously offended by my doubts.

"Hey, Vil? Who were all those people?"

His eyes narrowed behind his glasses. "What do you mean?"

"All those champions. That's way more than ten or twelve of us."

The geek frowned and shook his head. "You talk to Ivan about that. He has given instructions."

I didn't like that answer, but knowing Viljo's rabid devotion to our Ukrainian leader, I didn't think I'd get any more out of him.

It was dark by the time I got on the road. I'd forgotten how far into autumn we really were. Gone were the nine p.m. sunsets, the long summer days. Winter was knocking on the door, and I had to scrape a little frost off the windshield before I could get going. I was so not dressed for an early cold snap.

Getting out of Viljo's place was easy. Remembering which godforsaken back road led toward civilization, not so much. Twice, I got turned around in the dark, and had to backtrack, using the distant lights of Manitou Springs and the looming presence of Pikes Peak to guide me. And trust me when I say that turning a Suburban around on a narrow gravel road is *not* easy.

All the while, Cole's phone sat silently on the seat beside me. I tried to mentally will it to ring, to vibrate, something. Surely, they'd contacted Mira by now. Maybe I was just out of the service area, or Cole forgot his own number. (Hey, it happens. How often do *you* dial *your* own phone?) Whatever the excuse, I was a good three hours from being able to find out if the dill-wads didn't *call*!

This was how I felt last spring, I realized, and quite a few nights since then as I waited for some strange car behind me to run me off the road again. It was the feeling that something horrible was approaching, and I couldn't do a damn thing to stop it, could only sit and wait for it to land on me with both feet. Months ago, I was helpless to save Miguel and Guy. I was helpless now to produce Mira and her life-saving magic, helpless to reach out and protect the other people around the world who followed my same calling.

I hate being helpless. Even more than I hate zombies.

I won't say that my mind was entirely on what I was doing (driving a two-and-a-half-ton death machine) and I was probably going too fast considering the road and the unfamiliar vehicle. But when I say that someone appeared out of nowhere in the middle of the road, I mean literally *no*where. Suddenly, there was a tall figure in my headlights, arm raised to shield his eyes from the glare.

In that frozen "oh shit!" split second, I saw the blond Mohawk, the glint of too much metal in his face, and I knew in some back corner of my brain that it was Axel. But that couldn't stop my instinctive swerve, foot mashing hard on the brakes as the enormous truck pirouetted gracefully off the gravel road and into the ditch.

I came to a stop with a jarring metal crunch, establishing first that I didn't seem to be injured, and second that the truck was still running with no noticeable noises of impending death. The third thing that I established was that when I got out of the truck, I was going to kill Axel.

18

"Jesus freakin' Christ, Axel!" I hopped out of the truck, landing in ankle-deep, freezing muck, and slammed the door harder than I needed to in my frustration.

The demon appeared at the front of the vehicle and grimaced. "Again, can we not bring him into this?"

The left front fender was dented in, and I anxiously examined the truck for broken lights, happy when I found none. The fender damage was mostly cosmetic, and Marty could get it beat out in no time. That didn't make the accident any better, really, but at least I hadn't totaled someone else's truck.

"Have you ever heard of the phone? Or like . . . a singing telegram or something?" The demon actually looked a bit abashed when I turned my furious glare on him. "You could have gotten someone killed!"

"I needed you to stop. There was no time for a polite request."

I clambered out of the ditch, my feet making a nice "ssssshluck!" noise with every soggy step. As best I could tell in the dark, the rest of the Suburban seemed all right. "What's the freakin' emergency, then?"

"He's after the boy."

That made me stop, which was no doubt his intent. "The Yeti?"

The blond demon nodded. "At the hospital. If he touches the boy, it's all over."

"He's . . . in public? In full view of—" Axel was already nodding emphatically. "Why the hell would he do something crazy like that?"

"Because he knows you. He knows you'll do anything to protect that child." Axel's eyes glowed cherry red, beacons in the darkness. "He knows the only way for you to save the boy, from here, is to call him away. To call your challenge due."

"The guys are there. Are they all right?"

Axel shrugged his lanky shoulders. "They were when I last saw them." That wasn't an answer. He'd been giving me a lot of nonanswers lately.

"You could be lying."

"I could be. But think. Have I ever told you a lie? Even a little one?" He smirked and nodded toward the truck. "Try to call your friends. See if they'll answer their telephones while they're under attack."

I advanced on him and poked my finger into his chest, mostly to see if Mira's protective spells would trip. They didn't. Again. "You've been pushing me around like a damn pawn for the last week, for whatever agenda it is that you have, and I'm getting pretty tired of it."

He smiled at me, that slow sinister grin I was familiar with. This was an Axel I recognized. "Are you willing to let your friends die, the boy's soul be ripped out, over a sense of moral outrage, Jesse?" He *tsk*ed softly at me and stepped away, putting distance between us as he moved down the gravel road. "There might be hope for you after all."

"Does the Yeti have his little pets with him, attacking the hospital right out in the open?"

"Mmhmm. A few. He's become very short on cannon fodder, thanks to you." His boots crunched on the gravel, every step taking him farther and farther outside the reach of the truck's headlights.

"And if I call him away, those things will go apeshit again, like earlier."

"Mmhmm. But if you don't call him away, little Zane will be one of them. I wonder if he'll even realize when he's ripped his own father's throat out, eaten his tongue."

"If I call him away, I want something from you in return."

That made him pause, and he raised a pierced brow at me. "And what might that be?"

"Help them." The Yeti had rightful claim on my soul at the moment. I couldn't offer that to Axel and he couldn't ask. What was the worst that could happen? The demon pursed his lips thoughtfully, eyes narrowing as he looked me up and down. "C'mon, man. Whatever little spat you're having with your own kind, you've already picked a side by helping us earlier. Help them again."

He made a great show of thinking it over, rocking his head from side to side, going through the hemming and hawing. Finally, he smirked. "All right. *If* you call your Yeti away, I'll help them. But you will owe me a favor. Not your soul, I won't even try that. But . . . something. Something I'll ask for later."

"Fine." Part of me expected that deal to burn itself

black into my skin, like the Yeti's brand, but nothing happened. Maybe these ephemeral "rules" covered only set contracts, not vague favors.

"Decide quickly, Jesse. They don't have much time." He took two more steps backward, and the darkness swallowed him up. Sulfur wafted to me on the tiny breeze.

What else could I do but throw my head back and yell "FUCK!" at the empty night sky? Then I kicked one of the tires for good measure, mud splattering everywhere.

Well, I *could* try to get Cam—or anyone else for that matter—on the phone. Of course, every single number I tried went unanswered. It did occur to me at some point that Cole's phone was one of those fancy ones that would let me look up things, so I found the number for the hospital in Fort Collins. And that one went unanswered too. I hung up when it hit fifteen rings.

As much as I hated to believe that Axel might be telling the truth (and trust me, I *knew* he was doing it only for his own benefit), I couldn't think of any reason for a hospital phone to go unanswered, unless major shit was going down.

Sadly, I was in no shape to be fighting the Yeti. I had my sword in the truck, yes, but my armor was all the way back in Missouri. I threw open the back doors of the truck, pawing through what was left of my friends' belongings. They'd taken their packs at the hospital, and with them they'd taken their paintball markers. No holy paint for me.

As a last resort, I patted my pockets down, wishing

futilely for any of my little antidemon gadgets and doohickeys. I discovered something hard and flat in one pocket, and investigation revealed it to be a quarter. It tingled against my fingertips.

Great. One sword, and one holy quarter. This was my arsenal.

Second concern was location. Fighting in the middle of a blacked-out gravel back road was probably not the best idea. Not to mention that our terms said it had to be in the mountains. Immediately, my eyes lit on the peak, looming large over me. I grinned. Perfect. This time of year, any campgrounds would be deserted, and hopefully the park rangers would be long gone home for the night. If I was lucky.

With the judicious application of a *crap* load of gas and a colorful variety of curse words, the Suburban gave a lurch, a shudder, and then it was free of the muddy ditch, albeit quite a bit dirtier. I drove back toward the lights of the city until I found the first sign that pointed toward Pikes Peak, and I took that turn. Whaddya know, Marty's truck *will* squall tires. Probably shouldn't mention that to him.

I'd never actually been to Pikes Peak before this, but I knew you had to buy passes in order to drive up the mountain. And where there are passes required, there are gates. And where there are gates after closing time, there are gate crashers. Guess what I was.

I don't know if there was supposed to be some kind of barrier across the drive or what, but there wasn't. There was a light on in the little guard shack, but I didn't see anyone sitting in it as I blew right past it. I did hope briefly that: one, no one tried to chase me up the mountain, and two, that I didn't get anyone in trouble for not being at their post.

According to the posted signs, it was at least an hour drive to reach the tippity top of the mountain. The guys didn't have an hour. I'd have to make my stand somewhere lower down, preferably somewhere I could find cover, use the terrain to my advantage.

The road wound upward in sharp turns that seemed more about inconvenience than actual necessity. There were no guardrails on the serpentine highway, and I took the corners at unsafe speeds, straying dangerously close to the edge of the pavement. Each turn made my head swim, my damaged ears contributing a mild case of vertigo to all the other crap I had to deal with. The Suburban cornered like a brick, and my arms ached with fighting it, despite the power steering. No wonder the drive up took so freakin' long.

How long did I have? How much time had passed since Axel dropped his bombshell? Was I far enough up the mountain for it to count? Would Axel hold up his end of the bargain?

The tall trees that lined the road hid the top of the peak from view, and I kept my eyes open for anywhere I could pull off the road. Big trees were good; they gave me something to put my back against. Not to mention that they'd help hide the truck in case the absent guard actually saw me speed through.

When I spotted the roadside sign that jokingly indicated a Bigfoot crossing, I figured that was omen enough. Bigfoot, Yeti, same diff, right? I swerved the truck off the road, feeling the damp soil give under the heavy vehicle, and hoped vaguely that I'd be able to get the truck unstuck later. If I was alive to get it unstuck. I hopped out of the truck and didn't even stop to strap my sword on, just carrying the scabbard in one hand.

The trees there were mostly of the evergreen variety, their low-hanging boughs interlacing in places to provide an almost solid canopy. In the uppermost reaches, they were dusted with snow, fallen sometime during the day I guessed. For yards around, the only thing underfoot was dead pine needles, treacherously slippery to the unwary. That wasn't going to work.

The night was quiet as I jogged into the tall pines, lacking in the usual birds-and-bugs noises, but still within the range of "mundane and normal." I was just starting to wonder where the wildlife had gone, when I remembered that my ears weren't back to normal yet, hence the cone of silence effect. That was gonna suck quite a bit if the Yeti brought his little pets. I needed to be able to hear them coming. Last thing I needed was them dropping out of the trees onto my head.

Accordingly, I found a small area with relatively few low tree branches. The needles crackled under foot, faintly, and I strained my hearing to see just how impaired I was. The burble of trickling water reached me, proving that I wasn't entirely deaf, and I went to investigate.

It was a small stream, small enough that it probably wasn't even there all the time. A recent rain, or melting snow, or something, had given birth to the tiny trickle, no more than three feet wide and a couple of inches deep. The water ran swiftly, carrying needles and twigs with it, proof that the debris had existed here long before the creek.

On impulse, I fished Cam's holy quarter out of my pocket, eyeing it thoughtfully as I rolled it across the backs of my knuckles. Cam's magic smelled like Mira's, though I was willing to bet he'd argue that point with me. No matter the method—prayer versus spell casting—the effects had proven the same. And if his blessed coin was just like the magicked one she'd given me, so long ago . . . It had worked before. I just needed to get the big fur ball into the water.

Kneeling, I quickly buried the coin in the middle of the tiny stream, pressing it into the soft mud to keep it from flitting off down the mountain. The water was cold enough that a thin skin of ice had started to form at the very edges. My fingers went numb, and I tucked them into my armpits to warm them, wishing more than ever that I'd brought a jacket on this little vacation. Add the freak cold snap to the high altitude, and it was going to be downright frigid on this peak tonight.

How much time had passed? Fifteen minutes? Twenty? Thirty? My situation here wasn't going to get any better, and my friends' was only going to get worse.

I found a relatively empty place, where the trees were smaller, some of them growing directly out of outcroppings of the mountain's distinctive pink granite. Keeping the small stream at my back, I planted my feet and drew my sword. The scabbard I tossed away, honestly figuring I'd never be able to go look for it anyway. With both feet grounded against the solid mountain, my breath fogging the air before me, I opened my mouth to call the Yeti's name.

And choked.

It's not like I forgot his name. Trust me, those things get in your brain and live there like parasites, all coiled up and oozing ick. You don't get to just forget the demonic names you hear. You can't unknow, y'know?

But the moment I tried to say it, my throat closed up, and bile rose, strong enough that I really thought I was going to gag to death on my own puke for a second. My vision got all spotty and dim, and the faint ringing in my ears became a loud clamor as my heart tried to escape out that way and go fleeing into the trees.

I found myself on hands and knees on the forest floor, hacking up my sad little gas station cheeseburger. My throat burned with it, clear up into my sinuses. Oh that was *not* pleasant at all.

"Why the fuck do people do this on purpose?" I muttered to nobody as I struggled to my feet again. The universe tipped and swayed a bit, then steadied, and I was pleased to find that I was indeed upright, and that I'd never dropped my katana.

Properly forewarned and stomach empty now, I tried again. The name was there, at the tip of my bitter-tasting tongue. It was rage and jealousy, evil and venom, all rolled up into one garbled mash of consonants and vowels and razor wire and strychnine.

I forced every single cursed syllable out around a tongue that refused to cooperate, and a throat that was doing its level best to strangle me for my effort. The moment it passed my lips, a pall of silence descended over the mountain. And I don't mean "Jesse's ears are all broke" kind of quiet. I mean quiet like the whole world stopped to hold its breath, the water stopped flowing, the plants stopped growing, the stars stopped moving. That kind of quiet.

Goose bumps sprouted over my arms, my shoulders, and my stomach cramped painfully. Something bad was coming, and I'd invited it in, asked it to come have tea. I was gonna love him, and pet him, and call him George, right up until he ate my spleen.

I kept my eyes focused on the ring of trees around me, barely breathing myself as I strained for that first sound, the one that would tell me where he was coming from.

It turns out, that first sound was a chuckle somewhere behind me. I whirled and found the Yeti lounging quite comfortably on the far side of the tiny creek. He shook his horned head in amusement. "I knew you would call. You are predictably foolish."

"Yeah, and your mama dresses you funny." *Don't look at the water. Don't look at the water.* All I needed was for him to charge me, to run through what I really, really hoped was now holy water. "Where are your little pets?" That was the loophole I'd left in the contract. If he was gonna screw me, this was the point.

"I left two of them with your companions. They were hungry." The white-furred behemoth stretched then, rising to his full height. Pine needles rained down on him where his horns jostled the lower branches. Christ, he was huge. "But this one . . . she longed for your presence."

Dammit, I fucking knew it. "What the hell does it take to kill you?"

Handless emerged from the darkness behind the Yeti. Her left arm was gone at the shoulder, the bone a rather diseased gray color where it poked through. Putrid black fluid ran from the wound down her washboard ribs, and her right arm still ended in the jagged bony stump. Somehow, it didn't make her look any less dangerous. She snarled at me in her silent way.

This was not good. Even unarmed as she was, literally, I couldn't fight the Yeti-plus-one. Any lapse of attention was going to get me eaten. "Afraid to take me on by yourself, Fuzzy?" Maybe I could get Handless into the stream too? Or maybe I could convince them both to sit down for a game of cutthroat pinochle instead. Seemed just as likely. *Bet she'd have a helluva hand, har har har.*

"She will not interfere. Provided that you play my game."

"What game?"

"Any game I wish." The beast smiled, muzzle wrinkling to reveal those gleaming fangs that had ripped into me almost every night for the last four years.

I kept an eye on Handless, but she didn't seem inclined to move, just crouching at the Yeti's heel like a good little hound. "Then we're just burning moonlight. C'mon, Fuzzy. Give it your best shot." I had to hope that Cole and the others could hold their own against a few rabid zombies. There wasn't anything I could do but deal with what was right here before me.

"As you wish." He dropped to all fours, rocking back and forth on his clawed feet and enormous knuckles for a moment. I swear, as big as he was, the mountain actually rocked with him. Or, it could have been a bit of dizziness from the damaged ears. Whichever.

I settled into a ready stance, sword held low, and waited. *C'mon . . . go for a little swim . . .*

The Yeti opened his muzzle and roared, the sound echoing off the peak, crashing through the night air. The sound slammed into me like a tidal wave, and my head reeled with vertigo. The night tilted at off angles, and the ground seemed to ripple beneath my feet.

After what seemed like forever, the echoes died away and my brain corrected itself so that all down things were down and all up things were properly up. I blinked my eyes open in time to see him spring at me. Neatly up and *over* the goddamn stream.

Well, shit.

19

The Yeti crossed the distance between us in two giant leaps. The third one took him completely over my head. I dropped to one knee to avoid the claws, and his fur brushed across my face as he passed. It smelled of something musky and rank. A drunk goat swimming in a septic tank, maybe, with the distinctive undertones of sulfur and ozone. Futilely, I lashed out with my sword, trying to connect with anything solid, but the demon wasn't intent on attacking me. In a crash of brush, he bounded into the trees on the opposite side of the clearing and vanished.

"Oh, you have got to be kidding me." I hopped to my feet as quickly as I could, focusing on Handless who hadn't moved at all. She cocked her head to the side, watching me from her one-armed crouch. I didn't dare take my eyes off her, but . . . *Where did you go, Fuzzy?* I strained to hear any trace of the Yeti's passing, but between my ears and the oppressive demon stillness that had fallen over the area, there was nothing.

The guttural chuckle echoed out of the darkness, but I couldn't get a bead on the location. "Come find me."

"I did not sign on to play hide-and-seek!" My own voice bounced back at me mockingly. *Hide-and-seek!*

Hide-and-seek! It sounded odd to my abused eardrums, like the inside of a large glass jar.

It was eerily familiar, but I couldn't place just why. Not with more important things on my mind, like whether or not I was going to see the dawn with my internal organs inside me, or beside me.

To my left, up the mountain, a tree groaned and crashed down. I could see the new gap in the pine canopy twenty or so yards ahead of me. The newly revealed stars were so bright tonight, so far from the city lights.

I had two choices. I could stand here, and assume that eventually, the Yeti would get tired of his games and circle back around to me. Or, I could chase after him, which was exactly what he wanted. He wanted to play with me. I knew that about him, because I'd seen him do it before. It was just something he did, like being white and hairy or having really bad Hell-breath. Like that old story about the frog and the scorpion, it was simply his nature.

Handless shifted her weight, inching forward a few steps when I continued to just stand there. "That how it's gonna be? I either chase him, or you come for me?" She inched again and I leveled my sword at her. "Bad. Sit. Stay." I could take her. I was pretty sure of that. But I also knew that the second I committed to that fight, the Yeti was going to come back and dissect me.

And let's face it, pursuing him was my nature. Pretty sure he knew that about me, too. I gave Handless a small salute, and deliberately turned my back on her. Every step I took, I kept expecting to feel her slight weight land on my back, her blunt teeth tear into my neck. But she never moved. The last time I glanced back at her, she was still sitting on the far side of the stream, just watching me.

Running uphill is bad, m'kay? I wasn't that stupid. I set out at a determined walk, taking my sweet time in skirting around brushy turns or fallen limbs. Running pell-mell through the dark woods was only gonna earn me a broken leg, or worse. The Yeti couldn't have this little brawl alone, so he could by God wait until I got there.

I found the downed tree easy enough, the soil still damp around its old roots. It looked like it had been ripped out of the ground and tossed a few yards, even. Showing off? Trying to intimidate me? Or just happy to cause as much destruction as possible?

There was a tuft of white fur stuck to a branch, and even as I reached to pluck it off, it dissolved into a puff of black mist. I jerked my hand back and rubbed my fingers on my shirt, just in case I'd gotten any of the blight on me.

The Yeti hadn't been gone that long, then. He'd waited here, to see if I was coming. I could picture him in my mind, lounging here, dragging his head along the murdered tree trunk. Sure enough, my fingers found gouges in the bark, left by the massive curved horns.

Any other time, I'm sure Pikes Peak is beautiful. But I have to say that, in the dark of night, in the freezing cold, I wasn't that enamored of it. I passed my katana from hand to hand, flexing my fingers to keep them limber.

The roar came from my right, and I flinched into a defensive stance before I realized it had to be yards and yards away. Even with my less than functional ears, I could tell that much. The sound bounced up the mountain and back down, making it sound like a whole herd of mini-Yetis joining the chorus. I had to wonder what the sleepy denizens down below thought of this strange noise on their mountain.

Something landed in my hair and I reflexively ducked again, swiping with my free hand to discover only pine needles. Glancing up, I found Handless above me, balanced on a thin branch like a half-shattered gargoyle. "How did you even get up there?" Her mouth opened like she might speak, but only air came out, a warning hiss. "Yeah, yeah, I'm moving." Play the Yeti's game, I got the message. I set out again, pretty sure that having a chat with a zombie said some bad things about my sanity.

Three more times, we zigzagged our way up Pikes Peak. Each time, he lured me on with a downed tree, a roar, or even just the flash of white fur in the darkness. And each time, Handless was there, my zombie shadow reminding me what would happen if I hesitated.

As we climbed upward, and my lungs started burning with every breath, I realized exactly what he was up to. Lowlander that I was, the very altitude was going to work against me. The higher we went, the colder it got, and the thinner the air became. I stopped for longer and longer between each leg, concentrating on my breathing. I couldn't afford to get winded, or light-headed. I also couldn't afford to stop too long, lest Handless get antsy.

Luckily for me, the Yeti suffered from extreme predictability. Each jaunt was almost the same distance, crisscrossing back and forth up the mountain at almost the exact same angle every time. It wasn't hard to guess where I'd find him next, and I used the last two legs to prove myself right.

The tree line was going to end soon, leaving me on the bare mountain face. The next time the Yeti laid his little bread crumbs out, I got my bearings and chose a path straight up the mountain, fixing my mind on that point. That's where I'd meet him coming.

The Yeti's pet dropped from a tree only a few yards from me as if she too knew that she was going to run out of branches soon. "You gonna narc on me?" Her head swiveled almost a full one eighty as she tilted it, almost like she was pondering my words. "*Shh.* Don't tell." Her head swiveled the other way. Those glowing dark eyes watched me, but I got no sense of the Yeti behind them like I had before. He wasn't watching me, at least not through her.

After a moment, her face stretched, the tendons drawing her lips back from her teeth in a gruesome snarl. It took me a moment to realize that it wasn't a snarl at all. She was smiling. Smiling at me. Oh that was just . . . ew.

"Good girl. Stay." I had to hope she wasn't following me as I broke into a run, rushing through the trees to lay an ambush for my worst nightmare.

The wind was wicked, once I got out of the trees,

whipping my hair around my face hard enough to sting, and the terrain was treacherously rocky. There had obviously been a rockslide along this face sometime in the near past, and jagged chunks of pink granite stuck out of the ground like some giant kid's discarded building blocks.

I found a relatively flat place, and was just planting my feet when the great horned head broke through the brush at the edge of the trees. There was a brief moment of surprise, when his ears perked up and he got that comical tilt of the head like puzzled dogs do. It was almost cute. Then the large muzzle rippled into a low growl, and he prowled onto the bare rocks, nimbly clambering from one heap to another. His claws clicked on the hard granite. "Tricky, tricky . . . Ready to die, then?"

"I'm always ready to die." The way of *bushido* is death. I had no problem with that, so long as I could take this ugly mother with me. I was done with him hurting people I cared about. Hell, I was done with him hurting people I'd never heard of before.

"Wish granted." He sunk his claws into the boulder he was perched on and launched himself off it like a furry freight train.

It was different from the first time. I was more experienced, in better shape, more practiced. He was bigger, stronger. I had a slight speed advantage over him, and that was all that kept me one hair ahead of his swipes, dodging and parrying as best I could. Something that big should not be that fast. It simply isn't fair. I fully intended to file a grievance with the union, if we ever started one.

I briefly wondered where Handless was, but she was wiped from my mind in the face of the onslaught that was the Yeti. I couldn't even get a chance to go on the offensive with him. Every shred of my energy was poured into keeping those wicked claws away, into keeping those horns from connecting with my unprotected skull. The Yeti sprang from rock to rock, and I was forced to keep turning to face him, not giving any ground, true, but not gaining either. There was no way I could try to clamber after him and fight at the same time. He could dance around me all night, and all I was going to do was get tired.

Predictability. It led a demon to target a distraught boy, knowing that I'd come to his rescue. It almost got my friends killed. Might still, if things at the hospital were going poorly. It had me tracking a demon through unfamiliar territory, and it helped me catch up to the Yeti here at the end. It was the one thing I couldn't afford, anymore.

Being that you are samurai, be proud of your valor and prowess and prepare yourself to die with frenzy. Advice I could live by. Or die by, really.

The next time the Yeti landed, claws chipping shards away from the pink boulders, I was already on the move. I saw the demon's eyes widen as I charged him head on, roaring my own battle cry as I came.

It almost worked.

The first two slashes opened up blight-gushing cuts across one furry forearm and the thigh below it. The dark essence poured out, flowing down the jagged rocks like a deadly, life-sucking stream. It found a low spot and started to pool. The portal would form there, the doorway sucking the Yeti back to Hell.

The demon bellowed in pain, and I ducked under his arm to take a swipe at a hamstring, feeling my blade slide through thick fur into the solid muscle beneath. I let my momentum carry me off the rock, arms pinwheeling for balance as I landed on the next one below. A rank breeze ruffled my hair, the Yeti's backhanded swipe just missing my head as I dropped out of his reach.

Like I said, it almost worked. Before I could get my balance on my new perch, before I could turn around, I was bludgeoned across the back hard enough to send me hurtling through the air and into the rocks below. I went rolling down the jagged boulders, bruising and scraping every single part of me, and into the trees where the pine needles gouged at the already bloody places. Just as I came to a stop, I heard a distinctly metallic snap, and my sword hand came up empty.

Oh fuck.

I found the blade, easy enough. It was pinned beneath my body, and only kind fate had kept me from impaling myself on it. But it was snapped off neatly, just where the guard should have been, and the hilt was long gone, wedged somewhere in the rocks above me. If the Yeti didn't kill me, Marty was going to.

I scrambled to my feet, bare blade in my hands because hey, it was all I had. Holding it loosely was no problem, but the second I tightened my grip to strike, I was going to fillet my own fingers. Mentally, I did a quick check, cataloguing my other injuries from my tumble down the hill.

My back and both hips were bruised all to hell, I could tell that much. Something warm and wet was trickling down my left shoulder. I was scraped from knuckle to elbow on both arms and the back of my head throbbed dully. All in all, it could have been worse.

And where was my overly hirsute dance partner?

It was dark under the overhanging branches. I didn't realize how much I'd relied on the starlight above until it was taken from me. I blinked furiously, trying to will my eyes to adjust to the pitch blackness. I was blind here, cut off from sensation.

It also didn't escape my notice that I was in the trees again. Handless's turf. If she was going to get involved in this debacle, now would be the time. I could only hope I'd get some kind of warning before she pounced.

Nothing useful reached my ears. In fact, all sound seemed to be drowned out by my own panting breath, vibrating oddly in my damaged ears. Like a glass jar. Like a cave.

It occurred to me, in a flash of goose bumps and stomach cramps, that I'd been here before. Almost every night for the last four years, I had been in this place, surrounded by darkness and cold. My breath frosting the air, the sound distorted in my ears. The Yeti, hunting me.

"I know you're there." I couldn't stop myself from saying it. I always said it. It was always answered with a soft growl to my left, just out of my range of vision.

I turned, because I had to. Because in the dream, I always turned toward the sounds. God, I wanted to tell Mira about this. I wanted to ask what she thought of my dreams becoming reality, 'cause honestly it was freaking me out. "Come on . . . come get me," I whispered, my words echoing in the bell jar that was my skull.

A sound behind me, the faintest scrape of fur on stone. And I turned, because I knew I had to. Nothing faced me but the bare ghosts of pine trees, a lighter shade of gray in the black.

This was the moment, in every nightmare I'd had in the last four years. The moment when the sound stayed in front of me, but the attack came from behind. Always from behind, and I was always motionless, spellbound, paralyzed.

There came the faintest of clicking sounds from the darkness in front of me. The Yeti's talons . . . *Or Handless's long toenails?* I tasted the blood in my mouth, where I'd bitten my tongue.

This isn't a dream, dammit! "And I'll move if I fucking want to."

I reversed my grip on my broken sword and stabbed backward along my own rib cage, the blade slicing neatly through the first layer of my T-shirts. The point hit something solid, and suddenly the world lurched into motion again, like a film stuttering back to life. I never looked back. The blade bit into my palms as I slammed it home, then yanked hard to the left. I dropped to one knee, feeling the swipe that was meant for my throat pass harmlessly over my head, and with a heave, I dragged the naked metal to the side and out, ripping through the white-furred abdomen.

Blight poured out in place of glistening intestines. A river of black nothingness, it ran down the white-furred legs, visibly seeking to rejoin the part of itself that had already been shed. Still on my knees, the next two slashes opened up each massive thigh, severing what would be the femoral arteries in anything actually living. The blackness gushed out with force, washing over my hands, instantly numbing the searing pain I'd caused myself.

The Yeti roared but there was panic in that guttural voice. His claws flailed in the air, trying to connect with anything at all, but in his agony, they were blind strikes and came nowhere near me.

The wickedly curved horns went first, cracking and splintering into tiny shards, which in turn vanished into motes of blight, flowing against gravity and up the hill toward the waiting dark pool. Then the ears, crisping like they'd been charred in a fire, curling in on themselves. The bellow turned into a strangled gurgle, and only a quick roll saved me from being crushed as the Yeti pitched forward, his legs being eaten from the belly wound outward.

He writhed in the pine needles, hands grasping at the fleeing essence until his fingers melted away and he could only twitch. His glowing red eyes found mine, and what was left of his muzzle wrinkled in a silent snarl.

"Remember this," I told him. "Even on my knees, I killed you."

The last things to go were the wicked fangs, bared in

a defiant snarl to the bitter end. The stream of blight wafted its way up into the rocks, and I could smell the ozone. If I looked, there would be a pool of liquid demon up there, like black mercury in its pristine reflection. Even at that distance, I could hear the screaming, a sound just beyond my range of hearing, but something that I could feel in the back of my teeth. The unearthly call of Hell itself.

Just as suddenly, it was gone. It took the Yeti with it.

It did not, however, take his little pet. The brush to my right rustled and parted around a bald, filthy head. Handless hobbled her way into the open, settling on her haunches only a few yards from me. If I wanted, I could have reached out and touched her.

Even unarmed as she was—seriously, that joke never gets old—I wasn't sure I could take her in the condition I was in. I rose to a half crouch, blade cupped gingerly in my flayed hands. "You let him die. You could have stopped me."

She didn't move. For long moments we stared at each other across the six feet of intervening space. Then her cheeks stretched again into the mockery of a smile. The unearthly gleam of her black eyes betrayed how much hate she had for me, for all the living, but I understood. The only thing she hated more than me was him. She was free now. Free to rip my throat out, eat my flesh, feed. But I think in the end, she wasn't sure she could take me either.

She opened her mouth, and a man's voice came out. "Well, this is quite a pickle we find ourselves in, isn't it?"

I couldn't help but chuckle a little, bleakly. "Yeah, you could say that."

It was a woman's voice next, someone elderly perhaps. "I just don't know what I'll do without him. He always took care of everything."

She was doing it on purpose, somehow. Those echoes, those memories of long dead conversations, she was calling them up, using them to speak for her. "You go far, far away, where you can't hurt anyone."

A man's voice again. "A growin' boy's gotta eat!"

I forced myself all the way to my feet. "If you hurt anyone else, I will come for you. I will end you. You know that."

The next voice was John Wayne's, or a really good impression thereof. "A man's gotta do what a man's gotta do." Finally, she bared her rotting teeth at me in one last voiceless snarl, and started fading back into the trees. Her parting shot, though, chilled me to the bone. A deep gravelly voice emerged from the darkness. "You are to beink careful."

Ivan's voice. I'd know it, and his butchered English, anywhere. Somewhere, sometime, Handless had been close enough to Ivan to hear him speak.

About five minutes later, a bird chirped nearby, proving that she was truly gone.

I know I sat there for at least forty-five minutes, perched on the jagged pink boulders until my legs stopped shaking and my breath didn't burn in my lungs anymore. Idly, I peeled the flaking black skin off my arm, the demon tattoo erased with the contract I'd fulfilled. The sky was growing light in the east, false dawn heralding the passing of another night.

And I was still here.

I couldn't find the hilt of my sword, lost somewhere in the stones, but I carried the blade with me as I slowly picked my way down the rockslide. My hands were stiff, and the cuts across my palms seeped blood every time I tried to flex my fingers. I hurt everywhere.

I also had no idea where the hell Marty's truck was. How far had I come in my flight through the trees? But the great thing about being on a mountain is that down is usually the direction you want to go. So I headed down, my exhausted feet stumbling more than once on the uneven terrain.

Eventually, I found the plucky little stream again, and by following it I found the clearing in the trees where I'd first called the Yeti. Even just thinking of him brought a sour film to the back of my throat, and I wished vainly for something to drink.

I'm not dumb enough to drink out of a mountain stream. Duh. But I could wash the blood from my hands there. For some reason, the thought of staining Marty's truck with my blood was overwhelmingly unacceptable.

I knelt, noting which joints ached in all the wrong places. By morning, I'd barely be able to move. I dipped my hands into the ice-cold water, letting it run over the deep cuts and numb away the pain. I examined the injuries with a curious detachment, marveling that I still had motion in my fingers at all. I'd sliced my palms up pretty good.

Though . . . I gingerly wiped the caked blood off my left palm, letting the water carry away the grime, and realized that I couldn't see a cut at all. Looking at my right, I found the same there, my palm unmarred. Where my knuckles should have been scraped and bloodied, I found unbroken skin.

"Oh holy . . ." So, Cam's coin had worked after all. I knew I couldn't leave it there in the stream for just anyone to find. What if someone noticed this little creek suddenly had healing properties? I dug in the icy mud for a few moments, trying to find just where I'd buried the bespelled quarter, but I had no luck. Hell, I could have been yards off, in either direction. I finally had to resign myself to leaving it, and hoping that the spell would wear off before anyone noticed.

The Suburban was right where I'd left it, when I finally managed to make my way to the right location. I threw what was left of my katana in the back, and deep down I mourned my loss. She'd been good to me. She'd been there with me since the very beginning.

On the passenger seat, Cole's phone glowed, indicating a missed call and a waiting message.

"We're fine," were the first words out of his mouth. "Everyone's fine, and we got Mira on the phone. She was at the amusement park. Can you believe it? Zane's gonna be okay. Call me, big brother, soon as you get this. God, please call."

I would. I'd call him as soon as I got off the mountain, preferably before someone arrested me for trespassing. As soon as my hands stopped shaking. Maybe when the full-body shudders subsided. Definitely after my vision stopped being all black around the edges.

But first, I was going to call my wife, and I didn't even care what time it was back home.

She was expecting me. The phone rang only once. "Jesse??"

"Hey, baby." I couldn't help it. I had to smile at the sound of her voice, so thick with worry and tight with relief. "Did I wake you?"

Of course I hadn't woken her. She'd been pacing the floors, for the thousandth or so time, wondering if I was alive or dead, if the next phone ring was going to be *that* call. "Goddess, Jess. Where are you?"

"Um . . . somewhere on Pikes Peak? I paid Viljo a visit. He says hey."

"Are you all right? Cole said you were fighting."

How did Cole know . . . ? Oh yeah. The Yeti went bye-bye, and Zane's tattoo flaked off. That's how he knew. "Um . . . yeah, a little. It's all right. I won."

She took a deep breath, and I could hear the squeak of our bed as she sank down onto it. "How badly are you hurt?"

Good question. "Actually . . . not too bad. Gonna be a lovely shade of purple in a few hours, but nothing fatal. Nothing even debilitating." Sore and stiff and bruised was way better than filleted and bleeding and dying. Infinitely better. Hell, compared to my usual adventures, I'd come out of this one the rosy picture of health.

"You're sure? You're not . . . you're not lying to make me feel better?"

"No, baby. Promise." Of course, I'd lied to her about other things. Omitted. Dodged. It was no wonder she thought I might be fibbing now. I deserved her doubt too much to even be hurt by it. "Physically, I'm fine. Swear."

"And not physically?"

Ah, that was the question. For days, I'd buried my fear, crammed it down deep where no one else could see. I'd been running on adrenaline and instinct for three straight days now, wrapping myself in it like armor. But all of that was gradually washing away as I sat here, leaving me with nothing but belated terror. I rested my forehead on my knees when my vision started to swim again, my blood pressure humming in my ears. "It was him. It was the one in my dreams. He came back." God . . . he came back. And if he could come back once, he could come back again. That certain knowledge sent shudders through my body so hard I almost dropped the phone. "Are you all right there? You and the kids? Nothing weird?"

Handless had been near Ivan. Which meant the Yeti had. It wasn't unthinkable that he'd been near my wife and daughter too. Estéban.

Mira was exasperated when she answered. "We're fine. It's you I'm worried about. Do you need help? I can call Ivan, or Avery, or . . . Someone can come get you."

"No, I'll be fine. I'm gonna . . . just sit here a bit and catch my breath. Then I'm gonna go hook up with the guys again. We'll be home either late today or tomorrow, okay?"

"You call. You call every time you guys stop for something, all right? I want to know that you're coming home."

"I always come home, baby." Oops. There's that lie again. "Hey, I hear you got Zane all patched up."

"Oh, yeah. Cameron seems to have some basic magical ability. Enough that it worked. You're going to have to explain all that to me when you get home." She didn't want to talk about Cam and Zane, I could tell that much. "Are you sure you're all right?" she asked one more time. "Jess, if you need help . . ."

"Baby, I'm fine. And you should get some sleep. Anna's gonna drag you out of bed in a couple hours whether you want to or not. I'll see you both soon."

She heaved a heavy sigh. "I . . . Be careful, please. Come home."

"I will. Love you, baby."

"I love you too, Jess."

I hung up the phone and tried to muster the energy to get to my feet. The sun rose while I sat on the ground leaning on Marty's dented fender. It lit the world in shades of fire. It was beautiful.

20

There was a variety of interesting headlines in several news-type publications in the days and weeks following my pseudovacation.

The first one made national news, all the way from Fort Collins, Colorado. Apparently, an oxygen tank exploded in a storage room at the local hospital, damaging a hallway and causing the evacuation of the entire facility. Everyone was so thankful that it wasn't a tank in a patient's room, and that the injuries were minimal. No one could figure out just why the tank exploded, or what it was doing in the storage room where it didn't belong. Investigations were ongoing.

It took Cole a week (and most of a six-pack) to tell me what really happened.

"You're going to think I'm insane, big brother," he mentioned quietly one night. "Absolutely out of my ever-loving mind."

The Yeti had walked right into the ER in his human guise, like he owned the place. At his heels were two of his minions, scuttling along like the good little pets they were.

"It was like nobody saw them. Like they *couldn't* see them." Cole shook his head. "Why could we see them, and no one else?"

"People see what they want to see. You guys kinda

had it crammed down your throat." Really, I had no idea what I was talking about. Philosophy I could explain. Mystic shit, not so much. Despite my eerily accurate dream, I was not a magic user. I knew this. I *believed* this. *So what the hell had happened to me up there?*

"Anyway . . . I saw him come in, before they saw me, and I yanked the curtains shut around Zane's bed."

They'd retreated out the backside of the ER, into the maintenance hallways of the hospital, wheeling Zane's bed between them. Duke padded along silently, like he understood the risk they were taking.

Why no one stopped them, I don't think any of us will ever know. At Will's direction, they turned away from the patient room elevators and toward the operating rooms. There was only one way in or out down there, to keep it sterile, and Will figured there'd be fewer innocents present so late at night.

They might have gotten away clean, if the bed's wheel hadn't gotten caught on a sharp corner, jostling it. In his pained delirium, Zane moaned.

Demons track by sound, or so Axel said. I think he must have been telling the truth, because all it took was that moan, several hallways distant, to alert the Yeti and his zombie pets.

"We tried to stay ahead of them, but the kid was half awake by that point, and kept hollering. They came right to us. We could hear their claws, scrabbling on the floor tiles."

They weren't going to reach the operating suites in

time, so the guys crammed the bed into the nearest storage room they could find and barricaded the door with whatever they could get their hands on. They combined what little weaponry they had left—Cole's gun with two bullets, and one hopper full of blessed paintballs—and prepared to make their stand.

"He knocked on the door. Just tap tap tap, all polite like." Cole shook his head. "Cameron kept insisting that he couldn't hurt us, wasn't allowed to, and all I could do was look at Zane in that bed and think that Cameron was either crazy or stupid."

There were things Cole didn't say. Things that I maybe made up in my own head, but I could picture how it went so clearly. Oscar's hand, pressed so tightly over his son's mouth, trying to stifle the boy's cries. Will, pawing through the shelves of supplies to see if there was something, *any*thing there they could use. Marty with the loaded paintball gun, just waiting for the door to come flying open.

"He said, 'I'll give you two minutes to decide what to do with the boy, and then I'll send my pets in to retrieve him.'" My brother blinked a bit. "He really thought we'd give the kid up to save our own skins. What kind of person does that?"

"He's not a person, little brother. He's about the furthest thing from it."

The Yeti didn't give them two minutes. Almost immediately, they heard the ceiling tiles in the hallway go crashing down, and the minions were in the drop ceiling above them. The brackets that held the fiberboard tiles dipped and swayed dangerously, even the zombies' slight weight too much for the light support system.

"If they came through the ceiling, we were gonna be trapped in close quarters with them. But if we opened the door, the demon was gonna get Zane." Cole drained what was left of his beer and reached for another. "I took aim at the ceiling, thinking maybe I could shoot through the tiles and at least cripple them. We could let Duke finish them on the ground or something."

This was the part of the story where, unbeknownst to anyone at the hospital, I came in. There was a sudden silence above them, and out in the hallway, the Yeti chuckled. "I have been called away on unexpected business, gentlemen. I'll leave my pets here for your amusement." And just like that, poof, he was gone.

Of course, the guys had no way of knowing he'd really disappeared. They didn't know I'd just shouted out a name I'd sworn never to say, that I was about to fight for my life on a mountain far to the south. They *did* know, however, that the creatures in the ceiling paused for long moments, then exited the way they'd come in, tiles crashing to the floor out in the hallway. They heard the claws clacking on the floor, hurrying away.

I suppose it's possible the creatures remembered the guys. Maybe what little intelligence they had left recalled that tangling with my buddies meant excruciating, horrific pain. More likely, they just smelled the blood down in the OR and decided it was Zombie-Starbucks. Either way, once the Yeti wasn't there to boss them around, the two minions went scampering off into the hospital.

My brother knew they couldn't let those things go running off willy-nilly into the general populace. At the very least, having half-rotting animated corpses in the OR was *so* not sterile. I mean, there isn't enough hand sanitizer in the *world* to cover that mess.

So Cole left Marty and Duke to stand guard over everyone else, and went chasing off into the hallways alone, armed with two bullets. Yeah, I know. He's growing up to be just like me. Ain't I proud?

"I chased them almost all the way to the surgery suites, but I didn't realize until we were almost there that there was actually an operation taking place. I could hear the beeping machines, and people's voices." He paused there for a long time. "I knew I was gonna die, y'know. Knew I couldn't take them out with two shots, and it didn't matter. I had to stop them no matter what. Had to keep them from hurting anyone else."

He fired after those fleeing abominations, one bullet sending one of them cartwheeling into the wall. It didn't kill it, though, and they both turned on my brother, hissing as they bounded down the hallway toward him. With one bullet, he faced them both down and silently said his good-byes.

"I don't know what happened next, Jess. I mean, I can tell you what I think I saw, but . . ."

From behind him, a searing white light lit up the hallway, bright enough to blind him even with his back to it. He dropped to his knees, hands slapped over his eyes in agony, and the Yeti's pets shrieked in their

death throes. The light eclipsed everything, its bril-
liance so great that Cole couldn't make out the pattern
of the floor tiles, even with his nose pressed against
them. When he was finally able to raise his head, there
were only ashes in the hallway, drifting along in the
breeze from the air vents.

"And what do you think it was?" I had an idea. I'd
sent them help, after all.

"Honestly?" I waited while he mentally talked his
next words over with his beer. "I will swear to you,
Jesse. Swear until my dying day. I *swear*, in that hallway, I saw an angel."

I didn't believe in angels. Demons, yes. One demon
in particular. Axel had come through for me, and it
didn't seem important to tell my brother the truth.
He'd be happier, believing in angels. We finished our
beers, and neither of us has spoken of it since. That's
how we roll, my brother and I.

The next headline that caught my eye, though it
never progressed past a local piece in Fort Collins, was
the story of a teenager bitten by a rabid badger while
on a family camping trip.

You heard me. Somehow, some genius looked at the
human bite marks on Zane's arm and decided that it
looked like a badger. Trust me when I say that badger
bites don't even remotely resemble human. (I Googled
it.) I had to wonder if that was some deep conspiracy
cover-up, or just the human penchant for explaining
the unexplainable, no matter how ridiculous.

Zane was expected to make a full recovery. The guys
got Mira on the phone with Cam, and together, the two

of them magicked up a cure. The last I heard, he's had a full round of rabies vaccinations, and he's going to have to do some physical therapy to regain full use of the arm, due to muscle damage. It's been a while since I got an update, though. Oscar made it very plain that he doesn't want us (me) anywhere near his son, despite the fact that I saved the kid's soul.

I don't honestly care so much for my own sake, but I feel bad for Marty. The Quinns were longtime family friends of his, and it's my fault he's lost them now.

I haven't seen Marty in a few weeks either. He says I'm supposed to stay away while he works on this new sword he's started constructing for me. I can't tell if he's pissed or not. Guys, we don't typically sit around and talk out our feelings and stuff. Eventually, I'll head over to his house with a case of beer, and he'll either punch me, or he won't. Then we'll both know.

It's not like he doesn't have every right to be ticked. Stuff could have gone real wrong up there. Stuff *did* go real wrong up there. It would have been real easy for Mel to be a widow and a single mom, all in a split second. That's not the life she married for. Marty either. So . . . how do you blame the guy if he's a little skittish now?

At least I've still got Will. I mean, Will is Will. He takes whatever I throw at him, and he keeps on ticking, and cracking really bad jokes. I don't know what I'd do without Will, and it's more than his ability to tie a mean tourniquet. I have realized that I never gave him enough credit. He's good people.

The last headline made me laugh, and then glance

around sheepishly. It was a little blurb on the cover page of one of those supermarket tabloids. You know the ones. BIGFOOT AND SWAMP CREATURE ELOPE! Those kinds of stories.

Only this one was about claims that there was a miracle stream flowing down Pikes Peak. The creek wasn't always there, but when it appeared, it had healing qualities. Obviously, someone had stumbled across my little blessed stream after I'd left. Part of me hoped that anyone who could find it would find the cures to their health woes. The rest of me was pretty sure I was gonna get my butt kicked for violating some esoteric magic law I didn't even know about. Surely, leaving magic stuff lying around can't be proper spell-casting etiquette.

When Cameron showed up on my doorstep, I was pretty sure that was what he'd come to talk about. I was wrong.

Thankfully, my girls weren't home and Estéban was out on a date. I led Cam through the house and into the backyard. Call me paranoid, but I had no idea what was coming and I didn't feel like being confined.

"I owe you an apology," the priest began before I was ready, and the unexpected sentiment brought me up short. Cameron examined the stone chess pieces on my patio table—recently retrieved from storage—as he spoke. "I wasn't honest with you, or your friends. To say that I was only following orders is not a defense."

I folded my arms over my chest, curious to see where this was going. Cam talked like a man in need of confession, ironically enough. Men like that will spill all kinds of things if you just let them keep babbling.

"I told you I got in a car wreck last spring, right?"

I nodded. I vaguely remembered that conversation. That was how he got his limp, and the scar on his forehead.

He took a deep breath. "I hit you."

For a few seconds, that statement made absolutely no sense. My confusion must have shown on my face, because he went on in a hurry. "We were supposed to try and scare you guys off, see if we could get you to quit taking challenges. We thought it would eliminate you from the demons' hit list."

He picked up the bishop, turning it in his fingers. "I didn't know you were already contracted, at that point. I never would have tried . . . In all fairness, I didn't expect you to slam on the brakes. I wasn't going to hurt you, but *you* caused that wreck, and . . ."

And I remembered suddenly the sound of tortured metal, the squall of brakes, the pain as my head smacked into the window of my truck. "You hit my truck."

"Yes."

"You were in the blue Ford Escort that tried to run me off the road."

"Yes." To his credit, he didn't back up (much) as I came around the table, advancing on him.

"You *dented* my truck."

"Yes."

"I'm going to punch you in the face now."

"I thought you might."

And I did. If wagering my soul with demons doesn't cinch my place in Hell, I'm pretty sure punching a priest in the schnoz does.

By the time Mira and the kids got home, Cam was sitting on the patio with a bag of frozen carrots on his swollen nose, and I was doing my best to look perfectly innocent. Don't think my wife bought it, but she'd had a long time to get used to my quirks. She just shook her head and went back into the kitchen to start on dinner.

Things weren't all unicorns and rainbows between me and Cam by any means. As far as I was concerned, he and the Order both had a lot to answer for. Whether this prophecy thing was true or not, their Sooper Sekrit Book of Dooooooom meant that the Order had known about and believed in this impending crap for a long time. At the very least, they'd known since last spring, since they were trying to spook Ivan's champions into quitting, clear back then. Which meant that, for at least six months, they could have warned us, could have prepared us.

Instead, seven champions were attacked the same night that the Yeti cornered me and my guys in the cabin. Six of those champions had priestly shadows and managed to turn back their attackers. One of them did not, for the simple reason that Father Gregory didn't know about him. If the bastards had just *asked* for a roster, or even let us police our own . . . Scott Marks, formerly of Brisbane, Australia, might still be alive.

I didn't know Scott. I didn't even know *of* him until

after the fact. He was one of the champions I never even knew existed, one of Ivan's closely held secrets. Let me tell you, I was getting damn sick of them, and Ivan and I were going to have a very long talk when I could pin him down again. I think Viljo must have told him, 'cause both Ivan and the geek were avoiding my phone calls for the moment.

My other lingering grudge had to do with Cameron and Dr. Bridget.

The priest finally got up the stones to ask, "Are you going to tell her?"

"No." He looked surprised, behind the bag of frozen veggies. "She's happier now than I've seen her in a long time. I'm not going to be the guy responsible for fucking that up." Relief flared in his eyes (nicely blacked, thank you very much) then died as I shook my head. "You're going to tell her. It may be just a cover for you, but this is her *life* you're messing with."

He thought about that for a little bit, then nodded slowly. "I want you to know . . . for whatever it's worth . . . I didn't intend this. This thing with Bridget. And I have never lied to her about caring for her."

"No, you just lied to her about being a priest, ignoring that whole celibacy thing you're supposed to have going on."

He stiffened, jaw going tight. "I have remained faithful to my vows, throughout all of this."

Oh merciful Buddha, I didn't need to know that. "Yeah, good luck keeping that up. She's gonna expect *some* kind of something, eventually."

Cam dropped his gaze to his feet and sighed. "I know. I . . . don't know what I'm going to do, then."

"You're going to break up with her now, and save us all the trouble."

"Yes. It would . . . probably be best." He finally looked up again, meeting my eyes. "But if I was going to break my vows, it would be for her."

Another thing I didn't need or want to know. "Just remember, your biggest worry isn't me telling Bridge. It's me telling Mira."

Truthfully, I'd already told Mira all about Brother Lies-a-Lot and his order of backstabbing assholes, but what Cameron didn't know could terrify him. Really, after the hoodoo she'd walked him through with Zane, I wasn't going to be able to pass him off as just an amateur caster anyway. Much to my disappointment, she wasn't nearly as pissed off about the whole situation as I'd expected her to be.

"But he's *lying* to Bridget. He's using her."

Mira just shook her head at me, giving me that amused "I know more than you" smile. "I don't think he's lying to her about the important parts."

Still, I hoped he would just walk out of our lives. Yeah, Dr. Bridget would be heartbroken, but Mira could do that girl-bonding thing that women do when one of them gets dumped, and things would go back to normal-ish.

Speaking of normal-ish . . . Somehow, I expected Axel to waltz back into my life like he hadn't been gone the past six months. I left the chess set out on the back patio, thinking we could play again, or that it would at least give us an excuse to open up talks. He didn't show.

Often, when I came outside for my morning katas, I found the pieces moved. For a month, I played against a nonexistent opponent, attacking, feinting, countering, but the demon never showed himself.

But then, I suppose he was busy. No matter how things had turned out for me up on that mountain, stuff around the world wasn't any different. Winter was coming on, and the droughts had turned to blizzards. The wildfires had given way to mudslides, and the riots had become terrorist actions. Seemed like the entire human race was pissed off about anything and everything. Signs of the conflict seeping over into our world, I guess.

Halloween was looming on the horizon and I was out back bagging up pumpkin guts from our jack-o'-lantern frenzy, when Axel finally appeared. There was no fanfare, no flashing lights. He didn't even bother to hide inside a squirrel or other domestic pest. He was just there, at the edge of my water garden, when I looked up.

"Axel." I set the trash bag aside and wiped my hands on my jeans as I walked across the grass.

"Jesse." He offered a bit of a smile, but there was weariness to it.

"Kinda expected you sooner than this."

"Yeah, well . . . busy social calendar. You know how it is." He stuffed his hands into his pockets. If the chilly autumn air bothered him in his light T-shirt, it didn't show. "You've been well?"

"I'm still here. What's up with you?"

He shook his Mohawked head. "I can't stay long, Jesse. Don't waste your questions."

I nodded a little. I'd expected as much. "Fine. How about I start with telling you what I know, and you just say hot or cold, hm?"

After a moment, he nodded. "That could work."

"There's some kind of split Down There. Y'all are feuding amongst yourselves."

That earned me a nod and a "Hot."

"One side wants us champions out of the picture, for some reason."

"Hot."

"One side . . . wants us to stay?"

He frowned, mouth twisting as he tried to find an answer he could give me. "Warm."

"How warm?"

"Lukewarm."

This was getting us nowhere fast. "Look, are we still in danger? Are they going to come again?"

The demon kept frowning, and added pacing to his repertoire. "It's complicated, Jesse. Yes, someone, some-time, is going to come again. But you have to realize that you're dealing with creatures that have no sense of time. They could come tomorrow. They could come two centuries from now. And it would make absolutely no difference to them."

"Makes a helluva lot of difference to me," I muttered, and he smirked. "So what do we do?"

"What have you been doing for the last month?" He shrugged. "You go on."

"We go on, and just wait to see if some big fight that isn't even ours comes running over our head like a freight train?"

"Sounds like a plan." He scuffed the toe of his boots through my shaggy lawn, finding something on the ground suddenly fascinating. "There have been lines drawn over this, Jesse. Sides chosen. Things you didn't even see or know were happening. It's going to get much worse before it gets better."

"And whose side are you on, Axel?"

"Mine, of course. That was a foolish question." He smiled a little, never raising his eyes to meet mine.

Of course. It *had* been a foolish question. I'd known the answer before I ever asked it, and I expected nothing less of him.

The weird thing was, in all the years I'd known him, I couldn't think of a single time Axel had ever lied to me. Ever since he made that comment on that dark road, I'd tried to think back, wracked my brain to find a single instance. He omitted, yes. He evaded. But he'd never told me a straight-up bald-faced lie. And I had no idea what that meant.

"Hey, Jesse? Hold still while I try something, okay?"

Against my better judgment, I held still.

With a puzzled tilt to his head, Axel reached out and pinched my biceps *hard*.

"Ow!" I yelped, and reflexively socked him in the chest, hard enough to make him grunt. Then we both kind of stared at each other.

It was the first rule, the one inviolable rule that governed what we, as champions, did. A demon could not harm a human without that human's permission. That was the whole point of the contracts, of the bartering souls. It was the thin line of civility that protected us, the humans, against them, the demons.

But my arm hurt, and was going to bruise. He'd hurt me. And I'd hit him back with no mystical repercussions. "What does that mean, Axel?"

"I . . . don't know yet. But I'm going to find out." The fact that even Axel was flummoxed bothered me more than anything else. Before he faded out of view, he reminded me, "You owe me a favor, champion. Don't think I've forgotten."

Yeah. That. I had to wonder just how that was gonna come back and bite me in the ass later.

Cameron hadn't left town, of course. Big jerk. And as far as I knew, he was still dating Dr. Bridget, which was pretty high on my "not happy" meter. Still, it was handy to be able to ask him to dig through the Order's Library of Books Not Accessible to Mere Mortals. (I slay me, seriously.)

He found no trace of anyone named "Architect." No demon, no spirit. No angel either. Whatever Axel was, he hadn't been documented. Which meant he was either nothing notable at all . . . or he was some serious badass shit. I was starting to suspect it was the latter.

I couldn't help but think about what Axel had said. I had known the Yeti's name, and for whatever reason, that was threat enough for him to try to kill me. How many other names were swimming around in my brain? In my four, almost five years as a champion, I'd had fourteen challenges. More than any other champion in the same time period. Granted, two of them were with the Yeti, but that still left twelve other demons with some kind of special grudge against me. I needed to find out about this whole name thing, and fast.

I also knew that Handless was still out there. I suppose it was possible that she hobbled off into a hole and died, but . . . deep down, I knew better. She was out there, and she was something I'd have to deal with eventually. I entered everything I could remember about the Yeti's minions into Grapevine, so that any other champion who might run into them would have a fighting chance. I told them about Handless. I wouldn't be the only one looking for her now.

Ultimately, I could only take Axel's advice, scary as that was. I went on. Estéban kept taking lessons with me, sparring in the rain and the early-autumn snow. Mira renewed the protective spells on the house, and on all of our friends whether they wanted it or not. When my neighbor's mastiff had another litter, I took one of the puppies for Annabelle. Marty's Duke had proven invaluable against the Yeti and his minions. I wanted that kind of protection for my daughter.

He was a cute little fawn-colored thing, all paws and floppy ears. Anna named him Chunk.

ALSO AVAILABLE
FROM
K. A. Stewart

A DEVIL IN THE DETAILS
A Jesse James Dawson Novel

Jesse James Dawson was an ordinary guy (well, an ordinary guy with a black belt in karate) until one day he learned his brother had made a bargain with a demon. Jesse discovered there was only one way to save his brother: put up his own soul as collateral, and fight the demon to the death.

Jesse lived to free his brother—and became part of a loose organization of Champions who put their own souls on the line to help those who get in over their heads with demons. But now experienced Champions are losing battles at a much higher rate than usual. Someone has changed the game. And if Jesse can't figure out the new rules, his next battle may be his last...

**Available wherever books are sold or at
penguin.com**

ROC

JIM BUTCHER
The Dresden Files

The #1 *New York Times* bestselling series

"Think *Buffy the Vampire Slayer* starring Philip Marlowe." —*Entertainment Weekly*

STORM FRONT

FOOL MOON

GRAVE PERIL

SUMMER KNIGHT

DEATH MASKS

BLOOD RITES

DEAD BEAT

PROVEN GUILTY

WHITE NIGHT

SMALL FAVOR

TURN COAT

CHANGES

SIDE JOBS

GHOST STORY

Available wherever books are sold or at penguin.com

R0037